THE KEEPER OF STARS

A NOVEL

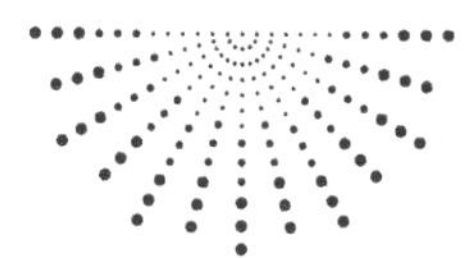

BUCK TURNER

❀ Created with Vellum

This book is dedicated to my grandparents, Ray and Muriel Cooper, with love.

Thank you for introducing me to the lake, and for providing me a glimpse into your world.

Though you may be gone, the memories I have of warm summer mornings spent trolling the waters of Douglas Lake remain, and I will cherish them all the days of my life.

THANK YOU FOR PURCHASING THIS BOOK

To receive the latest news and info, or to join Buck's team of beta readers, please go to:

www.buckturner.com

PROLOGUE

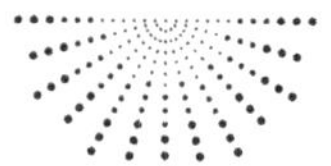

You don't find love. It finds you. It's got a little bit to do with destiny, fate, and what's written in the stars.

—Anais Nin

May 2020

They say our lives are written in the stars, that our fate is predetermined. But after the life I've lived and the things I've seen, I can honestly say that we are the authors of our own destiny, endowed by the Almighty with the power to choose our own paths, and, when necessary, to rewrite the stars.

Tonight, I sit alone under a chilly Tennessee sky. My only company, aside from a crackling fire and a glass of Jack Daniels, is a chorus of crickets and bullfrogs. It is a tune I know well. From the comfort of my rocking chair, I lean back and gaze deep into the heavens. Above me, the stars stretch to infinity like lighthouses on a thousand distant shores, waiting to guide my thoughts as they prepare to navigate the velvet sea.

But before they set sail, the sound of the telephone ringing brings me back to earth, so I push myself out of the rocker and shuffle into the house.

"Hello."

"Hey, it's me. It's done."

"Everything? Are you sure?"

"The moving truck is on its way to the storage facility, the door is locked, and the alarm is set. Sherrie will be by in the morning to stick the sign in the yard, so there's nothing left to do now but wait."

Between the alcohol, and the notion that the house that had known sixty years of love and laughter now sits empty, it takes me a moment to process.

"I can't thank you enough, sweetheart. I don't know what I would do without you."

"You're welcome, Daddy. I only wish I could do more. Speaking of that, I know you said you didn't want any company tomorrow, but I wish you'd reconsider. I could leave first thing in the morning and be at your place by noon. That way we could go together."

"Who would run the store?"

"Annalise can manage. She practically runs the place on her own as it is."

"I appreciate the offer, but you've more than held up your end of the bargain. The last mile is my cross to bear."

"Well," she says, sighing heavily into the phone, "if you change your mind, you know how to reach me. I don't mind dropping everything and leaving at a moment's notice."

"I know, and thank you. Oh, before I forget, did you find your mother's memory box?"

"No, I'm afraid not, and I searched every inch of the house. Twice in fact. The only thing I can figure is she must have moved it without telling you."

"You're probably right," I say, fearing it is lost forever. "I'll check again in the morning before I head out."

"Just promise me you'll be careful. I don't know what I'd do if I lost you too."

"I will. But try not to worry. I've been making this trip since before you were a twinkle in your mother's eye."

"Yes, but not like this."

I consider that, thinking that tomorrow will be one of the toughest days of my life.

After a moment of silence, she adds, "Well, I should go. I've been at it all day, and I'm exhausted."

"All right, darlin'. Tell Don I said hello, will you? Annalise too."

"Sure thing. I love you, Daddy."

"I love you too, sweetheart."

I mosey outside, add a log to the fire, and settle in for the long night ahead. "Now where was I?" At the bottom of my glass, it all comes back to me. "Now I remember." Leaning back in the rocker, I catch the glimmer of the North Star as the tail of a comet's light streaks across the sky.

PART I

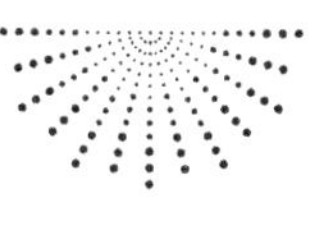

SUMMER

CHAPTER ONE

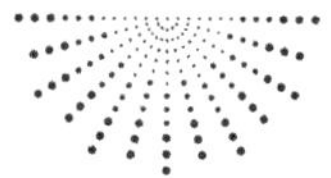

Gully Washer

May 1950

"Jack, if you get us killed, so help me God..."

The storm that had been building in the western sky rolled east, and a column of low, swirling clouds swept up the valley, blotting out the sun. By the looks of things, this was going to be a gully washer, which meant Jack Bennett had one shot at getting the motor to turn over. Otherwise he and his passenger would have to ride out the storm on Rock Island.

With the last bolt tightened, Jack turned and shouted into the wind. "All right, George, here goes nothing." Bracing himself, Jack pressed one hand firmly against the engine, grabbed the pull cord with the other, and yanked with all his might.

The engine spat and sputtered until finally, to Jack's delight, the steel beast gurgled to life as, from the bow, George Duncan put his palms together and raised his eyes to the heavens.

Jack grinned. But with a mile of open water between them and the dock, they weren't out of the woods yet.

* * *

A little while later, Jack and George huddled in the weathered shack at the end of the dock as rain fell in wind-driven sheets around them. Thunder echoed over the vast expanse, and like starlight pulsing through the graphite sky, lightning twisted and forked, bridging the gap between the heavens and the earth. It was as awesome a display of Mother Nature's power as either of them had ever witnessed.

As the dilapidated shack swayed and creaked around them, Jack took in a couple of deep breaths, smelled rain, gasoline, and the sweet aroma of chewing tobacco, then turned and stared out the window. "God must be angry today."

"I don't know nothin' about that." George lumbered to the icebox, plucked two beers from the top shelf, and tossed one to Jack. "But if we'd waited five more minutes, we could have asked him ourselves."

Jack smiled amusedly and opened his beer. "I ain't gonna let nothing happen to you, George. Besides, you keep forgetting I'm the best damn mechanic around. No one knows boats like me—or how to fix them."

"Speakin' of that, you should think about making a livin' out of it."

"What, boats?"

George shook his head as he took a long pull from his beer. "Bein' a mechanic. I mean, you can fix just about anything, and since there's no shortage of things breakin', you'd never run out of work."

Jack entertained the idea while he took a sip of beer. "Maybe you're right," he finally said. "I may look into that. Thanks, George."

"Don't mention it." George gulped his beer and drew a hand

across his mouth. "I'm sure glad to get outta that hot sun… and away from the storm. Now look at us." A smile worked across his weathered face. "We got a roof over our heads and somethin' cold to drink. A man don't need much more'n that." When he'd finished, he nodded toward the icebox. "There's more beer in the chest if you get a hankerin'."

"Thank you kindly," said Jack. "But you know I only drink one. I wouldn't want to get you into any kind of trouble, not on account of me."

George leaned back and let out a laugh that filled the small room. "The way I see it, if you're old enough to fight, you're old enough to have a beer. It's one of them rites of passage I heard the preacher talk about when I was younger. B'sides, there ain't nothin' wrong with it so long as you don't go burnin' up the roads. The water, on the other hand." He nodded toward the lake. "Why, you could go off course for pert' near an hour and not run into anything."

While George fetched another beer from the chest, Jack pulled out his wallet and counted the bills. *Thirty-five plus the four sixty-five I have at home makes...* He did the math in his head. *Five hundred big ones. Not bad.*

"Whatcha gonna do with all that cash?"

"I reckon I'll save it."

"For what?"

"Same thing as the last time you asked me."

"You mean that house on the hill?" Before Jack could respond, George shook his head in disgust. "Don't be a damn fool, boy. Like I told you before, only rich folks live on the hill. Folks like you and me—real folks—we ain't got no chance at a life like that. It ain't in the stars. We're lucky to scrape by down here at the water's edge. Which, if you wanna know the truth, ain't a bad deal."

George leaned in his chair and belched. Then Jack watched as a smile spread across his face.

"That's what you keep telling me. But even rich folks gotta start somewhere." Jack put away his money and stared out at the dark water, disinclined to accept the fate George had predicted for him.

"Think what you want, but someday you'll see what old George is talkin' about." George finished his second beer. After crushing the can and tossing it in the corner, he said, "Hey, listen. I appreciate you decidin' to stay on with me this summer. Honestly, I don't think I could run things without you. Not anymore."

Jack wondered if it was George or the alcohol doing the talking. Probably a little of both, he concluded as the man started on his third beer. "Aww, come on, George. That ain't no way to talk. You still got a few years left in you." He watched as George stared sullenly at the rain. "But in any case, I'm glad to do it and thankful for the work. Besides, it beats the hell out of working at the mill. I was talking to Ray Tucker the other day, and he said with all the windows they have in that place, it's like an oven in the summer. And in the winter you nearly freeze to death. That's no life I want. No, sir." He shook his head and glanced outside as the rain tapered off. "At least here I get to be on the water, and like you said, that ain't bad."

"Amen!" George slapped the table with an open palm. "I'll drink to that."

* * *

By the time Jack's house came into view, the storm had pushed east into the mountains, but evidence of its passage remained. The hike from the dock to his house, which was over a mile, took Jack along the lakeshore, through a dense stretch of woods, over a creek, and across a field of heather so thick he had to cut a path with his machete.

When Jack finally reached the porch, it was nearly suppertime, so he slipped out of his clothes, set them on the rail to dry, then pushed open the front door.

"That you, JB?"

"It's me, Mama," Jack answered wearily. He shuffled into the bathroom, washed his hands and face, and changed clothes before coming to supper.

"How was work today? You didn't get caught out in that squall, did ya? Donna Rae said Deep Springs Road is a mess."

"The woods too," said Jack. "On the bright side, there's a couple of trees down at the edge of the yard I can cut up and use for firewood. And to answer your question, me and George made it back just in time."

She looked at him dubiously. "You didn't pull that engine-trouble trick on old George again, did you?"

The fact that she remembered shocked him. "What if I did? You gonna to tell old George on me? I was only having a little fun." He rocked back in the chair, balancing on two legs. "Besides, I got us back with five whole minutes to spare."

Helen Bennett narrowed her eyes at him. "Jack Edward Bennett. I thought I taught you better'n that. And put that chair on all fours. If God had intended it to have two legs, he'd have made it that way." She shook her head in disgust. "You got too much of your daddy in you. That's your problem. If you ain't careful, one of these days you're gonna fool around and give old George a heart attack. How would you feel then?"

"I'm sorry." He set the chair right. "It won't happen again. Promise."

"Well, good. After all, George ain't as young as he used to

be. I reckon none of us are." She checked the biscuits. "You hungry?"

"Starving."

When the biscuits were golden brown on top, Helen took them out of the oven, covered them with a towel, and set them on the table to cool. Next, she brought over the jar of honey and a plate of fried bologna, put it beside the biscuits, and finally collapsed into her chair. "You wanna say grace or should I?"

"You go ahead. You're so much better at it than I am."

"Very well. Bow your head."

When the prayer had been said, Helen filled a plate and began eating while Jack poked and prodded at the fatty meat. Usually, he didn't mind bologna and biscuits, but this made the third day in a row. Even he had his limits.

"Mama, I wish you'd let me help with the groceries. I was counting my money this afternoon, and—"

Helen raised a hand, cutting him short. "Listen, I know you want to help, and God knows you'd give me your last dime if I asked you, but that's your money. You've worked hard for it, and hopefully someday it will help you get that house on the hill you're always goin' on about. So don't go wastin' it on me. B'sides, this may not be steak and potatoes, but it's nourishment to our bodies, and we got the good Lord to thank for that. Which is more than I can say for some folks."

Feeling a tinge of guilt, Jack dropped his eyes. "Yes, ma'am."

"But it's mighty kind of you to offer, JB. You're turnin' into a fine young man."

"Thanks, Mama." He took another bite of biscuit and chased it with a sip of tea. "Well, if I can't buy groceries, can I at least paint the kitchen? George has a couple of gallons of chiffon sitting in the shack that came from a man in White Pine. He said it's mine if I want it."

"Well, now." She chewed her lip for a moment. "I suppose there's nothin' wrong with that so long as it don't cost you nothin'."

"Not a cent," he said. "Cross my heart."

"All right, it's a deal—under one condition. You promise not to make a mess of my floors."

"Yes, ma'am."

After supper, Jack cleared the table and took the scraps outside to feed to the foxes and raccoons before drawing a bath. When he'd finished scrubbing the dirt from his body, he put on his pajama pants and opened the window to let in the cool breeze. The little house he and his mama called home was no mansion, and it didn't have any modern conveniences like a telephone or air-conditioning, but it had gobs of windows. Most nights they left them open to let in fresh air and be sung to sleep by the crickets and bullfrogs.

He spent a few minutes talking to God, then wrote in the journal Fleta Pickle had given him for his birthday.

Dear Lewis,

You should have seen the big storm we had this afternoon. The way the wind was howlin', you'd a thought the Rapture was coming. In all my days, I've never seen whitecaps like that. Luckily, I got me and George back in time without as much as a single raindrop hitting us. According to Mama, I nearly gave George a heart attack with that old engine-trouble stunt. Maybe she's right, and I should take it easy on him from now on. After all, I don't know what I'd do if anything ever happened to George. Anyway, when the storm passed, I dropped a line and caught a couple of crappies from the dock on some minnows I snagged with the net this morning. Neither of them any size but a promising sign. Maybe tomorrow I'll head up Flat Creek and see if I can't catch me a catfish for supper. I haven't had a good mess of fish in a while, and it'd sure beat having bologna again. Well, I gotta get some shuteye. Talk later.

Jack

CHAPTER TWO

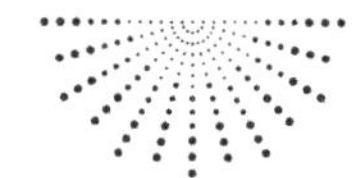

Room for One More

A rooster's crow woke Jack from a dream. Wiping the sleep from his eyes, he rolled out of bed and found a pair of work jeans, slid one leg in, then the other, and added a T-shirt and ball cap before stepping out into the hall.

After a search of the fridge, he found some leftover bologna and a couple of biscuits, wrapped them in cellophane, and shoved them into a paper bag before venturing out into the dark.

As he topped the hill, to the east the first rays of golden sunlight spilled over the mountains. Below, where the land met the lake, thick fingers of mist stretched across the surface of the water, blotting out the far shore. "God, what a view." It was the closest thing to heaven on earth.

By the time Jack made it to the dock, the tide had turned in the age-old fight between the fog and sun, and as rays of light bled through the thinning mist, he spotted George in his overalls and T-shirt.

"Gonna be another hot one." George raked a hand across his dark brow. "You ready to get after it?"

"Yessir." Jack stowed away his lunch, then went out to fuel the boat.

At the southeast corner of Douglas Lake, less than a mile from the dam, George and Jack ran a ferry service where tourists visiting the Smoky Mountains could stop and search the islands for arrowheads and other artifacts left behind by the Cherokee. They were an unlikely pair, George and Jack. George Duncan was a seventy-five-year-old Black man with a reputation for drinking too much. Bright-eyed, bushy-tailed, and unblemished, 18-year-old Jack Bennett was the antithesis of George. But despite their many differences, the one thing they shared was their love for the water.

"What time are you expecting the first group?" Jack asked as he cleaned the boat.

"Nine o'clock sharp." George finished sweeping the leaves from the dock. "And since I'm expectin' two big groups, there won't be no need for a third run."

Knowing what that meant, Jack felt a flush rise in his cheeks.

"I figure we'd cut out around four, which will give me time to make a beer run and you to get in some fishin' before dark. You can take the green boat if you want. I already gassed it up for ya."

"Thanks, George. I'll have to get some night crawlers from the corner store though. Forgot mine at home."

"I picked some up this mornin' on my way in along with a couple of sausage biscuits. You're welcome to the biscuits and the worms so long as you bring back what you don't use. The worms, not the biscuits." He chuckled.

"I promise. By the way, I'll be taking that paint if the offer's still good. I talked to Mama last night over supper, and she agreed to let me paint the kitchen for her."

"Fine with me. You need any help gettin' it home?"

"Nah, I'll manage."

Once they had the place looking spick-and-span, Jack and George sat down to breakfast.

"I was thinking"—Jack chewed and talked simultaneously—"about opening a fishing service."

"What happened to my mechanic idea?"

"I'm still mulling it over."

"So a fishing service, huh? You mean like takin' folks out and showin' them all the best spots?"

"Not the best ones. I'd keep those for myself. I'm just talking about the decent ones, where they could catch their limit."

George gave it some more thought. "Might work. Wait a minute. You're not thinkin' of strikin' out on your own, are ya?"

"Nah. I'm thinking about later, when I get older. If I'm gonna afford that house on the hill, I'm gonna need to make some real money."

George took a bite of biscuit and stared at the water. "Well, I like the way you think, JB. That's why you're the idea man."

It wasn't long before the guests began assembling on the hill. Jack went out to greet them while George stayed behind to collect the money.

"Howdy, folks," Jack shouted. "If y'all will make your way to the dock, I'll show you to the boat so we can get going."

Besides being on the water, meeting new people was the part of the job Jack enjoyed most. He found life outside Sims Chapel fascinating, so any chance he got to ask people where they were from or what they did for a living, he took it. Over the years, he'd talked to folks from as far away as California, but most came from Ohio and Michigan. They spoke with funny accents and had little experience on the water, which Jack found amusing. There was even one man the summer before who had lost his balance and fallen in, clothes and all. He and George still laughed about that.

* * *

When the morning tour had concluded, Jack sat down in the shack and had lunch. As usual, George had been right about the weather; it was hot as blue blazes. But after chasing his bologna biscuit with a glass of sweet tea, Jack was as good as new.

With the boat refueling, Jack wiped the hull and in no time had it shining again like new. And it wasn't long before the second crowd began to gather.

When everyone was aboard, Jack untied the lines and prepared for departure. But just as he was ready to shove off, he glimpsed something from the corner of his eye.

"Wait!" a voice echoed across the water.

Jack turned his head to find a young lady running toward him, frantically waving her arms.

"Wait for me!"

Upon closer inspection, Jack realized she was about his age. More importantly, she was pretty, which got his attention.

"Thank you..." She stopped to catch her breath. "Do you have room... for one more?" She smiled sweetly.

"I'm sorry, miss." He stared at the reflection of himself in her sunglasses. "We're already full. But I think we still have a few spots left in the morning if you'd like to go then."

She glanced at those in the boat, then reached into her

pocket and came back with a wad of money. "I'm willing to pay extra."

Up went Jack's eyebrows. "Whoa!"

"Please? I've come a long way, and I'd like to get out on the water this afternoon."

Usually unflinching, Jack found himself spellbound, stunned by her beauty.

Having heard the commotion, George lumbered out of the shack and assessed the scene before him. "What seems to be the trouble?" His gaze shifted from the young lady to Jack.

"She wants to go with us," Jack explained. "But like I already told her, we're full."

George counted the passengers, then noticed the wad of money she was holding. He stroked his chin. "I'm sure we can find a spot for her somewhere." He took the money and shoved it into the front pocket of his overalls. "Why don't you let her sit with you, JB?"

Jack glanced over his shoulder. "Where, on my lap?"

She pressed a hand to her mouth, stifling a giggle.

"You got a bucket, don'tcha?" said George.

"Yessir."

"Well, turn it over. It ain't the most comfortable seat, but it'll do in a pinch." He winked.

"You're the boss," said Jack. "All right, Miss...?"

"Spencer. Elizabeth Spencer. But everyone calls me Ellie." She presented her hand, palm down, so Jack took it and helped her into the boat.

"You'll be in the back with me." He showed her to her seat. "I'm Jack, by the way, but most folks around here call me JB. You ever been on a boat before, Ellie Spencer?" They eased away from the dock.

"First time."

"Welcome aboard. And don't worry," he said, sensing some trepidation, "you're in good hands. I may not look it, but I've been running these waters for forever and a day. So sit back, relax, and enjoy the ride."

* * *

The ride to the island took a half hour, during which Jack entertained the guests with stories of the Native Americans who had inhabited the land long before the river was dammed up by the TVA. It was all part of the experience. Jack's ability to spin a yarn was one of the reasons George had agreed to hire him in the first place. That, and he knew his way around the water.

When the island appeared, Jack cut the engine and glided to shore. After securing the boat, he helped the passengers onto the rocky stretch of beach.

"Watch your step," he warned.

Ellie waited patiently for the others to disembark before she made her way to the front of the boat. "You're not coming with us?"

He shook his head and helped her from the bow. "This is as far as I go. But I'll be close by if you need me. Oh." He noticed her shoes. "Those look new and expensive. Are they?"

"Yes. Is there something wrong with them?"

"That depends."

"On what?"

"On whether you want to wear them again." He grabbed a pair of waders from the boat and handed them to her. "Put these on."

Ellie turned up her nose. "Thanks, but I'll take my chances."

"Look, I know they're not the most glamorous things, but

you'll fare a lot better in these than you will those." He glanced at her shoes again. "Trust me on this." When she didn't object, he dropped to one knee and helped her out of her shoes and into the waders. "How do those feel?"

"Like I'm wearing someone else's bloomers."

He breathed an easy laugh. "Can't say that I've heard anyone describe it quite like that before." He looked up at her and smiled. "All right, off you go." He stood and pointed to an opening in the trees. "It's just through there."

While the guests scoured the island for artifacts, Jack drifted over to a familiar cove and put a line in the water. His odds of catching something in the middle of the afternoon were slim, but occasionally he'd get lucky and snag a carp or catfish feeding on the bottom.

The summer before, he'd brought a hammock to nap in the shade. Seeing it was still in decent shape, he stretched out and rested his eyes. After a catnap, he checked his line, then took out his journal and scribbled a few notes in the margin, documenting the lake level, the weather, and where he planned to fish that afternoon.

When the sun dipped below the treetops, Jack reeled in his line and eased over to the island. Sure enough, as he landed the boat, the guests appeared. He scanned the group until he found Ellie, covered in mud from the knees down.

"How was it?" Jack took Ellie's hand and pulled her into the boat, trying not to laugh.

She jammed her hands on her hips and glared at him. "I'll have you know I traipsed around this godforsaken island all afternoon, and the only thing I have to show for it is a sunburn and these mosquito bites." She scratched vigorously at her arm. "I demand a refund."

"Sorry, Miss Spencer, but all sales are final." It took every ounce of energy for him to keep a straight face. "On the bright side, at least you didn't ruin your shoes."

Her scowl loosened, if only a little. "Yes, I suppose you're right. Thank you, by the way, for the waders. They weren't as bad as I thought once I got used to them."

"You're welcome."

When everyone was aboard, Jack shoved the boat into the water, cranked the engine, and turned for home.

During the ride back to the dock, the guests talked among themselves, several showing off the arrowheads they found. But Ellie was quiet, choosing instead to concentrate on the scenery.

"Did you at least enjoy the fresh air?" Jack asked her as they motored south toward the dam.

She nodded once, looking glum. "But I had my heart set on finding an arrowhead."

"There's always next time. In fact"—Jack lowered his voice to a whisper—"if you're serious about finding arrowheads, I know a better spot than that old island."

She cocked an eyebrow. "You do?"

"Sure." He gave a nonchalant wave of his hand. "I've found dozens of them over the years. I could show you sometime. It's the least I could do since you didn't get what you came for."

Ellie cast a wary eye at Jack, seemingly unsure of him. "I'll think about it."

When they reached the dock, everyone got out and staggered to their cars. Ellie stayed back and returned the waders to Jack.

"Much better." She wiggled her toes, then dried her feet with a towel and slid into her flats. "Do you have another group coming in?" She took off her sunglasses, revealing a pair of mesmerizing green eyes.

"We're done for the day," he said, fighting the urge to stare. "George is closing early so I can get in a little fishing before dark."

"That sounds fun. I've always wanted to learn how to fish."

Sensing an opportunity, Jack said, "Why don't you come with me? I could teach you."

Her eyes met his gaze. "I would, but that's my ride." She nodded toward a green Chevrolet idling in the lot.

Jack glanced over her shoulder at the car. "Well, another time then." He tried to hide his disappointment. "But in case you're ever out this way again, I fish most evenings, so..."

She smiled at him with her eyes and shook his hand. "I'll keep that in mind. Thanks again for making room for me and for the waders. Even though I didn't get my arrowhead, I did enjoy being on the water."

"You're welcome," he said, then watched as she turned and headed for the car.

* * *

That evening while Jack hauled in a mess of bass and bream, he thought a great deal about Ellie Spencer, the girl with the fancy shoes and dazzling eyes. Reflecting on the afternoon, he realized she *was* the prettiest girl he'd ever seen. Which begged the question: What was a girl like that doing in Sims Chapel? And more importantly, would he ever see her again?

When night fell, Jack went home, ate, prayed, and dug out his journal.

Dear Lewis,

Don't ask me how, but I get the feeling today is the first day of the rest of my life. What am I talking about? An angel, that's what. And her name is Ellie Spencer. She's gorgeous, and I don't mean just a little. Think Jacklyn Carpenter, only prettier. And to top it off, she's nice, not like those girls from Knoxville, constantly thumbing their noses at guys like us. This one's different, I can tell. She's out of my league of course. You should have seen those fancy clothes all covered in muck. Do you think I'll see her again? If I do, you'll be the first to know.

Jack

CHAPTER THREE

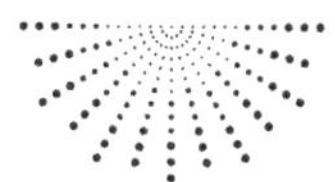

Rain Check

Much to Jack's chagrin, the next morning came and went with no sign of Ellie. Realizing the odds of seeing her again were remote, Jack figured she had likely stopped in Sims Chapel with her family on their way to the mountains or the beach. Given his luck, or lack thereof, she was probably halfway to the coast by now, never to return. Despite his disappointment, Jack went about his day like usual, running three tours to the island and back.

When the last passenger had cleared the dock, Jack unloaded the boat, carried everything—nets, oars, tackle—into the shed, and put it all away. After grabbing his fishing gear and a bucket of minnows, he locked the door and set off for the boat.

"Hey there."

Jack turned around at the sound of her voice. "Ellie."

She glided toward him, her feet barely touching the wooden planks.

"I was starting to think I'd never see you again."

A hint of a smile brushed her lips. "Why's that?"

"I figured you'd be visiting the mountains or on your way to the beach."

"I wish. Actually, I'm here for a few months visiting my aunt, so you'll likely be seeing a lot of me this summer."

His heart did a summersault. Taking inventory of her, Jack noticed her hair was up in a ponytail, and she had on a plaid shirt and had traded her expensive shoes for a pair of white Keds sneakers.

"She lives just there." Ellie turned and pointed to a white house on the far shore.

The house on the hill. The green Chevrolet he'd seen the day before. Jack connected the dots in his head. "You're Clara Sutton's niece, aren't you?"

"Guilty as charged." She reached up and brushed away a strand of hair that had blown onto her face. "Do you know her well?"

"Everyone around here knows Clara. I knew your uncle too before he passed." Jack dropped his eyes in reverence before speaking again. "Clara's been going on for weeks about you. I haven't seen her this excited in a long time."

"It sounds as if you know her better than I do." Ellie leaned against the railing, one leg over the other.

"Are y'all not close?"

"We were. She and Uncle Bill used to visit us every Christmas. But this is the first time I've seen her since the funeral."

"Then, if you don't mind me asking, why are you here?"

Ellie looked away before answering. "Mother says I've been in the North too long and thinks this will be a great opportunity for me to get back to my Southern roots." She sighed. "But I think it's just an excuse to get me out of the house."

"Southern roots?" Jack joined her at the rail, and they stared out at the water together. "Does that mean you were born around here?"

She shook her head. "Mother's originally from a little place called Sweetwater, but my sister and I were born and raised in Ohio. That's where my father is from."

"So what are your plans this summer—besides not finding arrowheads?" He teased her with a smile.

"Very funny." She nudged him playfully with her elbow in response. "I only arrived yesterday, so I guess I haven't figured that out yet. What is there to do around here besides go out on the water?"

He tried to think of something impressive to say but drew a blank. "Not much, I'm afraid, unless you go to Knoxville. There's plenty to do there."

She was quiet for a moment. "Well, what do you do besides ferry people to the island?"

"That's about it. I work six days a week from sunup to sundown. When I'm not working, I'm fishing; when I'm not fishing, I help Mama around the house and in the garden. Around here, work never ends."

"What about fun? They say all work and no play makes Jack a dull boy." She winked at him.

"You mean all that work doesn't sound like fun to you?" He waited until his sarcastic smile faded before going on. "But seriously, I have most of my fun on the water—fishing, swimming, and scouring the islands."

Ellie stared off toward the horizon. "What about that place you were telling me about yesterday, the one with all the arrowheads? Do you think you could take me sometime?"

That threw him for a loop. "It'd be my pleasure. Since you're here for the summer, just pick a day and we'll go."

She focused her gaze on him. "How about now?"

Her question put him on his heels.

"Unless you have plans," she added.

His head wagged back and forth. "No. No plans. Just let me grab a couple of things." He went to the door and fumbled nervously with the lock. Glancing over his shoulder, he saw Ellie watching him with amusement as he clumsily pushed his way inside.

* * *

They made it as far as the sand bar before a storm drove them from the water.

Jack unlocked the door to the shack, and they went inside. "Sorry." He offered her a chair at the table. "Sometimes Mother Nature cooperates, and sometimes she doesn't."

As if on cue, thunder rumbled in the slate sky above them. Jack removed his hat and checked the icebox.

"I've got sweet tea if you're thirsty," he said, finding the pitcher full.

"Yes, thank you." Ellie sat on a milk crate and let down her brown hair. "Is this where you and George hang out when you're not on the water?"

"Mostly." Jack filled two glasses with tea and handed one to Ellie. "I built this place myself a couple of summers back. It's nothing fancy, but it shields us from the elements." He sat quietly, watching her while she sipped her tea. "This place must seem foreign to you," he said after a minute.

"What do you mean?"

"Only that you seem citified, that's all."

She looked at him with folded arms and raised eyebrows. "I'm not uppity, if that's what you mean."

"I didn't mean it like that. I only meant that this way of life must seem strange compared to what you're used to."

Her expression softened, and her lips turned up in a half smile. "I won't argue with you there." She lifted the glass to her lips and took another drink. "But it's nice in its own way."

Outside, rain hammered down as the storm rolled on.

Ever curious, he asked her what life was like in Ohio.

"Not unlike here when you venture outside the city. My family lives on the outskirts of downtown, in Upper Arlington. Mother is a nurse, and my father is the president of a bank. I wish I could tell you it's a wonderful life, but the truth is it's rather exhausting. My parents, God love them, they're decent people, but all they care about is appearance and where they rank in Columbus's social circle. As for me, ever since I was little, my life has been very structured."

Her description of life in the big city surprised Jack, who had always imagined it far more glamorous. "What about school? Are you in college?"

She nodded. "I just finished my freshman year at Indiana University where I'm studying astronomy."

"You mean like the moon and stars?"

"Exactly."

"Interesting."

She beamed at his remark. "Oh, it is. Ever since I was a little girl, my dream has been to follow in Maria Mitchell's footsteps and become a professor of astronomy. Have you heard of her?"

Jack shook his head.

"That's okay. Not many people have. She was the first female astronomer in the United States," she explained. "But she's a tough act to follow. Most professors are men. Mother says I'll have to be twice as smart and work three times as hard just to have a chance, but I'm up to the challenge."

Jack found her ambition impressive. "Is that why your life is so structured, because of all the studying?"

She nodded, staring into her glass. "I realize part of it is self-inflicted, but my parents' expectations are just as high as mine, if not higher. Which is why I've been looking forward to this summer." She took a breath. "For the first time in as long as I can remember, I can finally let my hair down and have fun."

Jack couldn't believe his luck. Not only was Ellie gorgeous, but she was intelligent, easy to talk to, and enjoyed the water. And if that weren't enough, she didn't seem to mind his accent or the fact that he wasn't as educated as her. He pinched himself to make sure he wasn't dreaming.

Eventually, the rain slacked, but they waited a while longer on account of the lightning.

"Tell me about your parents," said Ellie, turning the conversation to Jack. "Are they any better than mine?"

Jack twisted uncomfortably in his chair, trying to suppress the emotions her question evoked. "Well, I only have the one," he admitted. "Mama works for a man in Dandridge named Cliff Sturgill who runs the largest produce business in the county." He swallowed hard, breaking the news to her about his father. "Daddy died in the war when I was ten."

"I'm sorry," Ellie said quietly. "I had a cousin who died in France. I guess the war touched us all in some way. Was it difficult growing up with only one parent?"

"At times, but I'm lucky to have someone like Mama. She's taken good care of me. That's why when I get a little older and start making some real money, I'm going to return the favor."

When the storm passed, Jack walked Ellie home and promised they'd resume their search for arrowheads another day.

CHAPTER FOUR

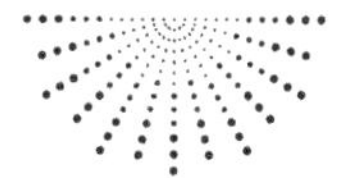

Blackberry Cobbler

Clara Sutton sat in the kitchen, eating blackberry cobbler, when Ellie walked through the front door. "Was that Jack Bennett I saw you with just now?"

"Yes, it was." Ellie moved into the kitchen and took a seat at the table. "He says he knows you."

Clara nodded. "I've known that young'un since he was knee high to a grasshopper."

Ellie laughed. "What can you tell me about him?"

"Well, for starters, you won't find a finer young man anywhere in Sims Chapel. But like most folks around here, he's had a difficult upbringing." Clara went to the sink and rinsed the saucer.

"Yeah, he told me about losing his father. By the way, I'm sorry for getting home so late. A storm ran us off the water, so we sat in the shack and talked and drank sweet tea while it passed."

"No need to apologize, Ellie." Clara cut the water and dried her hands. "Like I told you when you got here, I'm not your mother. That doesn't mean you can go hog wild, mind you, but you're a grown woman, for heaven's sake. Besides, if you were with Jack, you were in good hands." She put away the dishes in the cupboard, then leaned against the counter. "Speaking of your mother, she telephoned while you were out."

Her heart rate kicked up a notch. "What did she want?"

"To know where you were and what you were doing."

Ellie held her breath.

"I told her that you had gone next door to help one of the girls in the garden." Clara winked at her.

"You didn't have to do that, but thank you."

"Don't thank me yet. The reason she called was to see if I could arrange for a tutor to come by and help with your mathematics. She said you were having some trouble with algebra."

"If you call getting an A minus trouble." Ellie leaned back and folded her arms, irked that her mother, even from three hundred miles away, was still trying to control her life. "What did you tell her?"

"I told her what she wanted to hear, that I had the perfect person in mind. Her name is Sara Coffee. She's a mathematics major at the University of Tennessee. Sara lives up the road with her mother and father and is sweet as pie. I talked to her a little bit ago, and she said she'd be glad to help. Trust me. You two will get along splendidly."

"Can't wait."

Clara pulled out a chair and sat across from Ellie. "On the bright side, she'll only be here in the mornings, which means you'll have the afternoons to spend as you wish."

Ellie perked up. "You mean it?"

Clara nodded.

"I guess I can live with that," she said, thinking it could be worse.

Clara cleared her throat and looked earnest. "I don't mean to pry, Ellie, so if I'm overstepping, just say so. But for someone your age, who appears to have a good head on her shoulders, your mother sure keeps a watchful eye on you."

"You don't know the half of it." Ellie sighed, thinking how her relationship with her mother had deteriorated to the point that they hardly spoke to one another. "We were close once, but the truth is we rarely agree on much of anything these days. I suppose that's part of the reason I'm here, so she doesn't have to deal with me this summer."

"Come now. That isn't true, is it?"

"I'm afraid so. She and I have been at each other's throats for years."

"I hate to break it to you, darlin'," said Clara, "but every girl your age fights with their mother."

"They do?"

"Sure. When I was growing up, my mama and I fought like cats and dogs. You'd a thought we hated each other the way we carried on. And your mama was the same way."

"Now that I can believe." Ellie's body relaxed. "But she's only like that with me. She and Amelia hardly ever disagree on anything."

"And how old is Amelia now? Sixteen? Seventeen?"

"She'll be seventeen in October," said Ellie.

"Well, if I was a bettin' woman, I'd say her turn's coming. You see, in your mother's eyes, you're still her baby, and her maternal instinct is to protect you even at your age. But eventually she'll come around, one way or the other. They all do."

"I hope you're right." Ellie wondered what it would be like to be friends with her mother rather than enemies. "Thanks, Aunt Clara. I feel better."

"You're welcome, honey." A draft blew through the house,

so Clara got up and shut the windows. "Now that we've solved the world's problems, can I interest you in a piece of my world-famous blackberry cobbler? I made it fresh this afternoon."

"I'd love some." Ellie couldn't recall the last time she'd eaten cobbler. "I don't suppose you've got any vanilla ice cream to go with it?"

Clara went to the icebox and pulled out the container of homemade ice cream. "Darlin', you'll soon learn we do things right around here."

"In that case, make it two scoops."

"Now you're talkin'." Clara winked at Ellie, then grabbed a bowl from the cabinet. She cut a piece of cobbler and spooned out the ice cream. "I was thinking. Now that you're good and settled, how's about me and you plan us a trip to Knoxville?" She brought out the cobbler and a glass of milk and set them in front of Ellie.

"Thank you." Ellie took a bite. "This is amazing!"

"Ain't met no one yet that doesn't fall in love with my cobbler. Did you know I won three years in a row at the fair with that recipe?"

"I don't doubt it," said Ellie around a bite of ice cream. "What would we do in Knoxville?"

"Shop, eat, catch a movie. They got a theater on Gay Street that offers a twenty-five-cent matinee."

"Sounds fun." She set down the spoon, wiped her mouth with a napkin, and redirected the conversation. "You know, I'm glad I decided to spend the summer here. To be honest, I was dreading it a little."

"Why?"

"I thought I'd be stuck with no friends and nothing to do. But that couldn't be further from the truth because I have you and Jack. And then there's the water and everything it offers." Another thought struck her. "It might be hard for you to believe, but there's always been a part of me that wished I had grown up in a place like this." She let out a small laugh, then said, "Maybe Mama was right. Maybe I am a Southern girl at heart."

"There are worse things," said Clara. "Once you get a taste of this life—the water, the air, that feeling of being free—it's hard to let it go."

"Is that why you stayed... after Uncle Bill died?"

The smile ran away from Clara's face. "I suppose so. This was your uncle's favorite place in the entire world. He grew up in these mountains, spent his whole life here. Sure, I could have packed up and gone just about anywhere my heart desired, and for a while, I thought I wanted to. But when I sat and thought about it, there wasn't another place on earth I could have imagined myself besides here. This is the place where I fell in love, got married, and shared almost twenty years with the man I loved. And if I close my eyes, I can still feel him here with me. There aren't enough beaches and golden sunsets in the world to make me walk away from those memories."

Ellie digested her words, then said, "I admire you, Aunt Clara. Your strength, your independence. I hope someday I can be strong like you."

Smiling, Clara reached across the table and laid a hand gently on Ellie's arms. "Darlin'," she said, looking her niece in the face, "something tells me you'll end up being stronger than me or your mama."

CHAPTER FIVE

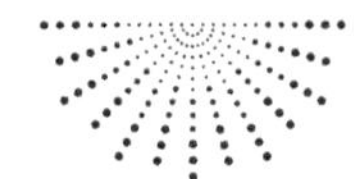

A Golden Opportunity

The next day, the weather took a turn for the worse. For two straight days and nights, the rain spilled down in sheets, which meant no tours and no fishing. But the break gave Jack ample time to think about Ellie. In fact, since the night he'd walked her home in the dark, he thought of nothing else.

To pass the time, he painted the kitchen, just as he'd promised. And while he waited for the paint to dry, he sat beneath the ancient oak that stood in the backyard and daydreamed while he listened to the rain sing on the red tin roof.

But all that daydreaming didn't go unnoticed.

"There you are," said Helen, finding Jack on the back porch late one afternoon.

"Oh hey, Mama. I didn't hear you come in. How was work?"

"Same as always. Everything all right?"

He nodded absently, watching a pair of squirrels playing in the oak tree. "Kitchen's done."

"I saw it when I came in. It's beautiful. Thank you." She

spent a few seconds inspecting the state of the garden before going on. "So what are you doin' out here all by your lonesome?"

"Thinking."

"About what?"

Jack stared silently at the rain, considering his answer. "Mama, how long after you met Daddy did you know you liked him? Was it love at first sight, or did it take time?"

She glanced at her wedding ring. "Oh, I don't know. I suppose I kinda liked him right off. Why?"

Jack jerked a shoulder in response. "I dunno. Just wondering."

Helen dusted off a spot beside Jack and sat down. "This wouldn't have anything to do with that young lady you walked home after the storm the other night, would it?"

Jack rubbed the back of his neck. "Possibly. Probably. Her name is Ellie. She's Clara's niece... from Ohio, and she's here for the summer."

"Let me guess. You're kinda sweet on her, aren'tcha?"

"I can't stop thinking about her."

Helen smiled briefly, then turned and stared out at the rain. "Well, it's only natural you start takin' an interest in girls. After all, I was married when I was your age."

"What if I said I wanted to spend time with her this summer? Would you be okay with that?"

"Do you promise to treat her like a gentleman?"

"I promise."

"And no fooling around neither," she warned. "You ain't in no position to be havin' no young'uns. God knows I can't take care of 'em. I can hardly afford to feed you and me as it is."

Jack's face burned red hot. "Yes, ma'am. I won't do nothing like that."

"Then I guess it's okay. But just remember this," she said, turning and looking at him, "I know Ellie's only here for the summer, but be careful who you give your heart to. Once it's gone, there's no takin' it back, no matter how much you might wanna."

* * *

When the weather finally broke, life returned to normal. Being cooped up in the house had taken its toll on Jack and Ellie, and they were anxious to get back on the water.

On Tuesday afternoon, they met at the dock and motored to the head of Flat Creek, where Jack kept his promise and taught Ellie how to fish.

"Most people don't know it," said Jack, "but there's an art to fishing. You gotta take into account the weather, color of the water, time of day, and so on." He rigged up a line for her, then spent a few minutes showing her how to cast and retrieve.

It wasn't long before Ellie caught her first bream.

Jack removed the hook, then released the fish into the water. "You learn quick."

"Maybe that's because I have a good teacher." She flashed a grin, surprising him. After adding more bait to the hook, she cast her line into the water. "You ever thought about doing this for a living?"

"What, teaching?"

She shook her head. "Fishing."

Jack wiped his hands on the towel and adjusted his ball cap. "It's funny you should ask. The other day I was telling George about this idea I had for a business. We're constantly getting outta-towners in here looking to catch big bass and catfish. With my knowledge of the lake, I could find the fish, and they'd be guaranteed to catch their limit. I think folks would be willing to pay for something like that, don't you?"

"So instead of taking people to the islands, you'd take them fishing?"

Jack nodded, watching his line.

Ellie thought for a moment and said, "Yeah, I think that's an excellent idea."

They drifted with the current, and the conversation came easy. Jack spoke of his love for the water while Ellie told him more about life in the city. Between them, they had enough stories to write a book. Before they knew it, the afternoon had gotten away from them, and as dusk approached, they eased toward home.

"See that rock?" Jack pointed toward a shallow spot a few feet from the bank. "There's an old stump between us and it, and at the base of that stump is a big bass I've been trying to catch since the spawn began. Why don't you give it a shot?"

Ellie reeled in her line and carefully cast it toward the rock. When the bait had settled to the bottom, she reeled slowly, just like Jack taught her. A few seconds later, the end of the rod twitched.

"I think I'm getting a bite."

Jack eyed the line and, in a quiet voice, said, "Just remember what I told you."

When the fish took the bait, Ellie jerked back on the fishing pole, just like Jack taught her. "I think I got one." For five minutes, she fought the fish, guiding it away from a fallen tree, out from under a rock, and finally to the surface. It was as if she'd been fishing all her life. When the bass was within arm's reach, Jack snagged it with the net, and grabbed the scales.

"Five pounds, four ounces," he said. "Golly, that's a whopper."

"What should we do with it?" she asked, eyes wide with excitement.

Jack scratched his head. "We could have it for supper," he offered, "but bass isn't the best eatin' fish."

"Or we could just let it go." Ellie looked as if the thought of killing such a beautiful animal broke her heart.

"I like your suggestion better," he said, sensing her apprehension, and got ready to release it back into the water.

"May I?"

"Be my guest." Jack handed the fish to Ellie. She took it by the mouth, leaned over the side of the boat, and lowered it gently into the water. It lay there for a second, motionless, then with a splash of its tail swam away and descended into the murky depths.

"What'd I tell you?" Jack beamed.

"You're amazing, you know that?" She sat down, and her eyes settled on him. "How'd you know there'd be a fish there?"

"I've been fishing these waters for as long as I can remember." Jack took off his cap and ruffled his hair. "From the time I was old enough to walk, I would go with my mamaw and papaw. In fact, I learned everything I know about fishing from them."

"Do they still fish?"

He shook his head. "They passed away a few years ago. But they loved being out on the water." A school of minnows caught his attention. "I guess that's why I like it so much." Jack was silent then, concentrating on catching a fish of his own.

* * *

The next evening, Jack and Ellie stood on the bank near the dam, skipping rocks. After the advice his mama had given him,

Jack was cautious around Ellie. The last thing he wanted was to fall in love only to have his heart broken at the end of summer. But it wasn't enough to dissuade him from spending time with her.

"Do you have someone special back home?" Jack asked as he hurled a stone across the water's glassy surface.

"You mean like a boyfriend?"

He nodded his head.

"Well, there's this one guy, Michael. He and I go to school together. We've gone out a couple of times, but he's not my boyfriend." She side-armed the last rock, watching it skip three times before disappearing beneath the surface. "What about you?" She set her gaze upon him. "With those eyes and that accent, I bet you have to fight the girls off with a stick."

Jack smiled, amused as he bent over and grabbed another handful of stones. "Nah. Girls around here aren't interested in a guy like me, except for maybe Sara."

"Sara Coffee?"

Jack snapped his head at her. "Yeah, how'd you know?"

"She's been helping me with my algebra," Ellie explained. "My mother wasn't satisfied with the A minus I got this year, so she thought having a tutor come over for a few hours in the mornings would be a good idea."

"Ouch," said Jack. "No offense, but your mother sounds like a drill sergeant."

"You have no idea." Ellie rolled her eyes. "So you and Sara, huh? Yeah, I can see that," she said after a moment. "The two of you would make a cute couple."

"If you say so. But in case you were wondering, we're not."

"Could have fooled me," she teased.

"What's that supposed to mean?"

"Nothing. It's just that the way she goes on about you all the time, I figured..."

"Don't get me wrong," said Jack. "Sara's a nice enough girl, but she and I are just friends."

"Sometimes being friends first makes for the best relationships, or at least that's what I hear. My parents were friends before they started dating."

"Come to think of it, so were my folks," said Jack. "But I don't see that happening with me and Sara. Besides, between work and helping Mama around the house, I don't have a lot of time for much else. And even if I did, most of the girls around here are looking for guys with money or a fast car or both. And I don't got neither." He skipped his last rock, then eased back toward the boat.

"Well, lucky for you, not all girls are interested in guys for their cars or money."

"Is that so?"

"Yeah, that's so." She looked up at him and batted her eyes.

"But I reckon it must matter a little, right? At least the money part."

When they reached the boat, Ellie turned to him. "Jack, why do you worry about such things?"

He dropped his eyes and spoke at the ground. "I don't know. I just don't want to end up poor like my mama. God knows she tries her best, but life hasn't been kind to her. Sometimes I feel like I'm headed down the same path. Then I look at you and see someone who will never know what it's like to be poor. And I don't blame you. It's just... my problems will never be your problems."

"Jack." Ellie took him by the shoulders. "Just because someone has money doesn't mean they don't have problems. They're just different kinds of problems. And just because you start off poor doesn't mean you have to stay poor. Why, there are plenty of stories about people starting with nothing that have made something of themselves, and vice versa. Just look out there." She pointed toward the western sky. "Our entire lives are before us, filled with endless possibilities. Who knows what the future holds?"

* * *

On a hot June evening while trolling a shallow stretch of water near the sandbar, Jack shouted, "Bite me hook, fishy."

Ellie laughed out loud at his choice of words. "Is that another of George's sayings?"

Jack shook his head. "Stole that one from my mamaw. She used to say it when the bite was slow."

"Your mamaw sounds like a real character."

"Oh, she was. I remember she used to sit quietly and fish from the back of the boat. That was her spot. She'd catch two or three fish before me or Papaw knew what was happening. But Papaw would just shake his head and smile."

"You miss them, don't you?" Ellie asked quietly.

"Every day. They meant the world to me. Still do."

For the next few minutes, neither of them said a word. Then a whooshing sound near the bank stole their attention.

"What's that?" Ellie asked, watching a blue-gray bird clumsily take flight.

"Shikepoke." Jack followed the bird with his eyes as it glided over the water's dark surface.

"What?"

"Well, technically, it's part of the heron family, but around here folks call them shikepokes."

She stared at him in silence, seemingly perplexed. "You know, you're different than I expected."

"Is that right? And what was it you expected?"

"I don't know. Where I'm from, we hear all sorts of things about people from the South, but I can see most of that isn't true."

"You mean like we're all ignorant, missing half our teeth, and married to our first cousins—stuff like that?"

She pressed a hand to her mouth to stifle her giggles. "Yeah, something like that."

"Well, as you can see, I have all my teeth, and while I may not be the sharpest knife in the drawer, I get by. And as far as the first-cousin thing, my parents were second cousins, so…"

Ellie's mouth fell open.

"I'm only kidding," he said, then laughed out loud. "And just so you know, you're not what I expected from a Yankee either."

Ellie swatted him playfully across the shoulder. "What's that supposed to mean?"

"That you'd have a funny accent and walk around with your nose stuck up in the air like you're better than everyone else. But that couldn't be further from the truth. Despite being the prettiest girl I've ever seen, you're very kind and funny and one of the most down-to-earth people I've ever met, and I really enjoy spending time with you." Jack looked away, watching the bird bank right and disappear behind the trees.

"Thank you," Ellie said thoughtfully. "That's sweet of you to say. And just so you know, I enjoy spending time with you too."

Meeting her gaze, something inside Jack shifted. The way she talked, the way she looked at him, deep into his eyes, gave him the impression that there was a genuine interest on her part, an interest that went beyond mere friendship.

When the sun went down, they returned to the dock and

put away the tackle. But instead of going home, they sat with their feet in the water, talking while the night closed in around them.

Ellie stared out at the water as pieces of silvery light danced on the surface. "Thank you for taking me on the water today and all the other days. I don't know what I would have done this summer if I hadn't met you."

"Don't mention it. Besides, I like having you with me. You're good company, Ellie, and I don't say that about many people. And just between you and me," he whispered, "you're a hell of a lot better to look at than George."

She laughed at his compliment, then, venturing a look in his direction, replied, "You're not so bad to look at either."

There was a moment when neither of them knew what to say or do next. Taking the initiative, Ellie scooted closer and held his hand.

Jack's pulse jumped. His eyes flickered to Ellie, then quickly away as all the blood in his body rushed to his head. At that moment, he wanted nothing more than to take her in his arms and kiss her, to tell her how he couldn't stop thinking about her, how when they were apart, his entire body ached. But when the courage wouldn't come, he sat there, staring at the water, realizing he'd let a golden opportunity slip through his fingers.

CHAPTER SIX

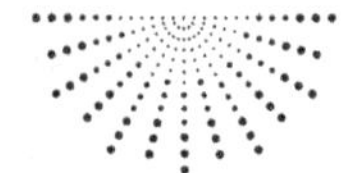

UNCHARTED WATERS

At first light, Jack went to see George.

"Mornin', JB." George opened the door ahead of him. "I wasn't expectin' to see you today. Everything okay?"

Jack nodded on his way in.

"There's some ham and a couple biscuits left if you want breakfast."

"You're not eating?"

"Already ate."

Jack fixed himself something to eat while George finished his coffee.

"So what's on your mind?"

"I was hoping to ask you a question, man to man."

George's brows shot up. "Sounds serious. Should I be sittin' for this?"

"Only if you want to." While Jack washed down the biscuit with a sip of tea, George leaned against the counter. "In your expert opinion, how do you know if a girl likes you? I mean, really likes you."

George's lips turned up in a smile. "First, let me be clear, when it comes to women, ain't no man an expert. Not even me. That said, the only sure-fire way to know if she likes you is to come out and ask, but I don't recommend that. I guess what I'm tryin' to say is, when it comes down to it, she either likes you or she don't."

Jack frowned. "So you're saying it's all about luck?"

"Luck ain't got nothin' to do with it," said George. "When it comes to likin' someone, to lovin' someone, it's all about what's in your heart. That don't mean we can't say and do things that push us closer together or further apart, but the attraction part, that comes natural, kinda like breathin'."

"So how can I tell if she's attracted to me?"

"I assume we're talkin' about Miss Ellie?"

Jack nodded.

"Well." George scratched his chin. "Given the time you two have been spendin' together lately, I'd say you got a better'n fifty-fifty chance."

Despite the odds being in his favor, Jack wasn't impressed.

"But if you want somethin' to really tip the scales, you gotta find the key to her heart."

Jack looked up. "How do I do that?"

"Well, for one thing, you can start by listenin'. When she talks, don't just pay attention to her words, but to what she's tryin' to tell ya. Women are complicated creatures. They speak a language few men understand. And second, you can't go wrong with an unexpected gift at an unexpected time. At least, that's what my daddy used to tell me."

"An unexpected gift at an unexpected time, huh?" Jack's mind went to work. "Thanks, George. I knew I could count on you."

* * *

Jack waited until church let out, then asked Ellie if she wanted to go to the island he'd been telling her about, the one with the arrowheads.

"I'd love to," she said. "Wait, I thought today was your day off."

"It is."

"Wouldn't you rather be fishing instead of wasting time with me?"

"Spending time with you isn't a waste, Ellie. And, no, there's no place I'd rather be."

Ellie took a moment to process. She'd received compliments before, mostly on her looks, but nothing like this. With his words, Jack had touched a place no hand could; he touched her heart. "Just give me a minute to get changed."

While he waited, Jack took in the view from Clara's back porch—the type of view he wanted for himself someday. But it would take more than ferrying people across the lake to make the kind of money he'd need to afford a place like Clara's.

"Well, well, well, if it isn't Jack Bennett. I was wonderin' when you might come around." Clara pulled him into a hug. "How are you, handsome?"

"Fine, Clara. How are you?"

"Fair to middlin'." She let go and gave him the once-over. "How's that mama of yours?"

"Fine. Thanks for asking."

"Still workin' for Mr. Sturgill, I gather?"

"Yes, ma'am. So how was church? Was Reverend Sykes spewing more of his fire and brimstone?"

Clara chuckled. "Not today. Believe it or not, today's message was about love."

Jack turned and stared at the mountains standing sentry over the blue lake waters below. "I'd almost forgotten how amazing the view is from here. Someday, I'm going to have me a view like this."

"I don't doubt that." She gazed out across the water. "So where are you and Ellie off to today? Flat Creek? Alley Ford? I saw George the other day, and he told me the stripe are runnin' over at Zimmerman's Shoals."

Jack shook his head and pointed north. "Muddy Creek. Ellie's been wanting to get her hands on an arrowhead ever since she got here, so I'm taking her to Parrott Island."

A crooked smile touched Clara's lips despite the wistful eyes. "Bill used to take me there when we were teenagers." She fell silent for a moment, then said, "Boy, do I have some fond memories of that island."

Ellie appeared then, stealing Jack's attention. "Ready?" She dropped the shades over her eyes.

Jack gave a nod and turned to Clara. "Well, it was nice seeing you again, and I promise to have her home at a reasonable hour tonight."

"You too, Jack. Y'all have fun and be careful."

Ellie then took him by the hand and led him off toward the woods.

"I had fun yesterday," she said when they were alone.

"So did I. And I have a feeling today will be even better."

Her eyes flickered to him. "Do you think we'll find an arrowhead?"

"Or two. Parrott Island is full of them. I can't wait for you to see it." He helped her cross the creek and led her out of the woods.

When they arrived at the dock, Ellie jumped in the boat and made herself comfortable while Jack grabbed the oars.

"How long will it take to get there?"

"An hour, give or take." Jack untied the lines and pushed off. "You okay with that?"

She leaned back on her hands and faced the sun. "I've got all day."

Jack started the engine and eased away from the dock. When they were a safe distance out, he increased the throttle. The nose pitched up, leveled out, and soon they were gliding effortlessly across the water.

They passed the point where Jack had caught countless striped bass with his grandparents, and Mama Holler where, when he was seven, he'd discovered schools of bream congregated around sunken trees. A little farther up, they motored past the island where he'd taken Ellie the first day they met. From there, the boat moved into uncharted territory, at least for Ellie. Jack had navigated that stretch of water many times, but not since the previous summer and never with a girl.

A little way up, where the channel narrowed, Jack eased back on the throttle. And as they coasted near the shore, something in the distance caught his eye.

"What's wrong?" Ellie asked as they turned and eased into the shadows.

"There," he whispered, pointing to a pair of birds hidden among the foliage. "Do you know what those are?"

She shook her head.

"They're mockingbirds. You can tell by the white on their belly and wings." He was silent for a moment, careful not to frighten them. "They're interesting birds. Would you like to hear about them?"

She nodded, transfixed by the pair.

"To protect their territory, mockingbirds mimic the songs

of other birds, not to mention insects, amphibians, and mechanical sounds."

Wonder filled her eyes.

"They're also excellent hunters, magicians in the air, and they mate for life. Even when they're apart for seasons at a time, they always find their way back to each other."

"How?"

"Some think it's the scent. Others believe they have an internal compass that guides them."

Ellie pulled her eyes away and looked at Jack. "What do you think?"

He grabbed an oar and pushed off the bank. "I think it has to do with the connection they make when they're young. Even though life takes them in separate directions, they always feel the need to return to one another. It's amazing if you think about it."

"And also kind of sad." Ellie glanced at the birds a final time. "But I guess that's life, isn't it?"

When the birds took to the sky, Jack started the engine and pushed farther upriver. A few miles ahead, a large island covered in tall trees grew out of the water.

Ellie put her palms on the hull and leaned into the wind. "Is that it?"

Jack nodded and maneuvered the boat into position. "Welcome to Parrott Island." He pointed the bow at a narrow strip of sandy beach. When he got close enough to see the bottom, he jumped out and guided the boat by hand. "It's peaceful here, isn't it?"

While Jack secured the boat to a nearby tree, Ellie pushed the sunglasses up into her hair and gazed out at the blue-green water. "It's beautiful. Thank you for bringing me here."

"You're welcome. Of all the islands on the lake, this one is my favorite."

"How'd you find it?"

"George sends me out exploring sometimes, looking for better places to take the tourists. I just happened upon this place by accident one afternoon and decided to check it out. So what would you like to do first?"

She glanced toward the woods. "How about we go exploring?"

"Okay." Jack took Ellie by the hand and led her up the hill to the woods. "Watch your step. This island's been known to have a copperhead or two."

"Copperhead? Are they poisonous?"

"Very."

They moved ahead, carefully stepping over rocks and branches. Ellie kept an eye out for snakes while Jack navigated the uneven terrain.

"Do you want to hear something crazy?" Ellie asked.

"Sure."

"Since I was a little girl, I've dreamed of getting married on an island like this."

"Really? I would have figured you for a church-wedding kind of girl."

"Don't get me wrong, church weddings are beautiful," said Ellie, "but also very traditional. An island, on the other hand, is exotic, adventurous, different. And it would have to be at night, a clear night, so everyone could look up and see the moon and stars."

"Of course." He mused that only she would come up with something like that. "But how would anyone see?"

"I don't know. Fire. Candles. I'd have to work out the details, but just imagine."

They walked on a few steps, side by side, while Jack considered the possibilities.

When they stepped into a clearing, Ellie broke from Jack. "Would you look at that? It's just like my dream." She ran ahead and stood beneath the gnarled branches of an old beech tree. "This is a natural arbor." She traced the shape of an arched branch that jutted from the trunk and extended to the ground. "It would be adorned with wildflowers, under which we could stand and exchange our vows." She grabbed Jack's hand and pulled him onto the small platform. "Do you, Ellie Spencer, take Jack Bennett to be your lawfully wedded husband? I do. And do you, Jack Bennett, take Ellie Spencer to be your lawfully wedded wife?"

"Um, sure," he answered awkwardly, playing along.

"And when there are no objections to us being married, the preacher will announce us as husband and wife." She gazed into his eyes. "Jack Bennett, please kiss your bride."

Jack hesitated, but only for a second. Summoning the courage that had eluded him the previous evening, he leaned forward and kissed Ellie as if they'd just been married—slowly, tenderly, lovingly.

When they parted, Ellie looked up at him, eyes wide with surprise. "That was... unexpected."

Jack's face flushed with embarrassment. "I'm sorry. I didn't mean to—"

"No, don't be. It was nice." A smile played about her lips.

Jack breathed a sigh of relief. "Has anyone ever told you that you have quite the imagination?"

Ellie cleared her throat. "As I said, it's only a dream." She stepped off the platform and stared longingly into the trees. "But dreams rarely come true, do they?"

Jack detected a hint of despair in her voice. "I suppose it

depends on the dream." He stepped off the platform and examined a pile of stones at the base of a tree. "Would you look at that?"

Ellie snapped her head around. "Is it a copperhead?"

Jack shook his head, recalling what George had told him about an unexpected gift. "Close your eyes."

"Jack, you know I don't like surprises."

"Trust me," he said.

When her eyes were shut, Jack placed a stone in Ellie's hands. "Now open them."

It took her a second to realize what she was holding. "Is that...?"

"An arrowhead." He smiled. "Told you we'd find one."

Ellie held it in the sunlight and examined the stone carefully, running her fingers along the chiseled edges. "A real true-to-life arrowhead," she beamed. "Just think. Someone was here, right here where we're standing. Gosh, I wonder what they were thinking when they made this?"

"The way you talk." Jack leaned against the tree, marveling at her.

"What, never heard a girl talk like me before?"

He shook his head, thinking that he wouldn't find another girl like Ellie if he lived to a hundred. "Never."

She smiled bashfully. "You're just saying that."

"No, I mean it. You're different, Ellie. Different in the most amazing way. I knew it the day we met. Sometimes when I'm around you I pinch myself to make sure I'm not dreaming."

She was quiet for a moment, then said, "You know I like you too, right? I realize we haven't known each other that long, but there's something about you that feels right."

"Must be the accent," he joked.

"That's part of it, no doubt." She took a breath, her expression shifting from cheerful to thoughtful. "But it's more than that. You're kind and gentle. I knew it the first time I looked into your eyes."

His brain fizzled. "Is that all?"

She took a step toward him, and he took a breath.

"And handsome," she said, letting her gaze linger over him.

His heart pounded in his chest. "And if I haven't said so before, I think you're the most beautiful girl I've ever seen."

She blushed. "Now I know you're joking."

He took her by the arm and looked deep into her eyes. "Not many people know this, but every night I go home and write in my journal. It's something I've done for years. And every night since we met, the only thing I write about is you. What I'm trying to say, Ellie, is that I think I'm falling in love with you."

Her face registered a look of shock. "Jack," she said breathlessly, "I—"

"It's okay. I don't expect you to feel the same way. I just know if I didn't say it now, I might not have the courage later."

"But that's just it. I think I'm falling in love with you too. And honestly, it scares me a little." She turned away.

"Don't be scared." He pulled her into a comforting embrace. "I'm right here, and I'm not going anywhere." Seizing the opportunity, he pressed his lips to hers, covering her in a long, warm kiss that left her short of breath.

When the kiss ended, Jack led Ellie to a bluff that overlooked a hidden cove. After stripping down to their bathing suits, they jumped in and spent the rest of the afternoon swimming in the cool water of the lagoon.

With the last rays of daylight dwindling, they toweled off and hiked back to the beach.

"Will we make it back before dark?" Ellie shimmied into her shorts and T-shirt.

Jack cast an eye to the west, noting the sun's position. "It'll be close, but don't worry. I know this lake like the back of my hand. Besides, if worse comes to worst, I'll use the stars as my guide."

As they pulled away from the island, Ellie looked back, reflecting on the afternoon. She'd gotten her arrowhead but also something far more precious. In Jack Bennett, she'd discovered her first true love.

CHAPTER SEVEN

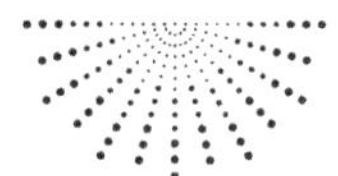

Afterglow

The following morning, Ellie looked up at the clouds that were threatening to rain at any minute and sighed. With her afternoon plans in jeopardy, she stayed in after her math lesson and waited for a break in the weather. Ellie had invited Sara to stay for lunch, so while Clara went to visit a neighbor, Ellie and Sara sat around the table, talking over a plate of deviled eggs and ham sandwiches.

"Are you enjoying your summer?" Sara asked.

"So far," said Ellie. "By the way, thank you for doing this. I'm sure there are a hundred things you'd rather be doing this summer besides helping me study."

"Think nothing of it. Besides, Clara is paying me, so it isn't all bad." She flashed a wry smile. "How are you keeping yourself busy in the afternoons?"

"Oh, you know, this and that. Clara's taken me to Dandridge a few times and to Knoxville, but mostly I stay around here."

"Have you been on the water yet?"

Ellie looked up sharply, wondering if Sara knew more than she was letting on. "A couple of times," she answered carefully.

"I may have told you, but Jack works down at the dock. If you're interested, maybe we could all go fishing sometime?"

"Um, yeah, maybe. So you and Jack are close?"

"Close as two friends can be. We've known each other since we were old enough to walk. I reckon he knows the water about as good as anyone around here. Says he wants to own his own business someday."

"You and Jack ever, you know…?"

Sara's face turned pink. "Heavens, no."

Ellie breathed a quiet sigh of relief.

"Well, I take that back. He did kiss me last summer, but I sort of got the impression he didn't like it much. He only did it once. I don't take it personal though. Jack's a bachelor, and I suspect he always will be."

"What makes you say that?"

"Jack's heart belongs to the water, always has, and probably always will. I'm not saying it's impossible, but I reckon it'd take a special girl to tear him away from it."

While Sara finished her lunch, Ellie turned and gazed out the window toward the water, wondering if she could be that girl.

* * *

The next morning while Clara was at the post office, Ellie received an unexpected phone call from her sister. She hadn't spoken to her since leaving for Tennessee.

"Amelia, it's good to hear your voice. How are you?"

"Good, sis. So how's Tennessee? Y'all bored yet?" A titter of laughter echoed through the phone.

"On the contrary." Ellie parted the drapes in the study, letting in a flood of bright morning sunlight.

"Do tell," said Amelia, her voice thick with intrigue.

"Well, for starters, I've been spending a lot of time on the water." Ellie gazed out the window toward the lake, peaceful and statue still. "They have a lake here that would take your breath away."

Amelia cackled into the phone. "You? On the water? Are you pulling my leg?"

"No. It's a lot of fun. I've been swimming, found an arrowhead, and there's this guy named Jack who taught me how to fish. He and I have been—"

"Hold on." Amelia stopped Ellie midthought. "Jack? Who's Jack? Is he cute?"

Realizing she'd said too much, Ellie tried to change the subject, but Amelia persisted.

"So he is cute," Amelia deduced. "All right, spill it."

"It's nothing... really." Ellie was thankful her sister couldn't see her face, which was now the shade of her dress. "Honest. Jack and I are just..." She wanted to say *friends*, but after professing her love for him on the island, she couldn't bring herself to lie.

"Just *what?*"

"Nothing." With a heavy sigh, Ellie plopped down into the chair behind the desk.

Amelia continued her interrogation. "Does this *Jack* have a last name?"

"Bennett."

Amelia mused aloud. "Elizabeth Bennett. Hmm. Does that make him your Mr. Darcy?"

"What?"

Amelia sighed. "Never mind. I forget you don't read

fiction." She went on. "So what else can you tell me about him? What does he look like? Is he tall? Is he handsome? I'll bet he has an accent. God, I knew I should have talked Mother into letting me come with you."

Ellie could hear the regret in her sister's voice as she tried to concentrate. But as the image of Jack appeared in her head, she found herself hopelessly lost in his hypnotic blue eyes.

"You still there?"

Ellie snapped out of it. "Hmm? Sorry. What were you saying?"

"I was asking what he looks like. Is he tall, short, skinny, fat? Is he like any of the guys around here?"

No, was Ellie's first reaction. "He's tall and strong," she finally said. "He spends most of his time on the water, so his skin is the color of summer."

"Sounds to me as if you like him?"

Ellie bit her lip to keep from smiling. "So what if I do? Are you going to tell Mother?"

"We're sisters," said Amelia, sounding as if Ellie's question had offended her. "I would never do that to you. So does this mean you have a crush on him?"

A crush. The thought seemed almost juvenile to Ellie. No, what she and Jack shared was more than just a crush. It was true love.

"I think it's more serious than that," she declared. "I think... well... I think I love him."

"Love?" whispered Amelia. "I've never heard you talk like that before."

"Which is why it must stay between us. If Mother finds out, there's no telling what she'll do." She took a breath and changed the subject. "Speaking of Mother, how are things at home?"

"You mean am I bearing the brunt of her fury in your absence?"

Ellie snickered. "Yes, that's exactly what I mean."

"She has her moments, but all in all, it's no worse than usual. Besides, I'm her favorite. It's you she doesn't like, remember."

Ellie cringed. "How could I forget?"

CHAPTER EIGHT

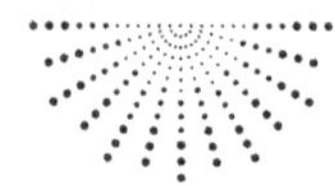

Dancing in the Dark

The next afternoon, Jack lay on his back, hands laced behind his head, staring into an endless blue sky. The day had been a bust all the way around. With enough passengers to fill only one tour, George closed early and lent Jack the boat. And since Ellie was out with Clara at the beauty shop, Jack drifted over to Finchum Hollow, where he anchored and swam alone. When he'd had his fill of the water, he catnapped in the shade and waited for the sun to go down.

As he lay there, drifting in and out of consciousness, Jack recalled the conversation with George at the beginning of summer. Despite George's prediction that Jack would never own a house on the hill, Jack was determined to prove him wrong. And now he had another dream to add to his list—someone with whom he could share the rest of his life. Someone like Ellie. And that's when an idea took root.

* * *

A few days later, Jack climbed the hill that overlooked the Union Grove Methodist Church and found a shady spot beneath a walnut tree. He took his time, enjoying a lunch of salt-cured ham with cornbread, and when he'd eaten his fill, he fed the rest to the birds, then leaned back against the tree and gazed at the cemetery below.

It wasn't long before he had company. "Hey there," Ellie shouted as she crested the hill.

"What a pleasant surprise. I thought you said you'd be in Dandridge this afternoon."

She stopped to catch her breath. "That was the plan, but we finished early, so I thought I'd come see what you were up to. I hope you don't mind. George told me where to find you."

"I don't mind." Jack offered her a spot on the ground beside him.

"What are you doing way out here by yourself?" she asked, taking in her surroundings.

"I come here to think," he said quietly. "And to talk to my brother." Jack raised his arm and pointed to a small headstone that sat in the shadow of an elm tree.

"You mean he's…" Ellie covered her mouth with her hand. "Jack, I-I didn't know. Would you rather I left you alone?"

He shook his head. "Actually, I'm glad you're here. I've been meaning to tell you."

Ellie was silent for a moment before speaking. "When did this happen?"

Jack drew a breath. "When I was twelve. Lewis—that was my brother's name—was nine at the time."

"So young. What happened to him?"

Jack took a breath before answering, steadying his nerves. "He drowned in the creek."

"I'm sorry, Jack. I can't imagine."

"The worst part is it was all my fault." Jack paused, recalling the events of that day. "When it happened, I was out there." Jack nodded toward the lake. "I was fishing with my mamaw and papaw. Lewis wanted to go with us, but I wouldn't let him because I thought he'd ruin my fishing trip. So he stayed behind and spent the morning playing in the woods below our house. When we got back to the dock that afternoon, George was on the verge of tears, and that's when I knew something was wrong. He pulled me aside and told me what had happened. After that, I don't remember much."

Ellie scooted closer and put her arm around Jack. They sat quietly for a few minutes, listening to the breeze as it shook the leaves above them.

"Don't be so hard on yourself," said Ellie. "Sometimes it's difficult for us to comprehend God's plan, especially when it involves the death of someone so young. But God put Lewis here for a reason, and he called him home for a reason, and if you believe there's a God in heaven, and I do with all my heart, you must trust that he knows what he's doing."

"Mama says the same thing," said Jack. "But I can't help but think that if I hadn't been so selfish, Lewis would still be here."

A few seconds passed. Then Ellie stood and gathered a handful of wildflowers. "Do you mind if I lay these on his grave to pay my respects?"

Jack shook his head and observed Ellie as she descended the hill. She stopped near the headstone, placed the flowers on the grave, appeared to whisper a few words, then returned to Jack.

"I'm sorry for being such a downer," he said. "Sometimes, I just need to be here, to feel close to him. I feel like I owe him that much."

"Don't apologize. He was your brother. Besides, if anyone

should apologize, it's me. If I'd known why you were here, I never would have disturbed you."

Jack circled his arms around Ellie's waist and pulled her close to him. "But I'm glad you did. Aside from me, Mama, George, and Clara, you're the only person that's come to see him since the funeral. That means more to me than you know."

* * *

The next evening, Ellie slipped out onto the side porch and read until sunset. Between tutoring, and running errands with Clara, these were the first moments she'd had to herself all day.

"Whatcha reading?"

Ellie looked up with a start. "Jack, what are you doing here?"

"You didn't think I'd let an entire day go by without seeing you, did you?" He glanced at the book in her hands. "Anything I'd be interested in?"

"Not unless you find a detailed scientific account of star creation fascinating."

"Can't say that I do." Jack cracked a smile, putting one foot on the step as he leaned against the porch post. "I don't suppose I could talk you into taking a break, could I?"

She felt the slightest twitch at the edges of her mouth. "That depends. What did you have in mind?"

"There's something I want to show you." Jack nodded toward the woods. "But if you choose to come with me you have to promise to be very quiet."

She could tell he was up to something. "Why not," she said, intrigued. "Just let me tell Clara where I'm going."

At the edge of the yard, instead of turning left toward the

lake, Jack veered right, venturing down a path unfamiliar to Ellie.

"I've never been this way before," she said as she followed Jack into the woods.

"Don't worry, it isn't far," he reassured her.

"I don't have to worry about copperheads, do I?"

"Not this time."

Deep in the woods, the path ended at the edge of a small pond surrounded by tall trees and thick brush.

"What is this place?" Ellie whispered.

"One of my favorite places in the whole world." Jack stepped forward and peered through an opening in the trees.

"Is this what you wanted to show me?"

Jack made a fist with his left hand, covered it with the right, then pressed them against this mouth. He blew into the opening between his thumb and forefinger until it produced a series of raspy, quacking sounds.

A few seconds later, a female mallard duck emerged from the thick cover and glided cautiously toward the center of the pond. A trail of ducklings followed in her wake.

"Look at them," said Ellie, leaning forward.

"Hold out your hand." Jack reached into his pocket and pulled out a bag of oats and cracked corn.

"No bread?"

Jack shook his head. "Believe it or not, bread can hurt them. This is more like the food they forage for in the wild." He grabbed a fistful of oats and corn and placed it in Ellie's hand. "Go ahead."

She took a step and tossed the mixture into the pond. Almost immediately, the ducks began pecking at the water.

"Watch them go," she beamed. "How did you find this place?"

While the ducks ate, Jack sat down in the grass and pulled his knees to his chest. "After Lewis died, I needed a place to hide, a place I couldn't be found. One day, while I was walking through the woods, I stumbled upon this place."

Ellie sat down beside him, keeping her eyes on the ducklings. "I can see why you like it here; it's so peaceful." She turned and looked at him. "Do you come here often?"

"A couple nights a week. The mama duck—Daisy—I rescued her a couple of years ago from the mouth of an old mutt and brought her here so she could heal. I fed her every night for almost two months. Ever since, she's come back here to lay her eggs, so I kinda feel obligated to make sure she and her ducklings are taken care of."

"That's awfully nice of you."

"It's the least I can do. Besides, it gives me time to sit and think about how I'm going to make my fortune, so I can afford that house on the hill."

Ellie cracked a smile. "Anyone else know about this place?"

Jack shook his head.

"Not even Sara?"

Jack shot her a look. "No. No one knows, except me, and now you." He stood and pitched the last of the feed into the water, then cast an eye to the sky. "It'll be dark soon. You ready to head back?" He pulled Ellie to her feet and led her out of the woods.

"Thank you," she said when they reached the porch, "for taking me to the pond."

"You're welcome." Jack stopped at the foot of the stairs. "I'm glad you're here, Ellie. Far and away, this has been the best summer of my life."

Ellie stepped off the porch and into Jack's arms. "I'm glad I'm here too," she whispered, then kissed him. "Listen, I know you have to get up early, but why don't you stay awhile? Clara made a cobbler just this afternoon, and there's plenty to go around."

"Cobbler, huh? What about ice cream? You can't have cobbler without ice cream."

A grin sprang across her face. "You know better than to ask a question like that."

Jack returned with a smile of his own. "In that case, lead the way."

Inside, Clara sat in the living room, listening to the latest broadcast of the *Adventures of Ozzie and Harriet*. "Evening, Jack."

"Evening, Clara."

"I see Ellie talked you into staying for cobbler and ice cream."

"Yes ma'am."

"It didn't take much convincing." Ellie flashed a grin at Jack on her way to the kitchen. After cutting the cobbler and spooning the ice cream into bowls, she handed one to Jack, then led him out onto the porch. "It's a nice night, isn't it?"

"Yes, it is." Jack took in the moon and stars. "Thanks again for asking me to stay. Clara's cobbler is hard to resist."

"My pleasure. Say, Jack, do you think it would be all right if I came to see you during the day, and maybe joined you for a tour or two? I promise not to get in the way."

He appeared thrown by her question. "I don't see why not. But why the sudden interest?"

"I don't know. It gets awfully lonely up here in this big house, and I figured it would give us a chance to spend more time together."

"Fine with me." He took a bite of cobbler. "Hey, do you hear that?"

Ellie listened quietly as *The Tennessee Waltz* played on the radio.

"That's one of my favorite tunes."

"Maybe we should dance."

"I would." Jack's face turned red. "But I don't know how."

"Don't worry. I'll show you." She took him by the hand and led him to the center of the porch. "Put your hands here," she said, placing them on her hips. "Yeah, like that. Now, eyes on me."

Jack raised his eyes and met her gaze.

When she'd circled her arms around his neck, she said, "Just do what I do, okay."

Jack followed her lead, moving as she moved, letting the music direct him where to go. It took a moment, but eventually he found the rhythm.

"See, nothing to it."

As they swayed to the gentle melody, Ellie realized for the first time that Jack was different from anyone she had ever met. He was wild, untamed. A little rough around the edges, but she figured these would smooth with time. In Jack she saw an equal, a partner, someone with whom she could share her most private thoughts without fear of judgment.

When the song ended, and they'd finished their desserts, Ellie walked Jack to the door. "I had fun tonight," she said, stopping on the porch.

"So did I." He gave a deeply contented sigh. "I wish every night could be like this."

She offered a sweet smile. "Maybe it can," she said, then kissed him goodnight.

CHAPTER NINE

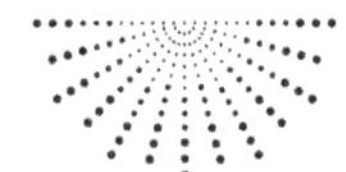

Lightning in a Bottle

The next evening, Jack and Ellie sat on Clara's swing, taking in the sunset.

"So what do you want to do when you get older?"

Jack considered that as he stared off toward the mountains. "I want to be a writer."

"Really? I would never have guessed."

"Why's that?"

"I don't know. I guess I picture writers as always so sad and serious."

Jack tore a few blades of grass, thinking that between the deaths of his father and brother, and the fact that he was poor as dirt, he had plenty of sorrow from which to draw. "My dream is to write the next great American novel, like *The Adventures of Huckleberry Finn* or *The Grapes of Wrath.*"

"So what is it about writing that interests you? The fame? The fortune? Both?"

"I'm not that interested in the fame, but the fortune sure would be nice. That way Mama could quit her job, and I could live right here on the hill, just like Clara. It's all I've ever wanted—that, and to be able to fish anytime the mood strikes me. Probably sounds boring to you, but to me it's heaven on earth."

Ellie looked east toward the mountains. "Actually, that sounds rather peaceful," she said, which caught Jack's attention. "But won't being a writer require you to go to college?"

"Not necessarily. William Faulkner didn't go to college. Neither did Mark Twain. And look what they were able to accomplish."

Ellie smiled amusedly. "I suppose you're right. But what if writing doesn't work out? What then? Would you ever consider something practical, like a doctor or lawyer?"

Jack frowned. "I don't got the money to afford the schooling for something like that, and even if I did, I doubt I'm smart enough."

"Don't underestimate yourself. I think you're a lot smarter than you give yourself credit for. Just because you're not filthy rich and haven't traveled the world doesn't mean you're not smart. Why, I know plenty of people where I'm from that have loads of money and have been all over the world, and they're as dumb as a sack of potatoes."

Jack chuckled. "So you really think I'm smart?"

"Yes, I do," she said, looking earnest. "And never let anyone tell you otherwise, you hear?"

As night fell, they got up and eased toward the porch.

"Did I tell you Clara's taking me to see the fireworks in Knoxville next week?"

"That sounds exciting." He walked on a few steps. "I've never been to see fireworks."

Ellie stopped and looked at him. "What? Well, that settles it. You're coming with us."

"Oh, I don't know. I wouldn't want to impose."

"You wouldn't be imposing," she insisted. "And I'm sure Clara wouldn't mind you tagging along. At least let me ask her. Please?" She looked up at him and poked out her lips.

"All right." Jack found her irresistible. "If Clara says it's okay, then count me in."

Ellie gave him a peck on the cheek. "Then consider it a date."

* * *

At supper, Jack hardly touched his food. He was too busy thinking about Ellie to concentrate on the meat loaf his mama had prepared.

"Is it not any count?"

Her words brought Jack out of his stupor. "Sorry, Mama. It's delicious."

"Somethin' on your mind, JB?"

He nodded.

"Ellie?"

He nodded again.

"I figured." Helen put down her fork and stared at him from across the table. "I remember what it was like when I first fell in love with your daddy. I don't think I ate or slept for a week."

"I just want to be with her all the time," said Jack. "And when we're apart, it's like every bone in my body aches." He stared at the floor, consumed by loneliness.

"I know the feeling. It's like being caught in a tornado, isn't it? One minute the world makes sense. The next you're spinning on your head. But Jack," she said, looking serious, "summer won't last forever. Have you thought about what will happen when she leaves?"

Jack wanted to believe that spending one summer with Ellie was enough to form a bond unbreakable by time or distance, but he wasn't naive enough to think that every guy with half a heartbeat wouldn't be chasing after her when she returned to school. Sure, she could fight them off for a while, but eventually, one of them would catch her eye, a guy who was better-looking than him, with more money, more education, more… everything.

"Honestly, I try not to think about it."

"I understand, but you need to prepare yourself. Whether you like it or not, the day is coming when Ellie must go."

The next day, Jack went to see Ellie during his lunch break. Despite the low odds of them staying together once the summer concluded, he wasn't ready to throw in the towel just yet.

"Morning, Jack." Clara came out to greet him. "What brings you by?"

Jack took off his ball cap and ran a hand through his hair. "I came by to see if Ellie was home. There's something I wanted to ask her."

"She and Sara are just wrapping up. You're more than welcome to wait for her."

Jack checked the time. "Thank you."

"George got you working hard today?"

"Yes, ma'am. I've already made one trip, and we got two more this afternoon."

"You keep that up, and you'll be a rich man, sure enough."

"Jack." Sara stepped out onto the porch, flashing a toothy grin. "What are you doing here?"

"Oh hey, Sara. Long time no see. I came by to talk to Ellie."

"Oh." The smile faded from her face. "I've been meaning to congratulate you on catching that lunker a while back. George told me all about it."

"Thanks, but I didn't catch it. Ellie did. First cast too."

"Is that so?"

Jack detected a hint of jealousy.

"I didn't realize she knew how to fish."

"She didn't until I taught her."

"How nice of you," Sara said with a mocking smile. "Well, perhaps you could show me where you caught it sometime. I've been dying to get out on the water."

"You know where it is," Jack said. "It's up at the head of Muddy Creek, near the bridge. I took you there last summer, remember?"

Sara frowned. "Oh yeah. Must have forgot."

When Ellie came out, Sara slipped away without Jack noticing.

"So what's the real story with you two?" Ellie asked as they stepped off the porch.

"What do you mean?"

"I see the way she looks at you when you come around, all googly-eyed."

Jack held her hand and rolled his eyes. "I made the mistake of taking her fishing last summer."

"Fishing, huh? Is that all?"

Wondering what she was driving at, Jack narrowed his brow.

They crossed the yard and stopped at the overlook. "I heard it was a little more than just fishing. Rumor has it you kissed her."

Heat flooded his face. "Is that what she told you? She's

lying," he said defensively. "I didn't kiss her. She kissed me. But it was just the one time, promise."

"Relax." Ellie lowered herself into the swing. "I believe you. Besides, I didn't even know you then, so what difference does it make?"

"I guess you're right." He breathed a sigh of relief. "Wait. She's not jealous, is she… of us?"

"If she is, she hasn't said anything to me. Not that she would. I mean, we're not best friends or anything. And besides, I never told her we were together. Did you?"

Jack shook his head. "But she's not blind either. I imagine she's put two and two together by now."

"Even so, a girl like Sara wouldn't say anything to anyone, especially not me. She'd just sit and stew over it. I don't understand folks like that, letting things eat away at them. I prefer to get it out in the open, attack it head on."

"I know what you mean," said Jack. "I'm the same way. Mama always says never to let things fester."

"Your mama sounds like a smart woman."

"She is. You'd like her." Jack paused as he tossed around an idea in his head. "Speaking of that, if I were to invite you to supper at my house, with me and Mama, would you come?"

Ellie beamed. "Of course I would, and I'd love to meet your mama."

Relief brought a smile to his face. "I was hoping you'd say that. How about this Friday?"

"Friday is good," she said.

"Great. I'll come by and get you around six."

* * *

Friday, after work, Jack escorted Ellie to his place for supper.

"I like your dress," he said as they walked up the drive.

"Thank you. My father bought it for me when I got home from school. This is the first time I've had a chance to wear it. I hope it's not too much."

"No, you look beautiful."

When they reached the porch, Jack jumped ahead and opened the door for her. "I'm back," he shouted.

Helen appeared then and greeted Ellie. "Well my, my, my. You must be Ellie, the one my JB keeps goin' on about."

"Yes, ma'am," said Ellie politely. "It's a pleasure to meet you, Mrs. Bennett."

"Please call me Helen." She pulled Ellie into a hug and then stepped back to admire her. "You're right," she said to Jack. "She's as pretty as a picture."

Jack flushed with embarrassment.

"Supper will be ready shortly," Helen said on her way back to the kitchen. "Why don't you show her into the living room, JB, and I'll call you when it's ready."

Jack did what he was told and offered Ellie a seat.

"I don't know why," Ellie whispered, pressing the wrinkles out of her dress, "but I'm nervous tonight."

Jack held her hand. "Don't be. It's just supper. Besides, I can tell she likes you."

"Maybe I should see if I can help her." Ellie stood and went into the kitchen. "I could help, Helen," Jack heard her say.

"You know your way around the kitchen?"

"Yes, ma'am. My mother says I'm an expert with a knife. I can peel, cut, chop, and mince."

"Well, all right. In that case, there're some potatoes on the counter that could use some attention."

While Ellie peeled and chopped the potatoes, Jack stood in the opening of the kitchen and quietly observed. Now and then, when Helen wasn't looking, Ellie would steal a glance at him and smile. And somewhere between the mashing of potatoes and frying of fish, Jack realized the feeling simmering inside wasn't just the excitement of his first kiss or the second or the tenth. For the first time in his life, Jack Bennett knew what it meant to be in love.

When the last piece of catfish finished frying, they sat down to supper.

"So Ellie, Jack tells me you want to be a college professor—something to do with the stars...?"

Ellie wiped the corners of her mouth before answering. "Yes, ma'am, I do. I've always wanted to teach, and given my fascination with the celestial, I figure it's the perfect occupation."

"Well, I don't know nothin' about bein' a professor, but seems to me it'd be pretty tough. How much schoolin' do you need for somethin' like that?"

"Quite a bit. Once I finish my undergraduate, there's two years of graduate school, and another year to get my PhD. So if everything goes according to plan, I should be teaching by the time I'm twenty-five."

"And how old are you now?"

"Nineteen."

"Six more years." Concern creased her forehead. "Well, God bless you, honey. I admire your ambition."

As the conversation continued, Jack listened quietly, contemplating where he fit in Ellie's plans. She had at least the next six years mapped out, if not more. He, on the other hand, couldn't say where he would be in six months. And for the first time since falling in love with Ellie, Jack wondered if he wasn't fighting a battle he was ill equipped to win.

* * *

After supper, Ellie joined Jack on a walk back to Clara's.

"You were right," she said as they strolled along the wooded path. "Your mama is a special lady."

"She sure took a liking to you," he said, taking in the moon and stars.

"You think?"

He nodded and his eyes drifted to her. "It was nice to see her enjoying herself. Sometimes I worry about her. She's had to deal with a lot in her forty years."

They walked on, her beside him.

"Can I ask you something?"

"You can ask me anything," said Jack.

"I noticed you had a lot of crosses on the walls at your place, but you don't go to church. How come?"

With a grimace, Jack said, "I used to, but after Daddy died and then Lewis, Mama stopped taking me. I guess she got angry at God."

"Were you mad at God too?"

Jack considered her question before answering. "I don't reckon so. After all, it wasn't God's fault they died."

"I know a lot of people back home who would disagree with you. They like to blame God for everything."

"The way I see it," Jack mused, "God gives us life and a brain in our head so we can make decisions. What we choose to do beyond that point is up to us, as well as the consequences that go along with it."

Ellie stopped and thought about that. "Does that mean you don't believe in fate or destiny?

"Daddy used to say that our fate was written in the stars,

but I don't believe that. I like to think we're the authors of our own destiny."

A smile brushed her lips. "I like that." Ellie walked on a few steps, then said, "I'm somewhere in the middle, I think. I believe in free will, but I also think some of us are destined to do certain things. Take me for example—I know I'm destined to be an astronomer. I can feel it in my bones."

"The same way I believe I'll have a house on the hill," said Jack.

"Exactly." They walked on silently before Ellie continued. "You were quiet tonight. Was everything okay?"

"Sometimes I get that way when I'm thinking."

"What were you thinking about?"

Jack stopped at a bend in the path and took Ellie by the hands. "I came to a realization tonight while I was watching you and Mama make supper."

"And what was that?" she said, gazing into his eyes.

"That you're the kind of girl I want to spend the rest of my life with."

Ellie was so shocked that it took several seconds before she could speak. "Jack, I-I'm flattered, but—"

"Relax, I'm not proposing, but I want you to know how I feel. All my life I've heard people talk about the feeling they get when they meet the person they're supposed to spend the rest of their life with. I never really understood what they were talking about until tonight. Watching you and Mama laughing and working together made me realize that I could search the rest of my life and never find anyone like you. You're one in a million, Ellie. One in a billion. And someday, when the time is right, I'm going to ask you to marry me."

Ellie's lip quivered, and she looked as if she might cry. "Jack, I don't know what to say."

"You don't have to say anything. Just promise me something."

"Anything."

"No matter what happens or where life takes us, you and I will always come back to each other, like those mockingbirds I was telling you about."

"Just like mockingbirds," she promised, then kissed him with tears in her eyes.

CHAPTER TEN

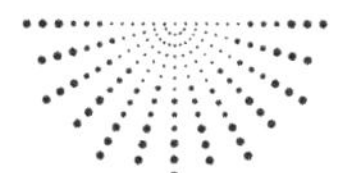

Fireworks

Jack stood in front of the mirror, debating whether the new outfit he'd bought the day before was adequate for his date with Ellie.

"Mama, what do you think?"

From the doorway, Helen took inventory of him. "Mighty handsome if I do say so myself. You look more like your daddy every day."

After dabbing on some of his daddy's old cologne, Jack stepped onto the porch just as Clara's green Chevrolet turned up the drive.

"They're here," he yelled back into the house. "Be back later."

Ellie opened the door from the inside, and Jack climbed in.

"Well, look at you." She gave him the once-over. "New threads?"

"Yep. Got them yesterday," he said as the car pulled away. "Do you think I look all right?"

"Better than all right." She gave him another look.

"That outfit must have cost you a pretty penny," Clara commented from the front seat.

"Eight dollars, after tax," said Jack. "Shoes and all. Muriel cut me a deal."

When they arrived at the fairgrounds, Jack grabbed the picnic basket and led them to a spot on the hill where they'd have a decent view of the fireworks.

"You two go and have some fun before the fireworks begin," Clara advised as she made herself comfortable.

"Do you want us to bring you anything?" asked Jack.

"I'll take a pop and a bag of kettle corn if you can find it." Clara reached inside her purse and handed Jack a ten-dollar bill. "Go crazy." She winked at him.

Jack took Ellie to the dunking booth, the carousel, and the Ferris wheel, and when they were done, they spent some time playing carnival games.

"I'm glad you talked me into this," said Jack as they strolled toward the concession area. "I'm having fun."

Ellie grinned. "So am I."

Jack found a quiet spot between the tents and pulled Ellie into a kiss.

"What if Clara sees?"

Jack scanned the crowd. "I think we're good," he said, then kissed her again.

Parting, Ellie checked the time. "Come on. The fireworks will be starting soon."

Jack found a stand selling kettle corn, so he stood in line while Ellie waited at the pavilion. When he'd paid for the corn, Jack circled back to get her, and as he approached, he noticed a young man—tall, broad-shouldered, wearing a letterman's jacket—hovering over Ellie.

"Can I help you?"

The young man snapped his head around at Jack. "Beat it, man. Can't you see the lady and I are having a conversation."

"The lady's with me," Jack said, stepping between them.

The young man appeared taken aback. "Who are you, her boyfriend?"

"As a matter of fact, I am." Jack took Ellie's hand and led her out of the pavilion.

But instead of ending there, the young man stalked them across the fairgrounds, taunting Ellie with whistles and catcalls.

"Just keep walking," said Ellie.

Jack tried his best to ignore the young man, but when he screamed an obscenity at them, Jack had heard enough. He turned on his heel and glared at the young man. "Didn't I tell you to back off?" He was angry now, unable to suppress the rage building inside him.

Ellie tugged at his arm. "Let's go, Jack."

The young man mocked him. "Yeah, Jack, walk away before someone gets hurt. And by someone, I mean you." He pressed a finger into Jack's chest.

But Jack had never backed down from a fight, and he wasn't going to start now. They stood toe-to-toe, the young man towering over him. Jack surveyed the crowd, which had taken notice. But before he passed the point of no return, Jack thought of Ellie, so instead of making a scene, he backed away, hoping that would bring the conflict to an end.

But the young man persisted. "That's right, Jackie," he mocked. "Walk away, you coward."

Jack stopped and glanced at Ellie. Seeing the fear in her eyes, he knew the only option he had was to fight. Jack turned around and rolled up his sleeves. When the young man was within striking distance, Jack threw a quick right that landed squarely on the side of his face. A gasp went up from the onlookers. The young man staggered back a few steps, shook himself, then returned with a right of his own. Jack took it like a man, but his mouth was numb from the impact. He drew a hand across his lip and saw blood. Shaking the cobwebs, Jack lunged forward and tackled the other man to the ground.

They rolled around, each struggling to gain the advantage. Finally, after outmaneuvering the young man, Jack got the upper hand and landed a flurry of punches. When it was all over, the young man lay unconscious, bleeding from his mouth and nose.

But Jack's victory was short-lived as the sound of police whistles stole his attention.

"Jack, come on," Ellie urged as the police converged on the scene. She pulled him to his feet, and they disappeared into the crowd.

By the time they found Clara, Jack's shirt was stained with blood. Ellie got a towel while Clara fetched some ice.

Exhausted, Jack sat down and shook his head. "I'm sorry, Ellie."

"Don't be. There was nothing you could do. I'm just sorry about your lip. Can I see?"

He removed the towel, and she examined the injury. "Does it hurt?"

"A little." Now that the adrenaline had worn off, there was an intense throbbing.

Clara returned then with a bag of ice and handed it to Ellie.

"Tilt your head back," Ellie directed him. "Mother's a nurse, and she's shown me what to do in situations like this."

Jack did as he was told and gazed into the darkening sky.

* * *

On the drive home, Jack felt better. But now that he'd had time to process, he regretted letting his temper get the better of him.

When Clara stopped in front of Jack's house, he got out, and Ellie walked him to the door.

"Listen," he said, when they reached the porch, "I want to apologize again for the way I acted tonight. I should never have let my anger get the better of me. You probably think I'm a heathen, don't you?"

Ellie laughed. "No. Besides, it wasn't your fault. That oversized buffoon is the one that started it. I know you were only protecting me."

"Still, I should have walked away. Fighting isn't always the answer."

"You're right," said Ellie. "It isn't always the answer, but sometimes it is. When we're pushed beyond our limits, fighting is the only option we have left. Anyway, I had a good time tonight, so if you're worried that you ruined the evening, you didn't." Ellie glanced over her shoulder. "I should go. I don't want to keep Clara waiting too long. Good night, Jack," she said, then kissed him carefully on his lips. "And take care of that lip. We've still got plenty of kissing to do before summer's over." She winked, then turned and headed for the car.

CHAPTER ELEVEN

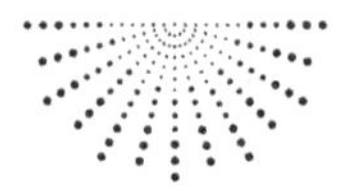

A Silver Lining

"Long night. You want a cup of tea?

"Thank you." Ellie discarded her purse in the living room on her way to Clara's kitchen.

"Coming right up."

Ellie took off her jewelry and changed into her pajamas before making her way to the back porch. When the tea was ready, Clara joined her.

"There we are," said Clara. She handed a cup to Ellie. "You might want to let that cool a minute." She sat down and kicked up her feet. "Tonight was fun, wasn't it?"

"Yes, it was."

"I haven't seen fireworks like that since your uncle Bill was alive."

"The grand finale was amazing," said Ellie.

"I wasn't talking about those fireworks," said Clara, eyeing her over the brim of her cup.

"Oh." Ellie's smile faded into a frown. "I feel terrible for Jack. His new shirt is probably ruined. Not to mention his lip is busted."

"Don't worry about Jack," said Clara. "He's tough. Besides, the blood will come out in the wash. And as far as his lip goes, it'll heal in a few days." She took a sip of tea before continuing. "So when were you going to tell me about you and Jack?"

"What do you mean?"

Clara raised an eyebrow at her. "This ain't my first rodeo, darlin'. Men, especially young ones, don't risk their lives for just anyone."

Clara was more observant than Ellie realized. After gathering her thoughts, she put down her tea. "I suppose it just sort of happened. Neither of us planned it."

Clara chuckled. "Well, of course you didn't. That's the way it works, hon. One minute you're riding around, talking, having a good time, and the next you've given your heart away without even knowing it. That's the magic and the misery of falling in love."

"Is that how it was with you and Uncle Bill?"

Clara nodded. "Your uncle was a wonderful man. Country as all get out, but a wonderful man. And crazy as hell about me. There wasn't anything that man wouldn't have done for me. You know, Jack reminds me a lot of him."

Ellie felt a rise in her cheeks. "He's special, isn't he?"

"Yes, he is."

"Honestly, I don't think I've ever met anyone like him. But I worry about what Mother and Father will think. He's nothing like the fellas back home."

Clara sighed. "It's funny. When I was your age, my mama and daddy wouldn't let me talk to a boy without one of them being present."

"That must have been awkward."

"Yes, it was. But there was this one boy I was fond of, and

he liked me too. He used to come by the house after everyone had gone to bed and throw rocks at my window. I must have been about seventeen at the time. In those days, your mother and I shared a room, so I'd have to get her to promise not to tell on me. Anyway, me and this boy would sneak out for a couple of hours and kiss in the woods behind the house. God, we felt so grown up. It was exciting doing something we knew was wrong."

"Whatever happened to this boy? Did your parents find out?"

"Eventually. And they forbid me from seeing him."

"What did you do?"

"The only thing I could do. I married him."

"You mean the boy was Uncle Bill?"

"That's right. When he found out what my parents had done, he got a ring and proposed the next day. I think he did it partially to snub his nose at them, but I also think he wanted to impress them, to show them he was serious about being with me. I'm telling you this because tonight I saw that same look in your eyes when you were caring for Jack. And in his eyes, I saw the same look your uncle used to give me. But your situation is different than mine," Clara added as her expression became serious. "You and Jack come from two very different worlds with different expectations. Your uncle and I didn't have those obstacles."

"What are you saying?"

"I'm saying you need to be careful. Jack Bennett is the kind of young man who would lay down his life for you and wouldn't think twice about doing it. I mean, look at what happened tonight. That boy was twice Jack's size, and things could have easily gone the other way. I just don't want to see him get hurt, not just physically, but in here." She put a hand to her heart. "Or you for that matter."

Ellie turned and stared into the darkness.

"I know you don't want to think about it right now, especially when you're having so much fun, but summer will be over in a few weeks. Before you know it, you'll be back in school, and Jack will still be here. Then what?"

Ellie shrugged without meeting Clara's eyes. "We can write and talk over the phone, and..."

"Sure, sure." Clara nodded along. "And how long will that last?"

For the first time since summer began, Ellie felt a pang of loneliness, as though everything she and Jack had worked to build was in vain.

"There's always next summer and the summer after that." Ellie was determined to remain optimistic. "And who knows? Maybe Jack could visit at Thanksgiving or Christmas or both." But even as she said it, she had the sinking feeling she wasn't being realistic, that her love for Jack Bennett, as strong as it was, might not be enough.

"I didn't mean to upset you," said Clara. "I wanted you to be aware, that's all. When it comes to matters of the heart, you can't be too careful."

CHAPTER TWELVE

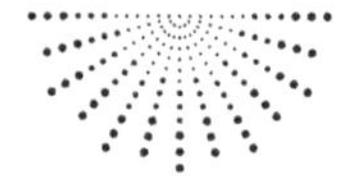

Stardust

One evening while drifting toward the dam, Jack watched Ellie twist her fingers together. "It won't do any good to keep it bottled up inside."

She looked up and grinned. "Sorry. I was just thinking."

He switched off the motor and let the boat drift with the current.

"There's something I've been meaning to talk to you about."

Jack scooted closer and waited for her to continue, not sure he wanted to hear what he feared was coming.

"It's just that summer will be over in a few weeks, and I was wondering what that means for *us*?"

"I don't know," he answered glumly. "I love you, Ellie, more than anything in the world, and I'd do anything to have you here with me all the time, but you've got your life to go back to. The only thing I know to do is write and talk over the phone."

"What about a visit? You could come see me at school.

Indiana isn't that far away, and who knows, maybe I can make spending summers here a regular thing."

"I'd love that," said Jack, though he couldn't trust her optimism. "But what happens when you meet someone new, someone better?"

"I won't."

"Come on, Ellie. We both know I can't compete with the fellas you go to school with. You said it yourself. They're destined to be doctors and lawyers. The only thing I'm destined to be is poor." Jack hung his head.

Ellie's face twisted in agony. "Just because you're not going to college doesn't mean you won't be a great man. My father once told me that a person's success isn't measured by money but by what his family thinks of him. Like I told you before, money and status aren't everything. Not to me." She took his hand in hers. "What you and I have is special, and I want it to last. And if you're worried about me being faithful, don't. My word is my bond, and I promise that no one will come between us."

And there it was again, the hope Jack had come to rely on Ellie for.

For the rest of the summer, Ellie and Jack were inseparable. During the day, she was by his side, joining him on his afternoon tours. And in the evenings, when work was over, they'd fish and scour the islands or find a secluded cove where they could be alone.

As July melted into August, Jack and Ellie realized their summer was ending, so they tried desperately to hold on to what time remained.

"When do you go to work at the mill?" she asked him one evening as they trolled along the edge of the sandbar.

"As soon as the weather turns." He checked his line. "When's the first day of school?"

"The twenty-first, but I'll have to move in a couple of days before just to get settled."

Jack was silent for a moment. "Did you ask your parents if you could come back next summer?"

"Not yet, but I will, when the time is right. Did you give any more thought to visiting me in Indiana?"

"I spoke to George about it, and he says I can catch a bus in Knoxville, and it'll take me all the way to Bloomington."

"Really?"

"Yep, and the best part is it'll only cost me twenty dollars for the round trip."

"That's not so bad," said Ellie. "Oh, I hope you can come. I can't wait to show you off to my friends. Marjorie and Susan will be green with envy."

Jack smiled, thinking of what it might be like to meet Ellie's friends. "That reminds me." He grabbed a bottle from beneath the seat and handed it to Ellie.

"What's this?"

"Just a little something to take home when you leave. I got one of George's old bottles and filled it with sand and pebbles from the lakeshore. That way, wherever life takes you, you'll always have a piece of this place close by."

Jack's gesture cost nothing, but it was the sweetest gift anyone had ever given her. "Thank you. I'll keep it with me always."

* * *

That night, the sky was clear, and the moon and stars shone brightly overhead.

"It's a perfect night for fishing." Jack reached into the live well and retrieved the box of night crawlers. Using the light from the lantern, he baited their hooks and dropped a line in the water. "Hang this lantern over the side." He handed it off to Ellie. "Fish are attracted to the light."

She did as he directed, and in no time, she'd caught a bass.

"You know, I had no idea I'd like this place so much," said Ellie. "It's so much different than home."

"How so?"

"Well, for starters, there's no lake, no mountains, and no…" She turned to face him. "You."

Jack smiled. "How do you spend your time, when you're not studying?"

"Well, Mother and Father entertain a lot, so there's always a house full of people. But I spend most of my time with friends or my sister. She and I are extremely close."

"Do you miss that world?"

"Not when I'm with you," she answered, staring at his face in the moonlight. "You make me forget all about my other life."

Jack stared into the darkness, recalling the day they met. "I'll never forget the first time I saw you. You were determined to get on that boat. I don't think there was anything I could have said that would have stopped you, was there?"

Ellie shook her head. "Probably not. When I make up my mind about something, I'm determined to get it." They sat silently until she asked, "Would you ever consider leaving this place?"

"I don't know. This is the only home I've ever known. I guess I'm not opposed to the idea, but it'd take a real good reason for me to leave. Why, what are you thinking?"

"Nothing. Something. I don't know. This whole business about us being apart has me troubled, and I've been thinking of a way where you could be closer to me. Since you're planning to go to work anyway, what if you moved to Indiana and found a job there? Bloomington has an RCA plant where they make televisions, and GE has a place there too. You could find work, no problem. That way, we could see each other anytime we want."

Her suggestion intrigued Jack. "Ellie, that all sounds great, and I'd do anything to be closer to you, but what about Mama and George? They depend on me. I can't just up and leave. And even if I could, what about the summer? I'd be there, and you'd be somewhere else."

"Well, it was only a thought."

Jack could hear the disappointment in her voice, so he offered a solution of his own. "I don't suppose I could talk you into transferring schools, could I? I'm sure the University of Tennessee has an astronomy program."

"If only it were that easy. Tell you what," said Ellie, "let's not talk about it anymore. Let's just enjoy the time we have left."

* * *

A week before Ellie's departure, she and Jack took the boat and anchored near Rock Island.

"It's so dark tonight." Jack was unable to see his hand in front of his face.

"Which is why this is the perfect night for stargazing. Did you know the stars appear brighter out here than they do in the city?"

"Why's that?"

"Cities produce ambient light, but out here in the country,

away from the hustle and bustle, it's clear. Look." She traced a cluster of stars with the end of her finger. "That's the Big Dipper. And over there is Orion."

"How'd you get to be so smart anyway?"

"I've been fascinated with the stars for as long as I can remember. When I was a little girl, my father would take me to the library, and I checked out every book they had on the subject. When I'd read everything there was in the library, we started looking for bookstores. In fact, there's one not far from campus where I spend most of my afternoons reading. I also work there on the weekends."

"I didn't know that," said Jack.

"You know, I'm really going to miss it here." She peered into the darkness. "I know it's only been a few months, but this place was starting to feel like home."

"Not as much as I'm going to miss having you here. You've become as much a part of my life as eating and sleeping."

Around midnight, Jack returned to the dock and tied up the boat.

"Since we only have a few days left, why don't we do something special?" Jack put away the life jackets and locked the door to the shack. "Whatever you want. Your choice."

Ellie thought about it for a minute, then made up her mind. "Why don't we go to the island one last time and sit beneath the stars?"

"Are you sure? We could do something more exciting, like go to Knoxville."

She shook her head. "That island means more to me than any other place, so I'd like to spend one last night there."

CHAPTER THIRTEEN

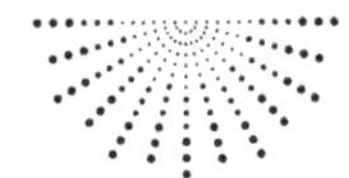

Heat Lightning

The next evening, Jack and Ellie met at the dock like usual. Ellie had come dressed in a blue sundress with her hair in curls. Jack couldn't recall a time when she looked better.

"You ready?"

She nodded, smiling, and he took her hand and helped her into the boat.

Easing away from the dock, Jack looked out over the lake, the calm water reflecting the soft violet of twilight. Entering the main channel, he directed the boat in a wide arc around the sandbar and sped north. In the distance, soundless flashes of lightning lit the sky like fireworks.

"It's not going to storm, is it?"

Jack shook his head as they motored into the deepening night. "Folks around here call that heat lightning. It won't hurt you."

When the silhouette of Parrott Island appeared, Jack moved the boat into position and landed it on the beach. Safely ashore, he got a fire going while Ellie spread out a blanket. They ate from the picnic basket and talked about life and what little they knew of it. And when they were finished, they lay on their backs and gazed up at the stars.

"Can I ask you something? Were you ever in love… you know, before me?"

Jack shook his head. "Never. You?"

Ellie didn't answer right away. "I don't know that it was love," she finally said, "but there was this guy, Daniel. We were sort of close for a while."

Jack listened quietly.

"We grew up in the same neighborhood, but his family moved away before the start of our senior year."

"I'm sorry to hear that," said Jack. "I know how difficult it can be to have someone taken from you unexpectedly."

Ellie rolled her head to the side. "But I want you to know that as much as I liked Daniel, my love for you is greater."

Her comment confused Jack. On the one hand, Ellie loved him more than any other. But, if she'd fallen in love once, or had nearly done so, what was to stop her from doing it again?

Jack lay quiet for a long time, listening to the gentle swoosh of waves lapping against the sandy beach. Staring into the heavens, he located the Big Dipper, Orion, and several other constellations Ellie had shown him. And when he observed a shooting star, he made a silent wish that he and Ellie would be together forever.

"We should probably be getting back soon," he said, noting the moon's position. "Otherwise, Clara will think we've run off together." Jack rolled over and got to his knees. But before he could stand, Ellie grabbed his arm and pulled him on top of her.

"Just a little longer?" Her eyes held him hostage.

Recognizing the mood had suddenly shifted, he swallowed hard. At the nod of his head, her legs parted, and Jack pressed his groin against her hips. His whole body quivered with a desire he'd never felt before.

Pulling him closer, Ellie kissed him softly, tenderly.

"Are you sure you want to do this?" he asked, staring into her eyes.

Without a word, Ellie rolled him over and sat on top of him. She pushed one strap of the dress off her shoulder, then the other, exposing her breasts.

For a moment, Jack stared, transfixed by her beauty. He had dreamed of this moment since the day they first kissed, but now that it was finally happening, his mind was a jumbled mess. Composing himself, Jack reached instinctively for her, his fingers tingling as they skimmed over her sun-kissed skin. Sitting up, his mouth went to her breasts, kissing them, caressing them with his tongue.

Clasping him to her, Ellie tossed her head back and whimpered. Every hair on her head stood at attention, every cell burned.

After working Jack's shirt over his shoulders, Ellie pushed him onto his back and took off his pants. And as her body sank into his, Jack felt the warmth of her skin against his own.

"I love you, Jack," she whispered as his body tensed with expectation.

"I love you more," he replied as they melted together.

* * *

Afterward, Jack put out the fire and loaded everything into the boat. The ride back across the water was quiet, tranquil, and

Jack held Ellie in his arms the entire way. After walking her home, they kissed good night and Jack returned to his house. For hours, he lay in the dark, thinking about what had happened on the island, realizing that his heart now belonged to another, never to be his own again.

CHAPTER FOURTEEN

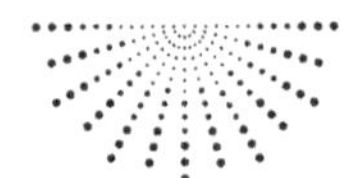

Chasing Rainbows

While sweeping out the shack the following day, Jack considered how he and Ellie could be together once summer was over. Now that they'd lost their virginity, they weren't just boyfriend and girlfriend. Where Jack came from, that meant something more. So when the thought of marriage entered Jack's mind, it wasn't completely unfounded.

That's it. He had an epiphany. *I'll ask Ellie to marry me.*

George appeared and caught Jack staring out the window. "You look deep in thought." He opened the register and placed the money in the deposit bag. "Everything all right?"

"Yeah. No. I don't know."

George chuckled. "Well, which is it?"

"I kinda got a situation," Jack said after a moment. "One I can't quite figure out."

George's brow furrowed. "That don't sound like you." He filled a glass with tea and sat down. "Lay it on me, kid."

"It's Ellie," said Jack.

"Somethin' wrong with Miss Ellie?"

"No. Nothing like that. It's just that she'll be going home soon, and truth be told, I can't stomach the thought of her leaving. I love her, George," Jack confessed. "I mean I really love her."

George's eyes widened. "Love? I ain't never heard you talk about a girl like that before."

"That's because I've never felt this way before."

"I see your predicament."

"But so far," said Jack, "the only solution I've come up with is to propose."

George choked down his tea. "Propose? Why you wanna go and do a thing like that?"

"Didn't you hear the part about me loving her?"

"Yes, but you ain't ready to be married. Not sayin' Ellie ain't a great girl, but you've known her for less than three months. Look, I know you're troubled about what to do, but gettin' married is a big step and not somethin' to be taken lightly. B'sides, I thought you was plannin' on stayin' here and helpin' me."

"I was. I mean, I am. It's just… I can't do nothing. Otherwise, she'll leave, meet someone new, and forget all about me."

George released an old man's sigh. "Listen, you ain't gonna solve nothin' sittin' in here. Why don't you get your tackle and head out on the water while I finish cleanin' up?"

"You mean it?"

George nodded.

Jack grabbed his rod and tackle and headed for the door. "You really think I'll find the answer out there, George?"

"Don't know, but it'll sure beat the hell outta sweepin' these floors."

That evening, Jack fished alone. Despite George telling him he wasn't ready for marriage, Jack wondered how hard it could be. He and Ellie loved each other, and that had to count for something. Sure, there'd be challenges, but considering the difficulties he'd already endured, Jack saw marriage as an opportunity rather than a risk.

* * *

With his mind made up, Jack borrowed George's truck and drove to Knoxville, stopping at Kimball's Jewelers on Market Street.

"Good evening, sir," said a well-dressed man standing behind the counter. "May I help you?"

"I hope so," said Jack anxiously. "I'm in the market for an engagement ring."

The man gave him the once-over. "You look awfully young to be thinking about marriage."

"I'm eighteen," Jack said firmly. "I got proof if you need to see it." He reached for his wallet.

The man held up a hand. "That won't be necessary. So what did you have in mind?"

Jack pulled the wad of money from his pocket and laid it on the counter. "Five hundred fifty-seven dollars. That's all I got. Do you think you could help me?"

The man smiled warmly. "I think we can find something. I'm Robert, by the way, but my friends call me Chappy." He introduced himself with a handshake. "I'm the owner of this here establishment."

"Jack Bennett."

"Nice to meet you, Jack." Chappy led him to a display where he kept the engagement rings. "These will be in your price range."

Jack perused the selection and spotted a diamond ring that

caught his eye. "How about that one?"

Chappy glanced at the price tag. "Six hundred."

Jack winced. "I don't suppose there's any room to negotiate, is there?"

"Make me an offer, and I'll see what I can do."

"This is all the money I got in the world," said Jack. "I've been saving since I was fifteen. I'll need a little gas to get home, so how's about five-fifty? That's the best I can do."

Chappy hemmed and hawed. "I don't know. Tell you what —let me check the books and see what I got in that ring. I'll be right back," he said, then disappeared behind the curtain.

While Jack waited, it dawned on him that his dream of having that house on the hill would have to wait. But at that moment, the only thing that mattered was what Ellie would say when he popped the question.

A minute later, Chappy returned. "All right, young man. You drive a hard bargain, but you got yourself a deal."

* * *

While Jack tried to keep his plans a secret, he and Ellie spent Thursday evening on the water.

"You're not yourself tonight," she said as they motored past the point. "Is everything all right?"

He nodded, staring ahead. When they reached Mama Holler, he cut the engine and dropped anchor.

"Are you still getting tutoring help from Sara?" he asked.

Ellie shook her head. "Our lessons ended a few days ago. Why?"

"Remember how you asked me once if she still had feelings for me?"

"Yeah."

"Well, she stopped by the dock yesterday evening. I had to run to Knoxville to get some... supplies. When I got back, she was there."

Ellie raised an eyebrow. "What did she want?"

"To know if we were together."

Ellie perked up. "What did you tell her?"

"I told her the truth. I mean, I had no reason to lie to her."

"And how did she take it?"

"Okay, I guess. But I could tell she was hurt."

"I told you she had a thing for you," said Ellie. "I'm usually pretty good at reading people."

When the sun began its final descent, Jack pulled anchor and headed for home. He cruised around the second point, crossed the main channel, then paralleled the other side as they slid off in the direction of the dam. The air was cool, the breath of fall signaling summer's end. Close to dark, Jack eased by the campground and glided over to Rock Island, where they sat and watched the sunset.

"I'm going to miss this," said Ellie. "The water, the sunsets, you." She took his hand in hers.

"Me too. It won't be the same here without you." He leaned over and kissed her, and they sat in silence until the sun disappeared. "Listen, I'm planning something special for tomorrow night. Are you available?"

She gave him a curious look. "I reckon. What should I wear?"

"Something nice. It's a surprise, but it doesn't involve fishing. Can you meet me at the dock at eight o'clock?"

"Sure."

* * *

After walking Ellie to Clara's, Jack went home and found his mama in the living room, reading the Bible.

"Can I talk to you for a minute?"

Helen shut the Bible and took off her reading glasses. "What's on your mind, JB?"

Jack took a deep breath and composed himself. "I've made a big decision, and I wanted you to be the first to know."

Helen straightened in her chair, her expression serious. "I'm listening."

Jack produced the ring and handed it to her. Almost instantly, her eyes filled with tears.

"Mama, you're crying. I've upset you, haven't I?"

She shook her head. "I was just thinking about the day your daddy proposed to me. He was about your age." A hint of a smile crossed her lips, and she returned the ring to him. "Jack, are you sure you've thought this through? You've only known Ellie since May."

"You and Daddy dated for less than that. That's what you told me."

"Yes, but your situation is different. Your daddy and I grew up together. We knew each other for years before he asked me to marry him."

"Is it Ellie?" Jack asked. "Don't you think she's good for me?"

"It's not that."

"Then what?"

"Well, it's just that Ellie's different," said Helen. "She isn't like the girls around here—not like me or Clara or Donna Rae either. She's smart, Jack, real smart. Not to mention ambitious. A girl like that requires things the rest of us don't."

"Like what?"

"Well, for starters, she'll need money. That's the world she comes from, and she's become accustomed to a certain lifestyle. Aside from that, she has her heart set on being a professor. She can't do that living in a place like this. Sure, she might be happy for a while, but what happens when she starts longing for her dreams again?"

Jack dropped his head and sighed. "So it's the other way around. You don't think I'm good enough for Ellie, do you?"

"I would never think that. Never. But even if she says yes, you won't be able to make her happy by staying here. Eventually, if you're to make it, one or both of you will have to give up something near and dear to your heart."

CHAPTER FIFTEEN

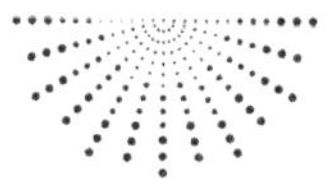

Stolen Thunder

"It's strange to see you here at this time of day." Clara found Ellie in the living room after supper Friday evening. "Normally, you're out on the water with Jack. Things haven't soured between you two, have they?"

"Everything's fine, Aunt Clara. Jack asked me to meet him at eight o'clock sharp—says he has something special planned."

"I see. Well, listen. I'm glad you're here because there's something I wanted to tell you."

Ellie closed the book and placed it on the table in front of her, giving Clara her undivided attention.

"I want you to know I've enjoyed having you here with me this summer. If Bill and I had been fortunate enough to have kids of our own, I would have wanted my daughter to be just like you."

Her comment caught Ellie by surprise, and it was only after swallowing the lump in her throat that she was able to respond. "Aunt Clara, that's sweet of you to say. And I've enjoyed being here as well. You've been kind to me, and I've fallen in love with this place. If it's all right with you, I think I'd like to return next summer."

"I don't see why not," Clara answered. "As far as I'm concerned, you're welcome here anytime so long as your mother doesn't object."

There was a knock at the door, and Clara got up to see who it was.

"Marie? What are you doing here?" Clara placed her hands on her hips and raised her chin.

Marie Spencer swung the door wide, stepped into the foyer, and immediately her eyes went to Ellie.

"Mother." Ellie was utterly confused. "W-What are you doing here?"

"It's nice to see you too, dear," she said mockingly. "I've come to take you home."

Ellie looked to Clara for answers.

"Why didn't you call?" Clara closed the door. "I wasn't expecting you until Monday."

"I apologize for the intrusion, but I've got a little surprise for Ellie."

"What kind of surprise?" Ellie asked.

"I thought we'd spend the weekend in Nashville, just the two of us."

Ellie felt as if something was amiss. "I appreciate the sentiment, Mother, but I'm not ready to go."

"Do you have other plans?"

She thought of Jack. "As a matter of fact, I do."

Marie raised an eyebrow. "Do tell."

"Well, I..."

"Doesn't sound that important to me." She glanced at her watch. "Go on and get your things. I want to be on the road within the hour."

"You're not staying the night?" Clara asked.

"I'm afraid not. I've already booked a hotel, and if we don't leave soon, it'll be after midnight before we arrive."

"An hour! But...?" Ellie thought about running straight to Jack. He'd know what to do. She checked the time. He'd be on his way to the dock by now. She felt trapped.

"Come along." Clara ushered her down the hall.

"Did you know about this?" Ellie asked Clara when she reached her bedroom.

"No, I didn't," she replied, looking irritated. "I'm just as surprised as you are."

"What should I do? What about Jack?"

"There's nothing you can do now." Clara spoke barely above a whisper. "Pen a note to Jack while you're packing your clothes. I'll make sure he gets it. Now go on before she gets suspicious."

Jack,

I'm writing this letter under duress, so I apologize for the brevity. Wouldn't you know, my mother is here. Three days early. Which can only mean one thing—she knows about us. I don't know how, but she does. I could see it in her eyes. I know I agreed to meet you tonight, but circumstances being what they are, it is impossible. You had something special planned, I just know it, so for that I am truly sorry. Mother says she's taking me to Nashville for the weekend, so I may not be able to reach you until next week. But rest assured, when I get the chance, I'll call or write. Thank you again for this summer. I had the time of my life, and if I live to be a hundred, I'll never forget it.

Love,

Ellie

After packing her suitcase, Ellie slipped the note to Clara when her mother wasn't looking.

"Stay strong, sweet girl." Clara hugged her at the door. "And stay in touch."

"I will." Ellie forced herself to hold back the tears threatening her eyes; she wouldn't give her mother the satisfaction. "Goodbye."

Under the cover of darkness, Ellie's mother drove her away from Sims Chapel, the streetlights flickering into the car. Ellie's jaw tightened as she watched Clara's house fall from sight, realizing that her summer, as wonderful as it had been, was over.

PART II

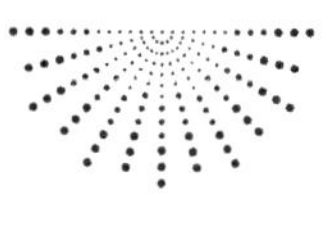

WINTER

CHAPTER SIXTEEN

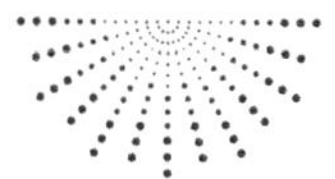

Dead of Winter

February 1962

Ellie navigated the snow and ice littering the sidewalk; her assistant, not so much.

"It's official," said Zora Wheaton, her words barely comprehensible through chattering teeth. "H-Hell has f-finally frozen over."

Ellie fought a smile, but in truth she couldn't recall a harsher winter.

Zora looked at her, bewildered. "It's winters like this that make me question my decision to move north. We don't get cold like this in Mississippi."

"So you've said."

They stopped briefly at the intersection, waited for the light to change, then crossed the street and started up the other side. When they reached the bookstore, Ellie asked Zora if they had time for a quick stop.

Zora pushed up her sleeve and checked the time. "Your next class isn't for another forty-five minutes, so yes."

"Afternoon, ladies." Sam looked up from behind the counter as they entered, cheerful as ever. "Can I help you find something, or are you simply seeking refuge from the cold?"

Ellie removed her hat and scarf. "Hi, Sam," she said with a smile.

"Dr. Spencer, my apologies. I didn't recognize you. And Ms. Wheaton," he went on, shifting his gaze. "How lovely to see you both. To what do I owe the pleasure?"

Ellie approached the counter. "You said you had a package waiting for me."

"Yes, I did." He reached beneath the counter and produced a rectangular box wrapped in brown paper. "This is for you."

She examined the package. "There's no return address."

"That's odd," said Zora.

Ellie looked at Sam. "Is this not the book I ordered on supernovas?"

"I'm afraid not. But I'm expecting it any day."

She frowned. "I was really counting on reviewing it this weekend. I'm already a week behind on my article as it is."

"Well, if you have a few minutes, I can check this morning's delivery." He cast an eye to the unopened stack of boxes behind the counter. "I can't promise you it will be in there, but it's worth a shot."

"Do you mind?"

"Not at all." He slid off the stool. "It may take a few minutes, so feel free to look around. Perhaps something will catch your eye."

While Sam checked the boxes, Ellie perused the nonfiction section. Zora, an avid reader in her own right, stayed at the front of the store, rifling through the classics.

"Sorry about the mess," said Sam as he opened the first box. "I'm in the process of reorganizing."

"Does that mean you've changed your mind about selling the store?" Ellie asked.

He began stacking the books on the counter. "I'm still mulling it over. We're waiting to hear back from the doctor on Alicia's condition. They say that sometimes being in a warmer climate helps slow the progress of the disease."

"How is Alicia?" Zora asked. "I haven't seen her since the New Year's Eve party."

"Fair. Some days are better than others, but we're trying to take it one day at a time."

Knowing how sensitive a subject this was for Sam, Ellie redirected the conversation. "This is new," she said, inspecting a display of classic romance novels.

"I'm glad you noticed. I just finished setting it up," Sam said proudly. "Apparently, in Chicago and Indianapolis, stores are selling out of them, so I figured I'd give it a shot."

Ellie glanced at Zora. "Still okay on time?"

Zora nodded and picked up a copy of *Pride and Prejudice*. "This is my all-time favorite. Have you read it?"

Ellie examined the cover and shook her head. "Is it any good?"

"Is it any good?" Zora cleared her throat. "'It is a truth universally acknowledged, that a single man in possession of good fortune, must be in want of a wife.'" Her voice was thick and dramatic. "That's how the book begins. Isn't it lovely?"

"If you say so."

Undeterred, Zora turned a few pages and read another passage.

"'Think only of the past as its remembrance gives you pleasure.'"

She skimmed ahead.

"'She was convinced that she could have been happy with him, when it was no longer likely they should meet.'"

Zora pressed the book to her chest. "How can you not be moved by her words—so beautiful, so elegant?" She swooned. "Do you know how many times I've read this book?"

"More than once, I presume."

"Eleven," Zora proclaimed. "Hands down, Jane Austen is my favorite author. Are you telling me that when you were in college you never read any of her books?"

Ellie shook her head.

"Charlotte Bronte?"

"Nope."

"Tell me you at least read something by Elizabeth Barrett Browning?"

"Sorry to disappoint you, Zora, but while you were reading about what love should be like, I was experiencing the real thing." She flashed a mischievous little smile.

"Aha." Sam pulled a hardcover copy of *Supernovas: A Detailed Look into the Death of Stars* from the last box. "I believe this is what you're looking for."

"Wonderful," said Ellie.

"Would you like a bag?"

"That won't be necessary." She returned to the counter. "Thank you so much for doing this, Sam. You're a lifesaver. What do I owe you?"

"Three dollars should cover it."

Ellie opened her purse and whispered, "And while I'm at it, add that one to the bill." She nodded in Zora's direction.

"Most certainly." Sam did the math. "That brings your total to five dollars even."

Ellie found a five-dollar bill and slid it across the counter, then tucked the package beneath her arm and headed for the door. "Thanks again, Sam." Zora opened the door. "And give me a call if anything else comes in you think I might be interested in."

"Will do. You ladies have a nice weekend, and be careful out there. Believe it or not, they're calling for more snow."

"Aren't you going to open it?" Zora asked as they set off for campus.

Ellie glanced at the package. "Eventually." She held the book tight and stepped onto the slushy sidewalk that wound along small shops between tall gray office buildings. "But it will have to wait until later. Otherwise, I'm going to be late." She walked on a few steps. "What's with you today anyway? I'm sure it's just another catalog."

"I don't know," said Zora. "I have a funny feeling. What if it's a gift from a secret admirer?"

Ellie rolled her eyes. "You've been reading too many romance novels."

"Very funny. Listen, I'm going to leave a little early today and meet Trey for dinner and drinks. I hope that's all right."

"Of course. With all the work I've had you doing over the past few weeks, you've earned it. I appreciate it though. I wouldn't have been able to finish the application without you."

"You're welcome. So I guess I'll see you tomorrow night, right?" Zora moved out of the way of a sudden splash of mud from an impatient driver.

Ellie drew a blank. "What's tomorrow night? Oh, Bill. I almost forgot. I can't make any promises, but I'll try my best."

"Please don't bail on me again. Bill is a good guy, and he's dying to meet you. Besides, you already know he's a patient man, which is difficult to find."

"And how do I know that?"

"Because"—Zora arched an eyebrow—"any man willing to give you another chance after standing him up twice must have the patience of Job."

CHAPTER SEVENTEEN

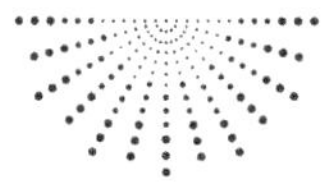

Out of the Blue

Ellie swayed to a Miles Davis tune as she reached into the kitchen cupboard for a wineglass. She glimpsed the package sitting on the counter. *What if Zora's right?* It wasn't out of the realm of possibility that Ellie could have a secret admirer. After all, there was much—intelligence, beauty, eloquence—to admire. "Don't be ridiculous," she told herself as she poured the wine.

Nevertheless, her curiosity had gotten the better of her, so she sat down at the table and unwrapped the package. Inside was a book with a note taped to the front cover. She glanced at the signature and caught her breath.

Dearest Ellie,

I hope this letter finds you doing well. I suspect you remember me, but in case you don't,

I'm the devilishly handsome man from Sims Chapel who one summer taught you how to fish and ferried you across the lake in search of arrowheads. Once upon a time, I told you my dream was to write the next great American novel. I'm not sure how great it is, but it's nonetheless a published work. Since I credit you as the inspiration for this story, I wanted you to have a copy as something to remember me by.

It's hard to believe nine years have come and gone since I last saw you, and while I realize we didn't part on the most pleasant of terms, I can only hope life has been as kind to you as you were to me that summer. And despite everything, I think of you often and wish you health, happiness, and love.

Sincerely,
Jack

When she finished reading, Ellie put down the letter and wiped her eyes. She was shocked at how easily his words stirred emotions she thought were nonexistent. Over the years, Jack had crossed her mind more than a few times, especially on warm summer nights. She often wondered what he was up to and if he had ever settled down with someone. Even once she'd considered a trip to Sims Chapel to see if he was still navigating the points and channels or scouring the islands. But something, be it her mother's voice in her head, her own stubbornness, or life itself, had always held her back. Suddenly all the loneliness and regret she'd been ignoring for years came over her in a flood. Ellie reached for the wine.

After composing herself, she cracked the cover and read the dedication.

To the one who holds my destiny in her hands, my keeper of stars.

Helpless against Jack's words, tears—the tears Ellie had been holding back since that night her mother had torn her away from Aunt Clara's house, from Jack—streaked down her face. She turned over the book and, through blurry eyes, examined his picture.

He was a man now. Hard lines had replaced the soft, rounded features of his youth, and his once long, windswept hair had been cut and styled to fit his face. Upon closer examination, she noticed a small scar above his left eye that made her wonder what he had been up to for the past decade.

But despite all that had changed about him, his eyes—those beautiful blue eyes—remained unblemished. If possible, he was more handsome now than the last time she saw him, making her wonder what he would think if he saw her.

She got up and examined herself in the mirror. She was older, of course, thirty now, and had filled out in the places most women do, but aside from her hair, which was a shade darker, and a few tiny lines on her forehead, her appearance was much the same as it had always been.

Physical appearance aside, Ellie had changed in other ways. After graduating college, she'd earned a PhD from Ohio State, then returned to Bloomington as head of the astronomy department following the retirement of her mentor, Dr. Stevenson. In terms of her career, Dr. Elizabeth Spencer was a smashing success, regarded as a trailblazer by her contemporaries and admired by faculty and students alike.

But for her many professional successes, Ellie's personal life was a disaster. Between countless hours of research, various speaking engagements, and teaching classes at the university, there was little time for meaningful relationships. Over the years, friends and family had encouraged her to find a decent man, settle down, and start a family. Some, like Zora, had set her up on blind dates in hopes she would find Mr. Right, but to no avail. Instead, Ellie poured herself into her career, thinking that once she had achieved her professional goals, only then would she consider settling down.

But now that she had firmly established herself as an expert in her field and had proven she had what it took to stand out in the sea of men dominating the scientific world, Ellie's biological clock began ticking. Everywhere she looked, women were starting families. Even Amelia, two years her junior, was married with one child and plans for another. While Ellie was busy chasing her ambition, everyone around her had moved on, leaving her to wonder if the best of her years were behind her.

Pushing the doubt out of her mind, Ellie dove into the

story, allowing Jack's words, like whispers in the dark, to resurrect memories long forgotten.

Before that day, I'd heard folks talk about love at first sight but never really believed it. But let me tell you, that's exactly how it happened. From the first moment I laid eyes on her I knew she was the one, and that summer would not be like all the others.

She also recalled that first meeting, seeing Jack in his ball cap, being captivated by his blue eyes and accent. And then how he had saved her from ruining her shoes. It wasn't love at first sight, but it was the next best thing.

Ellie put the book down and went to the window, realizing that this wasn't just any story. It was their story—a Northern socialite who had fallen in love with a backward Southern boy, had taken his virginity, stolen his heart, then fled North under the cover of darkness like a thief in the night.

After another sip of wine, Ellie returned to the couch, finding the place where she had left off.

I couldn't help myself. Falling in love with her came naturally, like breathing. Seeing her adapt to any situation made me love her even more. And that's when I knew I had found the girl with whom I wanted to spend the rest of my life.

She read on.

I stood on that dock beneath the moon and stars for what seemed like hours. I was as nervous as I'd ever been in my life. My knees and hands trembled. I must have looked at the ring a hundred times, wondering what she'd say, imagining the look on her face when I got down on one knee. Was I crazy? Yes. But I was in love.

After an hour, I knew something was wrong. It wasn't like her to bail on me. She'd never done it before. So I rushed to the house where she was staying, hoping to find her. But fate had whisked her away, ruining my chances of a happily-ever-after.

Confusion gripped Ellie. She read the passage again, wondering if it was real or fiction? Unaware of Jack's intentions, she wondered what might have been. She had loved Jack once, loved him with all her heart. But marriage? God, what would she have said? She tossed around the idea that she would have accepted his proposal and married him. Then what? Could they have made it work? She considered her family, education, and all she'd accomplished.

"No," she said to herself. "This was the way things were supposed to turn out. This was my destiny." And yet she wondered.

Opening the window, cold air rushed over her face. She took a deep breath and tried to make sense of things, but instead of clarity, an unsettling thought took root. If Jack had planned to propose, it now called into question the timing of her mother's visit, and she was reminded of a conversation she'd had with her mother shortly after arriving home from Tennessee.

* * *

August 1950

A knock on the door startled Ellie. "Who is it?"

Marie answered through the door. "It's me. May I come in?"

Ellie wiped the tears from her face and opened the door.

"Are those tears of joy or tears of sadness?"

Ellie sat on the bench beneath the window. "Both, I suppose," she answered glumly.

"I see. Well, at least part of you is happy to be home." After adjusting a pillow that was out of place, Marie sat down at the end of the bed. "And what about the rest of you?"

Ellie shrugged, not knowing what to say.

"I want to apologize for showing up out of the blue the way I did. Given our history, my actions must have seemed suspicious to you."

"I'd be lying if I said the thought hadn't crossed my mind."

"The truth is I was sitting here last week, all alone in this big house, thinking how quickly the summer had passed, and I realized that other than a few days after you got home from school, we hadn't spent any time together. I guess what I'm trying to say is I missed having you around."

Ellie cast a look of suspicion in her direction. "I figured you would have enjoyed the peace and quiet. Wasn't that the point of sending me to Tennessee in the first place?"

Marie's face registered a look of disappointment. "Perhaps." She drew a breath. "Look, I know we've had our issues, but that doesn't mean I don't love you."

"I never said you didn't. I just think you have a strange way of showing it."

"But we had fun this weekend, didn't we?"

Despite missing Jack, Ellie had enjoyed herself. "Actually, yes."

Marie chuckled. "Don't act so surprised. I can be fun when I want to be."

Ellie raised an eyebrow.

"You may not realize it, but we have a lot more in common than you think."

"So I've been told."

Marie tipped her head to one side.

"Aunt Clara," Ellie explained.

"Mmm." She pressed the wrinkles from her dress. "What else did your aunt tell you about me?"

"That you and your mother used to fight all the time, just like us, and it was only after you were grown and had moved away that you reconciled your differences." She thought for a moment before going on. "Do you think that's how it'll be with us?"

"I certainly hope not," said Marie. "Besides, I hate to break it to you, sweetheart, but you're already grown. I mean, look at you." She gestured with an open hand. "You're nineteen going on thirty. I'm sure Clara told you, but by the time we were your age, we were either married or engaged."

"She may have mentioned it."

"But times they are a changing," said Marie. "Women are starting to make inroads. You have opportunities I never had." She cleared her throat. "Tell you what, why don't we forget the past and start anew—right here, right now?"

"You mean it?"

"Yes. We'll never agree on everything, of course, but I think it's high time I started treating you like a woman rather than a child."

Ellie was at a loss for words. She had been at odds with her mother for as long as she could remember. Part of her wondered if Marie was being sincere or luring her into a trap. Regardless, if there was even a shred of hope that Marie was serious, Ellie was willing to take the chance.

"All right." She met her mother's gaze. "I'd like that." They embraced in a hug that left Ellie feeling hopeful. "Now that we've agreed to be amenable, there's something I feel I should tell you."

Marie stopped on her way to the door.

"I met someone… while I was in Tennessee. A young man. His name is Jack. I didn't mention it before because, well, I figured you already knew."

Marie appeared troubled by this news and hesitated a moment before answering. "I didn't," she said, "but I'm glad you told me. So does this Jack have a last name?"

"Bennett," said Ellie. "I met him on the water; that's where he works. He and his friend run a ferry service. I'm only telling you now because I want you to know we're in love. And I don't care if you approve or not because, like you said, I'm a grown woman and I can make my own decisions." She paused and took a breath.

"Well, I can see you wasted little time putting our agreement to the test. If you truly are in love, as you say, congratulations. Jack Bennett must be quite a young man to have caught your eye. As for whether I approve or not, you're right; it's none of my business. But if I might give you a piece of advice...?" She returned to the edge of the bed. "Since you were a child, you've dreamed of being an independent woman with a career as a college professor. As we've discussed, the deck is stacked against you, so you'll have to work twice as hard. But given your intelligence and determination, I have no doubt you'll achieve your goals."

"But?"

"But that doesn't leave a lot of time for much else, I'm afraid."

Ellie shuddered, despair creeping through her. "You mean for love, don't you?"

"Look, all I'm saying is that for you to achieve your dreams, love may need to take a back seat for a while, just until you're established."

That's all? Even in her wildest dreams, Ellie couldn't imagine her life without love, not now. And if forced to choose between Jack and a career, perhaps being a professor wasn't that important after all.

"I realize it's difficult for you to understand now, but someday when you're sitting behind your desk, staring at the name above the door that reads Dr. Elizabeth Spencer, you're going to thank me."

* * *

The clock struck midnight, bringing Ellie back to the present. After another glass of wine, she moseyed into the living room and added a log to the fire. Feeling the effects of the alcohol, her thoughts drifted to the weekend of Jack's surprise visit.

November 1950

After making love, Jack and Ellie lay naked in the motel room, the glow of neon lights filtering through the faded curtains.

"God, I've missed you," said Jack, wiping the sweat from his brow.

Ellie blew the hair out of her eyes. "Me too. Promise you won't wait three more months before coming to see me."

"You know I can't promise that, but I'll try my best."

"I still can't believe you're here." She traced a finger lightly on his chest.

"Neither can I. This is the furthest from home I've ever been."

"Really?"

"And it's all because of you. You give me the courage to do things I never thought I could."

"Go on." She grinned.

"I mean it," he said. "Without you, I don't think I would have ever left Sims Chapel, let alone the state. And look at me now, hundreds of miles from home. You're the best thing that's ever happened to me, Ellie. Sometimes, I think it's almost too good to be true."

"What do you mean?"

His mood shifted. "This. You. I just don't want this to end."

Ellie rolled onto her side, crooked her elbow, and rested her head on the palm of her hand. "It won't."

"How can you be so sure?"

"Because I know the way I feel about you, and I never want

that feeling to go away. I realize we don't come from the same places or have the same experiences, but I think that's what makes it work with us. We complement each other. And I don't know why God brought us together, but he did, and I'm grateful because you're the person I want to spend the rest of my life with. And even if that means we can't see each other every day, I'm okay with that because you're worth waiting for."

CHAPTER EIGHTEEN

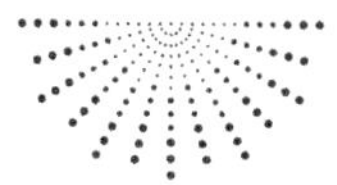

Snowed Under

Ellie woke the next morning, clinging to Jack's book. She had fallen asleep in the living room sometime after two. After a fresh cup of coffee, she curled up on the couch and picked up where she left off.

I woke to the sound of rain. The steady pitter-patter told me there'd be no tours today. Which was fine considering I was in no mood to face the world. She was gone, a notion that even the heavens seemed to echo.

When the last tour ended, I took a job at the mill. The work was backbreaking, the conditions deplorable, but it was honest work, and it paid better than anything I could have found at home. When I wasn't working, I passed the time by fishing. And as the lake levels dropped, the places she and I had visited—the places that bore my greatest memories—slipped further and further away.

Ellie put down the book and went to the window, finding fresh snow covering the ground. Lifting her gaze to the flat gray sky above, she longed for the orange and amber Tennessee sunsets.

Turning back, Ellie's eyes met the golden light of the fire, reminding her of something Jack had told her years earlier; that if you stare into the flames long enough, you'll find answers to questions you didn't know you had.

Questions? She had more than a few.

At the back of the closet, Ellie found her trunk that held her most precious memories and began sifting through old photographs, letters, and journals. Spreading the contents on the floor, she spent a few minutes thumbing through some pictures of her and Amelia from when they were teenagers. There was one at the beach and another on the steps in front of their house. She even found one from the trip they'd taken with their parents to Chicago. A jewelry box revealed more photographs: some of her roommates from college, and one of Michael, taken a few weeks before he'd broken her heart. Then, she found the memory box, the one that contained the artifacts from the summer when she fell in love with Jack. Lifting the lid, she saw the arrowhead, and the bottle of sand and pebbles Jack had given her. Biting back tears, she recalled how happy she had been that summer, and how her heart had broken when it all fell apart.

Resuming her search, at the bottom of the trunk, she found a journal she'd kept during the time she and Jack dated.

March 7, 1951

The clock starts now. Two years and counting. 24 months. 104 weeks. 730 days. God, that seems like a long time. Knowing Jack will be half a world away is enough to make me go mad. But as difficult as this is for me, I can only imagine what he's going through.

She thumbed ahead a few pages.

June 14, 1951

So far, so good. I received a letter from Jack in the mail yesterday, all the way from Korea. He seems to be in good spirits, which is more than I can say for me. Now that school is out, I find myself longing to be in Tennessee. Clara was right—when it gets in your blood, it's impossible to get it out.

September 10, 1951

Six months down, eighteen to go. Who knew two years was such a long time? I'm trying my best to remain strong, but at times I doubt my resolve. Maybe I'm not as strong as I thought. But Jack has been true to his word and writes often, so for him, I'll press on. Mother says I'm a fool for waiting when there are plenty of eligible young men at school. Marjorie says the same thing. Part of me hates them for saying such things. What do they know anyway?

December 24, 1951

Christmas Eve. Everyone keeps asking what I want for Christmas. But what I want can't be purchased at a department store. My only wish is to have Jack here with me. His letters keep coming but his tone has changed. Maybe the separation is taking its toll on him as well. Not much has changed here on the home front. School continues, and despite having friends, I find myself feeling increasingly isolated, withdrawn, finding little enjoyment in life. I don't know how much longer I can do this.

May 3, 1952

I've come to a crossroads. I'm reluctant to write these words for fear of where it will lead. This is terrible to say, but my memory of Jack has started to fade. Part of me feels as if I've lost him. God, forgive me for thinking such things.

Finally, she came to the entry she'd been dreading—a copy of the Dear John she'd written Jack. She drew a breath and braced herself.

Dear Jack,

This is without question the hardest letter I've ever had to write. Are you sitting down? If not, you should be.

By now, you've probably guessed the nature of this letter is an unpleasant one. Since we've always been honest with each other, I'll get right to it. Once upon a time, you and I enjoyed a magical summer beneath the stars; a summer I will never forget. And it was during that summer that we fell in love for the first time, kissed for the first time, and made love for the first time. Those are memories that I will carry with me for the rest of my life. But all that feels like a lifetime ago, and so much has happened since then. I've changed, and undoubtedly so have you.

I guess what I'm trying to say is I can't

do this anymore. I know I said I'd wait, but that's a promise I can no longer keep. Perhaps you're stronger than me, but the separation is simply too much. And though it breaks my heart to do so, for me to survive, I need to let you go. Despite my decision, I want you to know that I still love you, and I suppose a part of me always will.

I know this is hard. After reading these words, you'll likely hate me, but I can only hope that someday you will understand. In the mean-time, I will take with me the memories we made that summer and cherish them forever. I only hope you can do the same.

Sincerely,

Ellie

Ellie buried her face in her hands and wept, wishing she could go back. When her tears relented, she took the memory box and crawled into bed. Less than an hour later, she was awakened by the sound of the phone ringing.

"H-Hello."

"Hey, it's me. Are you getting ready?"

Ellie glanced at the clock—five thirty. "Ready for what?"

"Tell me you're joking," said Zora.

Suddenly, Ellie remembered the blind date she had agreed to. “Ugh. Zora, listen—”

“Let me guess. You’re not going to make it, are you?”

“I’m sorry, Zora. Truly, I am. It’s just...” She glimpsed the memories scattered on the floor. “I’m kind of in the middle of something. Cover for me, will you?”

Zora sighed into the phone. “I always do, don’t I?”

CHAPTER NINETEEN

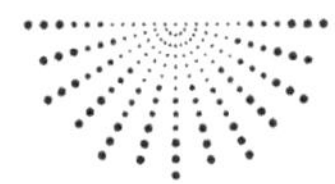

Cold Shoulder

When Ellie showed up for work Monday morning, Zora was waiting for her outside her office.

"What's with you?" Ellie asked, noticing the sour look on her face. When Zora didn't answer, Ellie pushed her way inside and flicked on the light. "Like I told you over the phone, I'm sorry, but I've got a lot on my mind right now. Maybe when things settle down, I can meet Bill for drinks."

"Too late," said Zora. "He was understanding about Saturday night but said if this is any indication of what it's like to date you, he's not interested. Congratulations, Ellie. You scared another one away."

In a way, Ellie was relived. Maybe now Zora would stop trying to set her up.

"You know, I don't get you. God knows I try to be a good friend to you. I go out of my way to find decent guys I think would be a great match for you, make you happy, but all I get in return are excuses and broken promises. I'm starting to think you want to be alone."

Ellie lowered herself into the chair and stared ahead. "Maybe I do," she finally said. "Or maybe I don't deserve to be with anyone."

"Relax," said Zora. "I was only joking. Besides, it's not the end of the world."

Ellie took a breath and exhaled slowly. "Maybe you should sit. There's something I need to tell you." When Zora had made herself comfortable, Ellie continued. "Shortly after you and I became friends, you asked me if I'd ever been in love. Do you remember?"

Zora nodded, a knowing look on her face. "I believe you said his name was Michael."

"Yes, but there was someone else... before Michael. His name was Jack Bennett. You've heard me mention my aunt Clara, from Tennessee. Well, when I was nineteen, I spent the summer with her, and it was during that visit that I met Jack. He was a year younger than me, working on the lake at the time. Long story short, the other day you said you had a feeling about that package I received at the bookstore, and..."

Zora's eyes widened. "It wasn't just catalogs, was it?"

Ellie handed Zora the book and watched as her eyes scanned the cover.

"Oh my God. He wrote this, didn't he?"

"Yes, and that's not all." She showed Zora the letter.

"It sounds like he knew you quite well," she said after reading it.

Ellie dropped her eyes. "Yes, he did. In fact, I think he probably knew me better than anyone ever has."

"Were you in love with him?"

Ellie nodded, the memory of that summer still vivid. "Very much."

"I take it he was the first man you ever loved."

"He was more than that," Ellie confided. "Jack Bennett was my first… everything."

"How come you never told me about him?"

Ellie shrugged. "It was a long time ago, and I guess I didn't see any reason to dredge up old memories."

"So what happened?"

"Summer ended, and we went our separate ways."

"And that was it? You never saw him again?"

Ellie looked at her, then away as the dread swelled inside her. "I saw him twice after that." She absently played with her earring. "Once that fall, and again after the war." And as she stared at his picture, she was reminded of the last time she had seen Jack. It was a meeting that still haunted her…

April 1953

"Hello. Earth to Ellie." Outside the beauty salon, Marjorie waved a hand in front of Ellie's face. But Ellie stared ahead, the way one does when observing a shooting star streaking across the sky, with silent reverence.

"Ellie?"

Finally, Ellie snapped to attention. "Hmm?"

"Is everything okay?" Marjorie gave her a funny look. "You look like you've seen a ghost."

"Yeah, you don't look so good," echoed Susan.

"I'm fine," she reassured them. "Why don't you go on ahead and get a table. I'll be along shortly."

"Are you sure?" Susan asked. "We could wait."

"I promise I won't be long."

When they were out of sight, Ellie took a deep breath and crossed the street.

"For a moment, I thought I was seeing things," she said to Jack, who sat at on a park bench outside the record store.

He stood and removed his hat. "Hello, Ellie." There was a moment of awkward silence, followed by a long embrace. "It's good to see your face again."

When Jack released her, she leaned away to look at him. "You look different," she said, surprised at how much he had changed. He was taller than she remembered, his shoulders broader. The once tousled locks of sandy-brown hair, which he used to keep hidden beneath his ball cap, had been cut to the scalp, revealing a thin and chiseled face. Before her was a man where once a boy had stood.

"It'll grow back." He looked at her with a penetrating gaze, nearly making her regret her decision to leave him. "I like what you've done with your hair."

Reflexively, she lifted a hand and touched the ends of her hair. "I just got it done this morning. I wanted to try something new."

"Well, it suits you." He met her gaze.

When the shock wore off, she asked, "What are you doing here, and how did you know where to find me?"

"Sam said you might be here. I hope you don't mind." He gave a tentative smile. "I probably should have called, but I didn't know I was stopping until this morning. I'd planned on going straight home, but since I was so close, I... well... I needed to see you—to let you know I'm back and that I'm okay."

"I'm glad." Her breath hitched a little. "That you're okay. I was worried about you."

"Oh, I almost forgot." He grabbed a bouquet of pink carnations and a book on stars and handed them to her. "I got these for you. Sam said that one just came out. You haven't read it, have you?"

She examined the cover and shook her head. "Thank you, Jack, but you really shouldn't have."

"I know, but I wanted to. Listen, I'm sure you're busy, but is there somewhere we could talk?"

Ellie hesitated, considering the consequences of dredging up feelings she'd spent the past year burying.

"Please? I've come a long way. All I ask is for ten minutes."

She agreed, feeling as if she owed him at least that much. "But I don't have long. I promised the girls I'd meet them for lunch."

They found a little café and sat at one of the outdoor tables. Ellie sipped on a glass of water while Jack drank coffee.

"This is nice," he said, taking in his surroundings. "Being here, seeing you again." His gaze drifted to her and wandered over her face. "You don't know how many nights I prayed for this moment."

But instead of returning his gaze, Ellie glanced absently at her watch.

"I know you don't have much time, so I won't beat around the bush." He set down his coffee and cleared his throat. "When I got your letter last summer, I was shocked, but in a way I wasn't. Maybe it was just me, but I'd felt for a while as if things between us had grown cold. I won't lie. It took me a while to come to terms with the fact that you had ended things, but eventually I put myself in your shoes, and I realized that being apart wasn't only difficult for me, but for you as well. Anyway, I just wanted to say that I understand why you did what you did. Neither of us asked to be put in that position, and we did what we had to—to survive."

Ellie looked up, surprised by his words. "Thank you, Jack. That means a lot."

Jack took a sip of coffee and went on. "But now that I'm back, I was hoping there was a chance for us to, you know, start over, maybe give it another shot? I realize it's a lot to ask, but being away for two years and seeing the things I've seen has taught me that life is short, and when we see something we want, nothing should stand in our way. So I guess what I'm trying to say, Ellie, is do you think there's still a chance for us?" He reached for her hand, but she dropped her eyes as a quiver of guilt rippled through her.

This was the part of the conversation she was hoping to avoid. Finally, she found the courage to look him in the eye. "Jack, I don't know how to tell you this, but I'm sort of seeing someone at the moment."

Taking back his hand, Jack was speechless for a long time as he processed her words. "How long?" he finally asked.

"Not long. A few months."

"I see." He took a moment to compose himself. "Is that the real reason you called things off, because you found someone else?"

"No. It's not like that at all. Being away from you was the hardest thing I've ever had to do. Everything I wrote in that letter was truthful—every word." Pain funneled into her heart. "Finding someone new wasn't part of the plan; it just happened."

Jack's shoulders slumped forward in disappointment. He glanced at the ground. "So who's the lucky guy?"

Ellie hesitated, knowing that the truth would break his heart. "Mike," she finally said, then studied his face carefully.

Jack's face flushed with understanding as he put two and

two together. "Mike Pearson?" He looked away, his face pained. "Is it serious? Do you love him?"

"I-I don't know. I've only ever been in love with you."

"And does it feel like that?"

There were times when Ellie thought she felt that spark with Mike, and others…

"You know what? Don't answer that." Jacked dropped a five-dollar bill on the table and walked away.

"Where are you going?"

"Home. I can see now that this was a mistake."

"Jack, wait!" She hurried after him. "I want you to know that I never meant to hurt you."

Jack took another step, stopped, and turned on his heel. "Hurt?" He scoffed. "What do you know about hurt?" He unbuttoned his shirt, exposing his bare chest. "See this?" He pointed to a scar just above his heart. "I took a bullet from a machine gun. And this…" He rolled up the sleeve to his shirt, revealing a jagged scar on his forearm. "Shrapnel from a mortar shell. Those hurt, Ellie. And telling my mother I had to go to war, not knowing if I would ever see her again, that hurt." He took a step toward her. "But what you did to me goes beyond flesh wounds. You literally reached into my chest and pulled out my heart. God, Ellie, you were the one I wanted to spend the rest of my life with. We had something special, you and me, and you threw it all away. And for what? So you could be with Mike? He doesn't love you."

"You don't even know him," she said in Mike's defense.

"I know all I need to know about him," Jack growled. "He's smug, arrogant, and as soon as something better comes along, he'll drop you like a hot rock. Just wait and see."

"You're wrong, Jack. Mike loves me. And you know what else, I love him too."

Silent tears clouded his eyes, concealing the look of a man who had just had his heart broken in two.

* * *

"I had no idea." A troubled look covered Zora's face. "But if you loved him so much, why did you end it?"

Ellie dried her eyes. "When Jack left, I had no idea how difficult being apart was going to be. I was sad all the time, to the point it affected every part of my life. If I hadn't done what I did, I would never have made it as far as I have."

"But at what cost? I mean, I get ambition and career and all, but Ellie, someday, when all this goes away, what will you have to show for it? Who will be there for you?"

And it was then Ellie realized that letting Jack go might have been the biggest mistake of her life.

"So you haven't spoken to him since that day?"

Ellie shook her head. "But I've thought about him, even asked my aunt about him once when she called to congratulate me on earning my doctorate. That's when I found out he had moved to the West Coast. After that, I assumed I'd never hear from him again. Then on Friday I get this package, and poof, it's like I'm nineteen again."

"Do you ever wonder what might have been if things had turned out differently?"

"All the time."

"Have you ever thought about seeing him again?" Zora asked.

Ellie shook her head.

"Why not? It's obvious this man still loves you. Why else would he send a book and write these words? He's probably thinking about you right now."

Ellie considered that. The gesture was more than just a token gift. Jack had taken the time to write a letter and an inscription. What if he *was* still in love with her? "But so much time has passed. I've changed, and undoubtedly so has he. And what if, by seeing him again, I somehow tarnished those memories I have of us when we were teenagers? Those are precious memories."

"I get your trepidation, but what if he's the man you're destined to spend the rest of your life with? I know we joke about it all the time, but what if the reason you're still single is because secretly, deep down in a place you keep hidden from everyone, including me, you've been holding on to a shred of hope that you and Jack would find each other again?"

Maybe Zora was right. Perhaps, subconsciously, Ellie had hoped she and Jack would someday reunite. If so, this was her chance to reach out, to see if he still had any interest in her. And it was at that moment she remembered the story of the mockingbirds Jack had once told her, and she wondered.

CHAPTER TWENTY

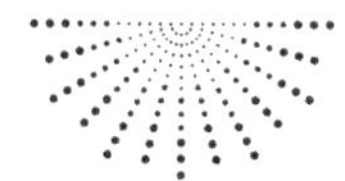

Tip of the Iceberg

On Tuesday, Ellie called in sick. With so much on her mind, she needed a day to sort through some things. Seeking clarity, she turned to the one person she trusted more than any other, someone who had been there for her through all the ups and downs.

"Ellie, what brings you by?" Amelia asked, greeting her at the front door.

"I was hoping we could talk. Is now a good time?"

"Yeah, come in. Just watch your step. I haven't had a chance to clean yet." Amelia showed Ellie to the living room, picking up toys and blankets as she went.

"Where's Christopher?" Ellie asked, thinking the house was too quiet.

"Across the street, playing with a friend. And Sean is at work, which means I have the entire house to myself." She put away the toys in the chest, then offered Ellie a seat.

"I could come back later." Ellie sensed the timing of her visit was less than ideal.

"Nonsense. Stay. I could use some adult conversation. Besides, when's the last time you and I had the opportunity to sit and talk in the middle of the afternoon?" Amelia eased toward the kitchen. "I was just about to put on a pot of tea. Would you like some?"

"Yes please."

Amelia filled a pot with water and put it on the stove to boil.

While she waited, Ellie picked up one of the most recent photographs of Christopher, proudly displayed on the bookshelf. "He's growing so fast." She marveled at the changes since she'd last seen him.

"Tell me about it. It seems like only yesterday we were bringing him home from the hospital." Amelia joined Ellie in the living room. "So how are you, sis?"

Ellie returned the picture and found a seat. "You know me —busy as a bee."

"Classes are going well, I presume."

"Couldn't be better. In fact, I received word last week that they're considering making me dean of the department."

"Ellie, that's great. You really have made a name for yourself."

The pot whistled, and Amelia went into the kitchen to prepare the tea. A minute later she returned. "There we are." She handed a cup and saucer to Ellie. "Chamomile tea with honey and milk, just the way you like it."

"Thank you." Ellie stirred the tea, then set it on the table to cool. "I apologize for barging in on you like this, but there's something rather important I wanted to ask you."

Amelia eyed her sister over the rim of her cup. "Sounds ominous."

"I wouldn't say that, but I am curious about something. It

has to do with the summer I spent with Aunt Clara. Do you remember?"

"How could I forget? That was the single worst summer of my life."

"What are you talking about? You and Mother got along swimmingly. It was me she hated."

"Hate is perhaps too strong a word. A general disdain is how I remember it." She flashed a wry smile.

"You always were one with words." Ellie took a sip of tea before continuing. "Regardless, Mother and I didn't get along. That much is certain."

A worried expression flitted across Amelia's face. "So what's your question?"

"It's not so much a question as it is a general observation. Something about that summer has always bothered me."

Amelia raised an eyebrow.

"If you'll recall, Mother showed up at Clara's three days early, claiming she had a surprise for me."

"You spent the weekend in Nashville if memory serves."

"Yes. I'll never forget it. We shopped, ate at the finest restaurants, even caught a show. In fact, it was probably the only time I can remember us ever getting along. At the time, I thought it was strange, but she explained it away, saying that she had missed having me around and wanted to do something special before I returned to school. I had no reason to doubt her, but now..."

"I know that look." Amelia leaned forward in her chair. "You think there's more to the story, don't you?"

Ellie shrugged, returning her attention to the tea in her cup. "I know it's been almost twelve years, but did anything happen in the days leading up to her leaving? Anything at all?"

Amelia took a moment as she tried to recall the events of

that summer. "Nothing comes to mind. Wait…" She put a finger in the air. "There was a phone call the day before she left. Yes, now I remember. After she hung up, I remember seeing her pale-faced and nervous, as if whoever had been on the other end of the line had told her something she wasn't expecting to hear."

"Do you know who made the call?"

Amelia shook her head. "You don't think it was Aunt Clara, do you?"

Ellie considered the possibility. "I doubt it, but I can't be sure."

"But if it was her, why would she want Mother to pick you up early? Did you and Clara have a falling out?"

Ellie shook her head. "On the contrary. In fact, we were in the middle of discussing my return the following summer when Mother knocked on the door. The only thing I can figure is it had something to do with the guy I met when I was there."

"You mean Jack?"

Ellie nodded and dropped her gaze. "I'm surprised you remembered."

"How could I forget? He was the topic of conversation for many months. But what's he got to do with this?"

"Nothing. Something. I don't know."

Amelia finished her tea. "What's brought all this on anyway? Did something happen?"

"Last Friday, I received this in the mail." Ellie took the book from her purse and handed it to Amelia.

Amelia examined the book. "So Jack's an author. Impressive. I guess that just goes to show you that Mother isn't always right. What is the book about?"

"His life, mostly."

"And I assume since you're here, he at least mentions that summer?"

She'd finally arrived at the heart of the matter—that summer.

"Yes. In fact, there are several chapters on the subject."

Amelia straightened in her chair. "So this book is about you?"

"Some of it."

"That must be difficult—to have the details of that summer out there for the world to read."

Ellie hadn't really considered that. "Now that you mention it..." She was overcome by a feeling of bewilderment. "But more than that, I get the sense Jack never stopped thinking about me."

"Does he say that?"

"Not in so many words, but..."

"And I take it you've read the entire book?"

Ellie nodded along. "I hadn't planned to, but I found myself hopelessly lost in his story, unable to pull myself away. And as I was reading, I came upon this one part..." Her throat tightened. "It talked about the day I left—the day Mother showed up unannounced. There's something you should see." She guided Amelia to a page with a dog-eared corner.

I stood on that dock beneath the moon and stars for what seemed like hours. I was as nervous as I'd ever been in my life. My knees and hands were trembling. I must have looked at the ring a hundred times, wondering what she'd say, imagining the look on her face when I got down on one knee. Was I crazy? Yes. But I was in love.

After an hour, I knew something was wrong. It wasn't like her to bail on me. She'd never done it before. So I rushed to the house where she was staying, hoping to find her. But fate had whisked her away, ruining my chances of a happily-ever-after.

"Oh my God, Ellie. Is this what happened?"

"I don't know. But if it is…"

"Did you know anything about this?"

"No, but someone must have."

Amelia returned the book to Ellie. "And you think that's the reason Mother showed up early, to stop him from proposing to you?"

"It must be." Ellie was now more convinced than ever. "Couple my suspicion with the phone call you say she received, and this has her fingerprints all over it. But for Clara to betray us like that would be out of character for her. She adored Jack. Still does as far as I know. Besides, unless Jack told her about his intentions, I don't think Clara knew."

"Have you asked Mother?"

"No. And even if I had, do you honestly think she would tell me the truth?"

"Good point. But why get all worked up about it now? I'm not trying to downplay what she may or may not have done, but that was twelve years ago. Everyone has moved on—you, him... You *have* moved on, haven't you?"

"Yes. I mean, I had. Or maybe I thought I had," Ellie said. "Anyway, when I saw his picture on the back cover, when I read those words, I don't know... Suddenly I was nineteen again, feeling things I haven't felt in a long time. Too long." She shook her head. "I know how ridiculous that sounds, but..."

Amelia joined Ellie on the couch. "No. It's not ridiculous. You were in love. He was your first love. That's a feeling that never goes away no matter how much time passes. I imagine seeing his picture has stirred those emotions that have been lying dormant all these years, making you feel things you haven't felt in a long time."

"I guess you're right." She forced a frail smile. "So what do you think I should do?"

"That depends," said Amelia. "When's the last time you thought of Jack?"

"Not since Christmas. I was going through some of my old things when I came across several artifacts—an old bottle, a ticket stub from a Fourth of July fireworks show, and an arrowhead—from that summer. I don't know why, but seeing those things again stirred some old memories."

"Well, the way I see it, you've got three choices. One, you can do nothing. Two, you can call or write him a letter. Or three, you can get brave and go see him."

See him? The thought was terrifying. "After the way things ended, I don't think seeing him is an option."

"Then write him. It's the least you can do. And in the meantime, if you really want answers, talk to Mother. Maybe then you'll have some peace of mind."

CHAPTER TWENTY-ONE

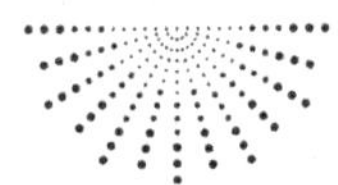

Snowball Effect

Despite her sister's advice, a month passed, then another, and Ellie still hadn't written Jack. Penning a letter to the man who had once stolen her heart proved more difficult than she imagined, so she decided to wait until summer, when she'd have more time to think.

* * *

The day before the end of the semester, Ellie was sitting in her office, grading final exams, when a call came in.

"No!" Ellie felt the air go out of her lungs. "What happened?"

"Heart attack. At least that's what it looks like." Marie sighed into the phone. "Apparently someone found her and rushed her to the hospital, but it was too late."

Ellie struggled to comprehend the news. "W-What about arrangements? There'll be a funeral, won't there?"

"Yes, but no plans have been made. I'm packing some things

as we speak and expect to be on the road within the hour. I'll know more once I get there. I spoke to Amelia a short while ago, and she's planning to leave in the morning."

"I'm coming too," said Ellie, thinking it was the least she could do.

"Are you sure? What about work?"

"Tomorrow's my last day. I'm proctoring an exam in the morning but can leave around lunchtime. I'll pack a suitcase tonight so I can go straight from work. I'll go ahead and reserve a room at the motel in Dandridge."

"Phooey," said Marie. "You can stay with us at Clara's. Besides, it will be nice to have both my girls under one roof again, even if it is under less-than-ideal circumstances."

Ellie considered that, picturing the weekend ending in disaster. "If you insist."

"Well, I need to go. Drive safe, Ellie, and I'll see you tomorrow."

When Ellie hung up the phone, she sat in stunned silence, still trying to process Clara's death. It had been years since she'd last spoken to her aunt, but the time apart did little to dull the sting of her loss.

PART III

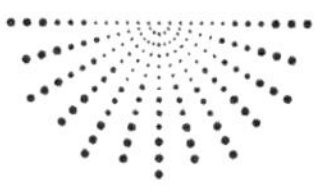

SPRING

CHAPTER TWENTY-TWO

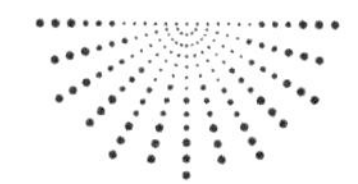

Thunderstruck

May 1962

Cresting the hill, a scene from a postcard unfolded before Ellie's eyes. Rolling emerald fields dotted with pines and oaks sloped gently toward the blue-green water of Douglas Lake. And in the distance, rising in undulating waves of purple and green, were the Smoky Mountains, their rounded peaks shrouded in mist. The view nearly took her breath.

Twelve years had passed since she'd seen anything like this, and all it took was one glimpse for the memories to start flooding back.

Descending the hill, she noticed a marina where once there had been pristine farmland. Scanning the horizon, she spotted a house, then another, and a half dozen more on the far shore. Apparently the once well-guarded secret had finally gotten out.

At the stop sign, she made the right onto Deep Springs Road. She knew this stretch like the back of her hand, and as she paralleled the shoreline, she was transported back to the summer when she was nineteen.

Turning up Clara's drive, Ellie's mind drifted to the last time she'd been in Sims Chapel. Armed with the knowledge that Jack had been waiting to propose, Ellie felt the fury twist inside her, reinforcing her belief that someone had betrayed her.

She pulled into the side yard and parked beneath the shade of a majestic elm. How it had grown since she'd last seen it. Taking a moment to settle her nerves, she prepared herself mentally. The funeral alone was stressful enough, but the possibility of seeing Jack coupled with an extended stay with her mother was enough to push her over the edge, and it would take every ounce of strength and restraint she had to survive the visit.

When she was ready, Ellie grabbed her suitcase and headed for the door.

"Ellie." Marie welcomed her inside. "It's so good to see you, dear. I'm glad you could make it."

"Good to see you too, Mother. How are you holding up?"

"Fine." Marie's stoic features gave no hint of what was on her mind.

Ellie addressed her with a cordial smile before stepping into the foyer. Taking a moment to let her eyes wander, Ellie found things nearly the same, down to the position of the chairs in the living room. "It's like I never left," she muttered.

"I thought I heard your voice." Amelia suddenly appeared and pulled Ellie into a long hug. "How are you, sis?"

"I'm okay." A wave of emotion swept over her. "How long have you been here?"

"A couple of hours. Mom got here last night. This has really done a number on her," she whispered so Marie couldn't hear. "I don't think I've ever seen her like this."

Ellie glanced over her shoulder, surprised that her mother had any feelings.

After exchanging pleasantries, Ellie found her old room and made herself at home while Amelia whipped up something to eat. When it was ready, the three of them sat down to dinner and discussed plans for the funeral.

"I have a meeting with the funeral director tomorrow morning at nine," said Marie. "Amelia has agreed to accompany me. I figured you might want to visit the lawyer regarding Clara's will," she said to Ellie.

"Wouldn't that be the responsibility of Clara's executor?"

"Yes." Marie gave her a look. "It would."

It took Ellie a few seconds to make the connection. "I'm Clara's executor?"

"So it would appear." Marie averted her gaze. "Clara didn't want a gathering of friends, so we'll have a service and the burial Monday morning at the cemetery. Which means there's much do between now and then."

That night, after Marie had gone to bed, Ellie and Amelia sat on the back porch.

"I spent more than a few nights out here," said Ellie, gazing up at the moon.

"You never talked much about that summer. Why?"

Ellie shrugged without looking at her. "I don't know. I thought if I said too much, Mother and Father would find a way to ruin it for me. Which in the end is exactly what happened."

"I take it you haven't spoken to Mother about what you and I discussed?"

Ellie shook her head. "But given the circumstances, that conversation may be unavoidable."

"Maybe that's a good thing," said Amelia. She leaned against the rail, one leg over the other. "At least then you'd have some clarity."

Clarity was the one thing Ellie seemed to lack in several areas of her life. "I still can't believe Clara's gone," she said, struggling to comprehend her loss. "Earlier, when I walked through the door, I expected to find her standing in the kitchen, making one of her famous blackberry cobblers."

"I wish I'd known her better." Amelia's expression turned wistful. "From the stories Mother was telling me before you arrived, Clara sounds like a real firecracker."

The thought brought a smile to Ellie's face. "Yes, she most definitely was."

Silence descended on them, and it was several minutes before either of them spoke.

"Do you ever stop and think if you'd done something as simple as going left versus right, how different your life might be?"

Amelia considered that. "I suppose at one time or another everyone thinks about the choices they've made and what might have happened if they'd done things differently. But I try not to dwell on such things." She rolled her head to the side and looked at Ellie. "Are you having regrets about something?"

Ellie stared into the darkness, reflecting on the decisions that had led her to this point. Was it fate that had brought her here? No, she thought, laying the responsibility at her own feet. She had chosen this path, and it all began when she decided to leave Jack. "I keep wondering what would have happened if Mother hadn't shown up when she did."

"So this is about Jack? Did you ever write him?"

"I wanted to," Ellie answered with regret, "but I could never think of the perfect thing to say."

"Well, you'd better think of something, and fast," said Amelia. "Be it fate or destiny or something else, you're here, back where it all started, and if he was as close to Clara as you say, it's only a matter of time before you run into him."

At the mere thought of seeing Jack again, Ellie's stomach clenched tight.

That first night, sleep was nearly impossible. For Ellie, returning to Sims Chapel was bittersweet. Some of her most precious memories had been made on its sandy shores but had also given rise to some of her deepest regrets.

Lying in bed, listening to the chirping of crickets and katydids, the events of that summer—hot days, cool nights, and stolen kisses in the dark—played inside her head like a movie reel. Twelve years had passed since she and Jack had navigated the coves and channels of the lake, yet it felt like yesterday.

Unable to sleep, she slipped out of bed and stood by the window, peering into the darkness, and thinking of Jack. With his newfound success as an author, she imagined him traveling the country, visiting the places he'd talked about when he was eighteen. Or perhaps he was married, living in North Carolina. He'd mentioned having family there. Either way, she couldn't imagine him in Sims Chapel. Not anymore.

The next morning, Ellie woke to the smell of bacon frying.

Shrugging into her robe, she shuffled down the hall toward the kitchen and found her mother preparing breakfast.

"Someone's up early." Ellie found a seat at the table and sat down.

"Morning, dear," said Marie. "I couldn't sleep, so I figured I'd get up and start breakfast."

"That makes two of us." Ellie pressed her palms against her temples. When the throbbing in her head ceased, she offered to help with breakfast.

"You still remember how to make biscuits, don't you?"

"You forget who you're talking to." Ellie rolled up her sleeves and gathered the ingredients—flour, baking powder, salt, and sugar—then checked the fridge. After grabbing the buttermilk and a stick of butter, she found a bowl and sifter and began mixing the dry ingredients. Pressing a fist into the center of her mix, she added the buttermilk a little at a time, then rolled the biscuits by hand.

"I see you haven't lost your touch," Marie noted as Ellie placed the biscuits in the skillet. "You always were a whiz in the kitchen."

Ellie reached for the knob and turned on the oven. "Still am."

When the oven had preheated, Ellie put the biscuits in and closed the door. "Where's Amelia? I figured she'd be the first one up."

"I would have if I'd gotten any sleep." Amelia shuffled into the kitchen, smothering a yawn. "But between the crickets, bullfrogs, and whatever was scratching outside my window last night, I'm surprised I got any sleep at all."

Ellie laughed under her breath, recalling how those sounds had once serenaded her to sleep.

After pulling her hair into a ponytail, Amelia offered her assistance.

"Think you can handle scrambled eggs?" Marie asked.

"Piece of cake."

Soon the three of them were working together.

"When's the last time the three of us cooked breakfast like this?" Marie leaned against the counter.

"Probably not since Ellie and I were teenagers." Amelia cracked the eggs into a bowl and began whisking them rapidly.

"Thanksgiving, 1954," said Ellie. "I was working on my master's degree at the time."

"That's right," said Amelia. "That's when you were still seeing Michael, wasn't it?"

Ellie raised an eyebrow.

"Whatever happened to Michael anyway?" asked Marie. "He was a real go-getter."

"Last I heard, he took a job in Kansas City," said Ellie, hoping they wouldn't dwell on the subject.

"Has it been that long?" Amelia switched off the burner and set the eggs aside to cool. "Time really does fly, doesn't it? But look at us now, all grown, successful women. It's just a shame that it takes a tragedy to bring us together."

When the biscuits were ready, they each filled a plate and moved to the back porch to take in the fresh air and morning sun. Above them, a few wispy clouds drifted overhead on their way to the mountains, but otherwise, the sky was clear.

"I'd forgotten how lovely this place is," said Marie, taking in the view.

"You've been here before?" Ellie asked. "In the daytime, I mean."

Marie nodded, observing a pair of mockingbirds singing in the oak tree at the yard's edge. "Before you came along, your father and I visited Clara and Bill often. Believe it or not, the four of us were the best of friends."

"What happened?" Amelia asked.

"Life, I suppose." Marie looked wistful. "Once you start having children, everything changes."

"I can attest to that," said Amelia before taking a bite of eggs.

Family? Children? Sadly, Ellie knew nothing of that life. Not that she hadn't dreamed of getting married and starting a family. She'd had it all planned out: graduation at twenty-two, a doctorate at twenty-four, married by twenty-six, and a mother by twenty-eight. But as she'd come to learn, the best-laid plans often didn't materialize, at least not in the way she expected.

When breakfast concluded, Marie and Amelia set off for the funeral home, leaving Ellie to deal with the attorney. After ensuring the paperwork was in proper order, she was off again. Knowing that her mother and sister wouldn't be back for a couple more hours, she drove around for a while, reminiscing about the past.

Turning onto the old highway that circumvented the lake, she rolled down the windows and let the warm breeze blow through her hair. It reminded her of the times she and Jack had ridden around in George's truck, spending hours talking and laughing without a care in the world.

But her trip down memory lane ended abruptly when she passed Jack's old house.

"Oh no!" she cried, finding only charred remains where once the house had stood. Curious, she went to take a closer look.

Peering through the windshield, she realized something

terrible had happened. Her thoughts went immediately to Helen.

She got out and walked to the backyard. The oak tree, beneath which she and Jack had once sat and dreamed of the future, was gone, along with the garden, and Helen's rose bush. *What happened to this place?*

Carefully navigating the tall grass, she reached the house's outer wall and peered into the space where the kitchen had been, recalling the night she and Helen had prepared dinner for Jack. It was the same night he'd told her he would someday marry her.

Her lip quivered, and a sob threatened to choke off her voice. But before she shed a tear, the sound of tires on gravel caused her to look up. A truck was barreling up the drive. It came to a stop, and a second later, a man emerged, his identity concealed by the sunlight at his back.

"I'm sorry, miss." He strode toward her. "You can't be here. This is private pr—" He stopped dead in his tracks. After what felt to her like an eternity, he said, "Ellie?"

The sight of him took her breath. For several long seconds she stood there, frozen in time. "Hello, Jack," she finally said, finding her voice.

He stared, seemingly unsure if she was real or a figment of his imagination. "I-I'm sorry if I startled you." His tone softened. "I got a call from Mrs. Myers saying someone was snooping around. I figured it was some of the local kids again. You don't know how many times I've had to run them off." His eyes were on her again.

"That's all right. I didn't mean to cause a fuss, it's just that when I drove by and noticed the house, well..." She glanced at the ruins. "I didn't know you still lived here." Her mind was reeling. "Last I heard you were in Arizona. Or was it California?"

"Oregon, actually."

"Oh." She held his gaze for a moment before looking at the ruins again. It was easier to think when she wasn't looking directly at him. "What happened here?"

"A storm." He eased toward her. "Remember that old oak tree, the one we used to sit under? Lightning split it right down the middle. Half of it fell on the garden, the other half on the house, which is what started the fire. Fortunately, no one was home when it happened, but by the time help arrived, it was too late to save the house."

"Thank God your mother wasn't home."

There was a moment of silence, during which Ellie could feel Jack's eyes on her.

"Listen," he said. "I'm glad I ran into you. Given the circumstances, I figured you'd come, and I wanted to tell you how sorry I am for your loss. Clara was… well, she was a fine woman, and she'll be sorely missed."

"Thank you, Jack. That means a lot. I was just telling Amelia last night how I still can't believe she's gone."

"Neither can I." He took a breath. "I only wish I could have gotten to her sooner. Maybe she'd still be alive."

Recalling a detail from her conversation with her mother, a chill climbed Ellie's spine. "You mean you're the one who found her?"

Jack nodded, looking solemn. "I had come to repair the back porch. When I arrived, she was sitting in that old rocker of hers, facing the mountains. At first, I thought she had fallen asleep, but…" His expression grew grim.

Ellie put a hand to her throat and blinked back tears. "Jack, I'm so sorry. I can't imagine what that must have been like for you. Thank you for trying to save her though. I know how much she meant to you."

He stared silently ahead, looking as though the enormity of the moment was too much for him. "I should go." He took a step back. "Feel free to stay as long as you like." He turned and headed for the truck.

"What's your hurry?"

He stopped at the truck and pivoted slowly on his heel. "Work. I told Matthew I'd only be gone a few minutes."

"Work? Where?"

"At the dock, same as before. You remember the place, don't you?"

"Sure, but..." She scratched her head. "You still work there?

"You sound surprised."

"It's just that I figured you would have given all that up, what with the success of your book and all."

Jack climbed into the truck and rolled down the window. "It's only one book, Ellie. Besides, even if I write a hundred books, it won't change me or my love for the water." He turned over the key and started the engine. "Well, it was nice seeing you again. Take care."

"Wait," she said before he pulled away. "How do I find you... in case I want to see you again?"

He stared at her for a moment before answering. "You're a smart woman, Ellie. I suspect if you want to find me bad enough, you'll know where to look."

CHAPTER TWENTY-THREE

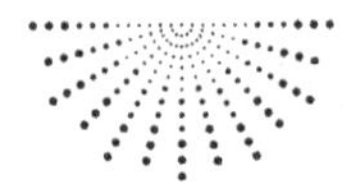

The North Star

After Ellie had eaten dinner, she stood on the back porch, watching dusk fade to a night sky filled with stars. With the anxiety of seeing Jack now behind her, she was free to focus on whatever came next. And although their exchange that afternoon, albeit brief, had been cordial, she didn't get the impression he was overjoyed to see her. Either way, she was happy they talked, and equally satisfied to have seen his face again.

Hearing the door behind her creak open, her thoughts evaporated as she turned to find Amelia slipping out onto the porch.

"How is she?"

"Sleeping… finally," said Amelia, exhaustion showing on her face. She shut the door and joined Ellie at the rail. "This has been an emotional day for her."

"I'm a little surprised." Ellie couldn't recall a time when she'd seen her mother display any emotion other than anger or disgust.

"I suppose none of us are impervious to the effects of

death," said Amelia. "Not even our mother." She leaned against the rail and drew a deep breath of the cool evening air. "Besides, Clara was her sister. I know I'd be devastated if anything ever happened to you."

Amelia's words left Ellie feeling hollow. "You know I feel the same about you, right?"

Amelia nodded knowingly. "But it wouldn't hurt you to say it sometimes." She grinned, then set her gaze upon the water below. "You weren't lying when you said this place was gorgeous. How come you never came back after that summer?"

Ellie considered that. "I had planned to," she said, recalling the promise she'd made to Jack about returning, "but after Jack went to war, I couldn't stomach the thought of being here without him. Then after we broke up, I tried to forget about this place. I suppose I could have come back to see Clara, and in retrospect, I should have, but it would have been too hard. This is a small town, and sooner or later, I would have run into Jack. And what do you say to the man whose heart you broke?"

Amelia cast a look of suspicion in her direction. "I thought you said Jack left you?"

Ellie averted her eyes. "That's what I told everyone, but the truth is I'm the one who ended it."

"Why? What happened?"

Stricken by remorse, Ellie hesitated before answering. "From the moment I returned home, Mother was in my ear, trying her best to convince me that I should forget about Jack and focus on school. But I was stubborn and refused to give in. Determined to prove her wrong, my love for Jack strengthened, and for a while, things were great. Despite the distance, we wrote almost every day. I was convinced we were going to make it, that once school was over, we would get married and spend the rest of our lives together. Then in November of that year, Jack came to visit, and something happened that caused a fracture in our relationship."

"What?"

Panic stirred inside Ellie as she recalled the details. "Considering it was Jack's first time in Bloomington, naturally, I wanted him to meet my friends. I thought they'd love him for all the same reasons I loved him, but I was wrong. Anyway, Jack and Michael got into an argument, which led to Jack leaving a day early. I was devastated. In the days that followed, all I could hear was Mother's voice inside my head, saying told you so." Ellie paused as a wave of agony tore through her. "A few weeks later, Jack received his draft letter. Things were never the same after that. We hung on for another year, but eventually, I think we both knew our time had come and gone, so in the summer, I decided to end it. I felt terrible for breaking his heart, especially considering he was at war, but I felt as if I had no other choice."

Amelia took a moment to process Ellie's words. "I didn't realize you had gone through all that. Why didn't you come to me?"

"I was hurt and ashamed," she said, fighting tears. "I loved Jack with all my heart, and breaking up with him was the hardest thing I've ever had to do. Over the years, I've tried to forget about him, to move on, but I can't. A piece of my heart remains with him."

"Do you still love him?"

She dissolved into tears.

Amelia comforted her until she stopped crying.

"You must think I'm a fool, carrying on like this." Ellie dried her eyes.

"Of course not. This is an emotional time. Honestly,"

Amelia said, releasing her, "I'm relieved to see that you still have feelings."

"What?"

"Well, it's just that normally nothing seems to affect you. You're very..." She seemed to be searching for a word. "Stoic. At least now I know you're not completely heartless. For a while, I was starting to think you were turning into Mother."

They burst into laughter.

"I needed that." Ellie took a moment to compose herself. "You don't know how much I've missed this."

"What?"

"Talking, just the two of us, like we did when we were teenagers. I don't know if I ever told you, but growing up, I had this vision in my head of what our lives would be like when we got older. I figured we'd both be married, live in the same city, maybe even on the same street, and have children that grew up together." She frowned. "But that couldn't be further from the truth, could it?"

"We can still have those things," said Amelia. "But that would require a rearranging of your priorities, and I'm not sure you're ready for that."

After another sleepless night, Ellie woke the following morning with the sole purpose of finding Jack. Emotions held captive for the past decade had broken loose at the mere sight of him, filling her with a sense of hope—and dread. She loved him, of that she was certain. The only question was: did he still love her? Moreover, she hadn't noticed a wedding ring, which made her wonder why, after all this time, he hadn't married.

"Where do you think you're going?" Marie looked up from the morning paper, stalking Ellie with her eyes.

"If you must know, I have a few errands to run," she said as she crossed the foyer to the front door. "But don't worry. I'll be back in plenty of time to help with the arrangements."

She was on the road in less than a minute, speeding toward the dam. With each passing mile, the memories came, one after the other, flooding her senses with the stickiness of warm summer nights.

When she reached the dock, Ellie parked the car and took a moment to reacquaint herself with the area. At the end of the ramp, around a new section of dock, a half dozen silver boats bobbed, their hulls gleaming in the sunlight. Off to the left were anchored a dozen more boats, all bearing the name J&G CHARTERS. And in the center of the complex, where the little shack had once stood, was a newer, larger structure.

Ellie searched for the johnboat she and Jack had used to navigate the lake, but it was nowhere in sight. Summoning every ounce of courage she had, Ellie got out, took a breath, and descended the hill. When her feet touched the wooden planks, she recalled the day she and Jack first met. And when she passed the spot where they used to sit with their feet in the water, tingles ran down her spine.

"May I help you?"

Ellie turned to find a good-looking man in his early thirties standing in the doorway. "Yes." She slapped on a smile. "I'm looking for Jack Bennett. I believe he works here."

A smile ruffled his lips. "That's one way of putting it. Jack owns this place, and I work for him. You must be Ellie."

"Yes, how did you—?"

"Jack talks about you all the time." He gave her the once-over. "He was right; you're beautiful."

Heat touched her cheeks.

"I'm sorry, where are my manners? I'm Matthew Malone. Jack and I served together in the war." He introduced himself with a handshake.

"Nice to meet you, Matthew. Is Jack around this morning?"

He nodded toward the water, then glanced at his watch. "He's out making sure everything is ready for our charter, but I'm expecting him anytime. There's some fresh coffee inside and some rocking chairs at the end of the dock if you'd like to wait for him."

Ellie thought for a moment, still trying to grasp that Jack often talked of her. "Yes, I think I will. Thank you."

She filled a cup of coffee and strolled to the end of the dock, letting the cool morning air fill her lungs. Relaxing into the rocker, she turned her eyes toward the water. And as the sun topped the trees, she pulled the sunglasses from her hair and slipped them on.

* * *

Less than a mile away, Jack rounded the point. Scanning the horizon, he noticed someone sitting at the end of the dock. He leaned forward in his chair, looked closer, and felt his heart jump. "I'll be damned."

"Got room for one more?" She lifted herself out of the rocker and offered a cheeky smile.

Seeing Ellie with her shades on took Jack back to the day they met. He watched her for a few seconds, wondering why she'd come. "Hop in," he finally said. He helped her into the boat, and they set off for open water.

"Things sure have changed around here," she said, breaking the ice.

"Twelve years is a long time. You didn't expect it would be the same, did you?"

At his abrupt tone, she lost her smile. "No. I suppose not." They eased along the shoreline, hardly making a wake. "Does it ever get old, trolling these same waters?"

Jack shook his head in a swift arc. "Never. Lakes are like people, ever-changing, which means there's always something new to discover." Talking about the water was far easier than dealing with his feelings, but when Ellie looked away, he couldn't help glancing at her hand. She wasn't wearing a wedding ring. "Are you still teaching at the university?"

She nodded as her gaze returned to him.

"Is it everything you hoped it'd be?"

Lines pulled at the corners of her mouth. "Yes, I love it there."

"I'm glad," he said, responding with a smile of his own.

"So what are you up to these days besides fishing and writing?"

"Isn't that enough?" He bit back a smile. "Actually, I fish less than I used to. Nowadays I mostly scout and run the business side of things. It's all thanks to George. You remember George, don't you?"

A smile breezed over her. "How could I forget? Is he still around?"

"No," Jack muttered, before glancing away.

A hushed silence fell over them.

"I'm sorry. I know how much he meant to you."

"Thanks. When he died, he left his business to me, so I took it over and transformed it into what it is today. We still run a few tours to the islands now and then, but mostly we cater to folks looking for trophy bass or crappie."

"Just like you said you wanted to. It sounds like you're happy."

"For the most part," he said, nodding along. "What about you, are you happy in Indiana?"

"How happy is anyone, really?" she mused. "Content is perhaps the best way to describe it."

"What about a family—a husband, kids?"

She turned her face away. "Someday, maybe."

He sensed there was more to the story but decided not to press his luck.

"I don't see a ring on your finger," she said, turning the tables. "No woman ever tied you down?"

Jack quirked his lips. "Someday, maybe."

"Any particular reason?"

Jack eyed her narrowly. "I guess I haven't found the right woman."

"Now that you're rich and famous, I figured you'd have every eligible bachelorette from Nashville to Charlotte knocking on your door."

He breathed a laugh through his nose. "Hardly. Besides, you know me. I prefer to keep a low profile."

They motored around Rock Island to the head of Flat Creek where Jack had first taught Ellie how to fish.

"This feels familiar." Her eyes gave a sweeping glance. "Over there is where I caught my first fish. And there," she said, pointing to a rocky outcropping, "is where I caught that lunker, remember?" She ran a hand through her hair and rested her gaze on him. "God, that seems like a lifetime ago."

"It was." Jack locked eyes with her. "And it wasn't. Time is a funny thing. Sometimes when I'm out here on the water, I'll hear or see something that makes me think of you, and for a moment I'm eighteen again." He eased along the shore, letting the wind ruffle his hair. He watched Ellie's face, her hair, her everything. Despite the walls he'd spent years constructing and reinforcing, she had managed to breach them in two days. How weak he felt in her company. And his heart, which had waxed cold long ago, beat once more.

"Your accent," said Ellie. "Where did it go?"

Her question amused him. "This place isn't the only thing that's changed since you been away. There's a lot you don't know about me, Ellie."

"Care to enlighten me?"

Jack smiled, realizing little about her had changed. He considered telling her everything that had happened since she last saw him but opted to reveal only the details he thought she needed to know. "I'm not sure we have enough daylight." He chuckled, then went on. "But to answer your original question, most people don't take you seriously when you talk like you have your mouth full of rocks."

Ellie uttered a hushed laugh.

"When I got out of the service, they told me I'd earned a free education, so I took advantage of it and enrolled at the University of Tennessee, where I studied literature and linguistics. It was a slow process, learning how to speak correctly, but by the time I graduated, my accent was almost entirely gone."

"It's amazing how much you've changed."

Jack smiled and they drifted with the current, neither saying anything for a long time.

"I read your book," Ellie said, breaking the silence.

"All of it?"

"Every word."

"What did you think?"

"It was emotional but wonderful at the same time. Your

words captured the essence of that summer nearly perfectly. You must be proud."

"I am. It was a labor of love." He was quiet for a moment, then went on. "If you read the book and got my letter, why didn't you call or write?"

His question seemed to take her by surprise. "I wanted to... was going to..."

"But?"

"Honestly, I didn't think you'd want to talk to me, not after..."

Jack found a quiet place and switched off the engine. For nearly a decade, he'd wondered what he might say at this exact moment. "This might come as a surprise, Ellie, but I harbor no resentment toward you."

She raised her eyes as a look of shock scrawled across her delicate features. "You don't?"

Jack swung his head in a no. "When I came back from Korea, I was in a dark place, not just because of what happened with us, but because of the war and the things I'd seen and done. The doctors call it combat fatigue. As it turns out, a lot of us who served suffer from the same condition. I tried to pick up where I left off, to acclimate to life away from the battlefield, but I found no joy in anything. There were times I'd sit and stare at the water for hours, just trying to feel something. Then when I'd lost almost all hope, my doctor suggested a change of scenery, so I went out west for a while and stayed with a buddy from my platoon. He and I ran a mechanic business, working on cars and trucks. I had only planned to stay for a few months, just long enough to clear my head, but I ended up meeting someone while I was there. But eventually, I started longing for home, for the mountains and the water. And since I couldn't convince her to move to Tennessee, we ended things." He paused, gathering his thoughts. "I say all this because I want you to know I understand why you did what you did. We were kids back then, Ellie, forced into a situation that neither of us wanted. The only difference is you had options, and I didn't."

A relieved look washed over her face. "You don't know how glad I am to hear you say that. And I'm sorry about all you went through. I had no idea."

Jack smiled at her, thinking how beautiful she still was. "That's okay. I'm doing much better now."

"And I'm glad you got over me," she added. "I was afraid you hadn't."

"Over you?" Jack suppressed a laugh. "Is that what you think? That I got over you? Hell, Ellie, I moved on, that's all. Not because I wanted to but because I had to—to keep from going crazy. But I never got over you, and never will. You were the one I was supposed to spend the rest of my life with. How does anyone get over that?" His words left her speechless. While she composed herself, Jack started the boat and motored around the next point. "Listen. I realize it's only for a few days, but I'm glad you're back. This place hasn't been the same without you."

Ellie's expression lifted into a smile. "Honestly, it's good to be back. I've missed this place, more than you know."

Jack looked up as a thick cloud shuttled across the sky.

"So how long are you in for?"

"The funeral is Monday, but since Clara appointed me her executor, I have to stay at least another day or two to take care of some paperwork."

"What about work?"

"The quarter just ended, so I'm off for the summer. I still

have research to do, but I'll probably take a few weeks off before I dig in again."

When Ellie had finished, Jack checked the time. "Listen. I hate to cut our conversation short, but I have a group coming in at ten. Perhaps we could continue this later?"

She nodded. "Yes, I'd like that."

When they reached the dock, Jack helped Ellie out of the boat. She wobbled for a second, then steadied herself.

"Easy," he said.

She put a hand on the rail. "I guess I'm out of practice."

Jack grinned. "It takes some getting used to, but don't worry. You'll have your sea legs back in no time."

After a friendly goodbye, Jack stood in the doorway to his office and watched Ellie until her car faded from sight.

Matthew appeared then and said, "Looks like you were right. She came back, just like you said she would. Now what?"

Jack shook his head, wondering if it was coincidence or fate that had brought her back into his life. "I don't know, but she's back, and for now that's all that matters."

CHAPTER TWENTY-FOUR

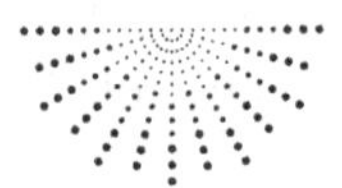

Fireball

At dusk, Jack left work and stopped at the cemetery, processing his conversation with Ellie. Seeing her again had resurrected old memories—some pleasant, some painful—so instead of going straight home, he needed a moment to gather his thoughts.

When he finally got home, night had fallen, and Sara was there waiting for him.

"You're late," she said as he walked through the front door. She handed him a glass of sweet tea and kissed him on the lips.

Jack eased his tired bones into his favorite chair and attempted to push Ellie out of his mind. "Sorry. I stopped at the cemetery."

"Everything okay?"

Jack tipped his head in a yes.

"Are you hungry?"

"Starving."

"Supper's almost ready. We're having your favorite, pot roast with potatoes and carrots."

Jack's stomach rumbled.

Sara went to check on supper then returned a moment later. "So," she said, lingering in the doorway, "a little birdie told me Ellie's back in town. You haven't seen her, have you?"

Jack looked up and eyed her suspiciously. "No, but you knew she'd come... for the funeral."

"Nevertheless, I imagine it's only a matter of time before she comes looking for you."

Jack narrowed his brow at her. "What makes you say that?"

"I may be a lot of things, Jack, but naive isn't one of them. I remember how crazy she was about you."

Jack upended his tea glass before responding with an edge in his voice. "That was a long time ago, Sara."

"Regardless, you know what they say about old habits."

"Are we really going to have this conversation again?" he asked, pressing down his irritation. "Like I've told you countless times, Ellie and I are ancient history. Whatever fire may have existed burned out long ago." But even as he said it, his thought betrayed him.

"Let's hope you're right." She shot him a look of warning. "For her sake, and for yours."

The following morning, Jack ate breakfast while Sara slept in. Far from a superstitious man, even he recognized the timing of things—Clara's death and Ellie's subsequent return—as an omen. The only question was—was it a good omen, or did the future hold more heartbreak for him?

Leaning in his chair, Jack's thoughts drifted to the woman with whom he now shared a bed. Over the years, Sara had waited patiently for her turn to be with him. She had been there when he returned from war, calmed him when the night terrors came, and waited for him while he went out West to clear his head. So despite his feelings for Ellie, Jack kept them hidden, unwilling to risk his relationship with the woman who had loved him through it all.

He dipped his biscuit into the gravy as Sara walked in. "I was thinking," he said as he chewed, "maybe after the funeral we could get out of here and spend a few days in the mountains."

Her eyebrows went up. "The mountains? What brought this on?"

He gave a half shrug, attempting nonchalance. "We've both been busy lately, me at the dock and you with your mother. I just thought we could use some time away, that's all."

She cast a look of suspicion in his direction. "And you promise this has nothing to do with Ellie?"

"Promise." He finished his coffee.

"In that case..." Sara came over and sat on his lap. "Some time away would be nice." She circled her arms around his neck and pulled him into a long kiss.

That afternoon, Ellie was on her way to the kitchen when she heard someone knocking at the door.

"Sara," she said, swinging the door wide. "I almost didn't recognize you. Golly, what a nice surprise. Please come in."

"Are you sure? I don't want to impose."

Ellie gave a dismissive wave. "Nonsense. You're no imposition, and it's nice to see a familiar face." Ellie showed her inside and offered her a seat in the living room. "My mother and sister won't be back for a while, so we have the place to ourselves."

"I can't remember the last time I was in this house." Sara's eyes wandered around the room. "I'm terribly sorry for your loss. Miss Clara was a wonderful woman."

"Thank you," said Ellie. "That's sweet of you to say. I was just about to sit down to lunch. Care to join me?"

"Yes, thank you."

Ellie offered Sara a seat at the table, then brought out a plate of sandwiches and two glasses of tea. "I didn't realize you still lived around here." She relaxed into the chair. "What brings you out this way?"

Sara set her glass on the table. "To offer my condolences and to speak with you about Jack."

Ellie's eyes narrowed. "Jack? What about him?"

Sara stiffened under Ellie's gaze, her expression becoming determined. "I know you went to see him yesterday."

Ellie detected a hint of jealousy in Sara's voice but took it in stride. "Yes. I went by the dock to see the changes he'd made. It's a first-class operation now."

Sara nervously sipped her tea before responding. "Did he happen to tell you he and I are together?"

Ellie felt the air leave her lungs but held it together. "No, he didn't."

"Figures."

"How long?"

"Six weeks tomorrow," she answered proudly. "That may not seem like a long time, but when you've waited as long as I have for Jack..."

Ellie mustered a smile. "Well, I'm happy for you. You're a good person. I've always thought so."

"Thank you," she said with a smile of her own. "And don't

worry, someday you'll find that special someone too. I just know it."

Ellie thought she detected a hint of malice in Sara's voice, but ignored it, thanking her instead.

When they'd finished eating, Ellie walked her to the door. "So I'll see you at the funeral tomorrow?"

"Of course. Jack and I wouldn't miss it."

* * *

Needing to clear her head, Ellie went into town to pick up some essentials. Sara's visit had left her rattled, and as she walked the supermarket aisles, she wondered why Jack hadn't mentioned his relationship with Sara the day before.

"Hey there, stranger. Fancy running into you."

Ellie looked up at the sound of Jack's voice. "Hey," she said, and kept walking.

"Everything okay?"

She stopped and took a breath. "Sara came to see me this afternoon." She watched as the color drained from his face. "How come you didn't tell me about the two of you?"

Jack rubbed the back of his neck. "I was going to, but then we got to talking, and... Anyway, I'm sorry you had to find out like that, but I'm glad you know."

"That's all right. You didn't exactly owe me an explanation." She reached for a cabbage head and placed it in the shopping cart. "It's funny, I don't remember Sara being so forward."

"Typically, she isn't, but you bring out a different side of her."

"Because you and I share a past?"

"That, and because she knows in my eyes, she'll always be second to you."

His comment caught Ellie off guard.

"I only mean that she knows how things were that summer and how in love I was with you," he clarified. "Anyway, I'll have a talk with her before she leaves. The last thing I want is her causing trouble for you and your family."

They walked to the end of the aisle, and Ellie got in line.

"Listen," said Jack, "I was serious yesterday when I said we should continue our conversation. I know you've got a lot going on, but maybe we could take another ride around the lake, or you could come over to the house and let me show you what I've been working on."

Knowing Jack was in a relationship made her hesitate. "I don't know if that's such a good idea."

Jack gave a half-cocked smile. "Is this about Sara? Because if it is, you have nothing to worry about. Her bark is worse than her bite. Besides, she'll be at her mother's place in Rogersville tonight. Come on, what do you say to supper at my place? I'll cook."

A voice inside Ellie's head screamed no, but she agreed anyway, thinking anything—even something as risky as supper at Jack's—was better than time with her mother.

"Great. We'll eat like kings, and I can give you a tour of the house. I think you'll be impressed."

Matthew then popped his head inside the store and told Jack it was time to go.

"A man's work is never done." Jack paid for the ice, then jotted down the address and handed it to Ellie. "Come by around seven. I should have everything ready by then."

CHAPTER TWENTY-FIVE

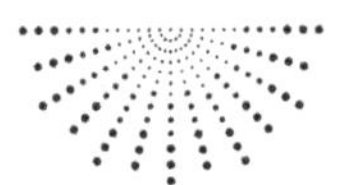

Event Horizon

Amelia stood in the doorway to Ellie's room, picking lint from the sleeve of her blouse. "I think since tomorrow is going to be a long day for us all, I'm going to take Mother to dinner in Knoxville this evening, if only to take her mind off things for a few hours."

"Good idea," said Ellie, who sat by the window, watching the birds and the squirrels play in the yard. "She'll enjoy that."

"I don't suppose I could talk you into joining us, could I?"

Ellie was quick to say no, likening a night out with her mother to beating her head against the wall. "I appreciate the invite, but I have plans of my own."

Amelia took a step inside the room. "Anything you care to share?"

Aware of her mother in the next room, Ellie kept her voice down. "I ran into Jack this afternoon, and he invited me to dinner at his place."

"Just the two of you?"

Ellie nodded.

"Are you sure that's a good idea?"

"A girl's gotta eat, doesn't she?"

Amelia raised an eyebrow. "You know what I mean. Besides, after what you told me about Sara, I can't imagine her being supportive of this."

"Who said she was?" Ellie went to the closet and rifled through her outfits, choosing a red-and-white polka-dot dress with the plunging neckline. "She'll be at her mother's this evening, so she won't be around."

Amelia eyed the dress, then cast a wary glance at Ellie. "I hope you know what you're doing."

"Actually," said Ellie, shaking her head slowly, "for the first time in my life, I don't know what I'm doing." She laid the dress on the bed, then set her gaze on Amelia. "But I know how I feel. God knows I don't want to be the type of woman who breaks up a relationship, especially after what Michael did to me, but I need to know if Jack still has feelings for me. Besides," she said resolutely, "they've only been dating for six weeks, so as far as I'm concerned, he's fair game."

Amelia grabbed Ellie's black heels and set them on the bed beside the dress. "In that case, wear the pearls," she said, then winked at her. "Men are suckers for pearls."

Ellie's brows went up in astonishment.

"What? How do you think I landed Sean? Just promise me you'll be careful and that you'll think with your head instead of your heart. You deserve to be happy, Ellie, so the last thing I want is to see you get hurt again."

"Thank you. You're the one person I can always count on to be in my corner." Ellie stepped forward and hugged Amelia. "And I promise I'll think with my head instead of my heart. I'm a scientist, remember? Thinking is what I do best."

"Speaking of thinking," said Amelia, giving the outfit

another look, "I wonder what Jack will think when he sees you in that dress?"

Ellie offered a mischievous smile. "I can only imagine."

When Marie and Amelia were gone, Ellie slid the dress on over her shoulders, put on her heels, did her hair and makeup, and added a spritz of perfume on her wrists and neck. Lastly, she put on the pearl necklace as Amelia had suggested and stepped back to examine herself in the mirror. She couldn't recall a time when she'd looked so good. After putting on her favorite red lipstick, she grabbed her keys and headed out the door.

The sun hung low in the western sky when she pulled up in front of Jack's house.

Jack greeted her on the porch. His eyes traveled the length of her body and back again, ending at her eyes. "You look incredible."

"Thank you," she said, watching his lips curl into a smile. "So this is your new place?" Ellie took a moment and stared at the old mansion, its facade awash in golden sunlight.

"I bought it last November, just after the book started selling."

He gave her the nickel tour of the grounds, then led her inside and lit a fire. "Can I get you something to drink? Tea? Wine?"

"Let's start with tea and see how it goes," she said, thinking the wine might lead somewhere she wasn't ready to go.

While Jack poured the tea, Ellie eased into the living room, taking in the rest of the house. "Is this the original brickwork?"

"Yes, it is." Jack brought her a glass of tea, then told her to make herself at home.

After checking out the rest of the main floor, Ellie joined

Jack in the kitchen. "I've got to hand it to you. This place is incredible."

"Thank you," he said as he finished dicing the carrots and celery. "It predates the Civil War. It was in rough shape when I bought it, but it had good bones."

Ellie leaned against the doorframe, sipping her tea, and watching Jack. "How'd you get your hands on it?"

Jack dropped the vegetables into the water and set the timer. "Funny story... I ran into this fella at the dock one day who had recently inherited this place from his uncle, who was recently deceased. He was from Wisconsin or Michigan or something. Anyway, we got to talking, and he said he had no interest in keeping the home and wanted to know if I knew anyone who might want to buy it. I played it cool of course, and after a little haggling, we struck a deal."

Ellie shook her head. "Only to you can something like that happen."

"Lucky, right? Anyway, I sold my place to this fella who was looking to make a fresh start, and here I am."

Yes, here you are. "I almost can't believe I'm standing here talking to you."

He looked at her with wonder in his eyes. "Neither can I, but I'm glad you're here. There are so many things I want to tell you."

She watched him move about the kitchen with the ease of a French chef, grinding spices, filleting fish, and preparing a salad. Where had he learned all this? He had all the qualities of a worldly man, a traveler, someone who had seen and done things that exceeded her own experiences. Yet something about him felt comfortable, familiar.

He'd mentioned in his book traveling when his time in the service was over. He talked about London, Paris, and Lisbon, places she had only dreamed of seeing. And she marveled at the man he had become.

While waiting for supper, they moved their conversation into the living room, where they sat in front of the fire.

"Life is funny, isn't it? A week ago, I had all but given up on ever seeing you again, and now..."

"I know what you mean. This time last week I was grading papers and wondering how I was going to spend my summer. Not in my wildest dreams did I imagine a week later I'd be sitting here, talking to you."

Jack smiled briefly before turning serious. "Can I ask you something?"

"Anything."

"If Clara hadn't... That is to say, if she was still around, would you have come?"

His question surprised her, and she took a gulp of tea before answering. "Yes, at some point—at least I think so," she said, conflicted. "After I read your book, I struggled with what to do. I considered writing or calling, but it seemed so impersonal. Plus I could never think of the right words to say." She paused, taking a moment to think. "After reading what you wrote, I... It caught me by surprise, that's all."

Jack's eyes tightened at the corners. "Which part?"

"The part where you were going to propose. I had no idea."

Jack went to the fireplace and stood with his back to her, staring into the flames. "Not having the opportunity to ask you to marry me is still the single biggest regret of my life. You don't know how many times I've replayed that night in my head, wondering what went wrong." He turned and looked at her. "If I had it to do over again, I would have driven from the jewelry store straight to Clara's and asked you right then and there."

They hadn't made it to dinner, and already Ellie had the answer she'd come for. If there was any doubt before, now there was none. Despite Ellie having broken his heart, Jack Bennett was still madly in love with her and had likely been the entire time.

"I'm sorry too," she said, feeling a sharp pang of remorse. "Ever since I read those words, I've wondered what I would have said, what I would have done. We were so young back then, so naive."

He came back to her. "But we were in love, weren't we?" he asked earnestly.

"Yes, very much in love. Jack, I—"

The timer went off, cutting her short.

"Hold that thought." Jack went to check the fish. When he returned, he noticed that Ellie's glass was empty. "More tea?"

"Actually, I think I'm ready for that wine now."

They sat down to supper, and the conversation came easy. Ellie told him about her career and the successes she'd had, and when she was done, Jack regaled her with stories of fishing and the sights he'd seen while traveling. They spent the evening getting caught up on each other's lives, and when the meal concluded, they continued their conversation on the porch.

"This has been fun." Ellie peered into the darkness. "I was hesitant about being here, but I'm glad you talked me into it."

"So am I." Jack took another draw from his beer and eased into the rocker. "So tell me more about Indiana, about your life outside work."

Ellie leaned against the porch post, staring into her wine. "It's rather lonely, I'm afraid. Between lectures and the endless hours of research, there isn't a lot of time for much else."

"That surprises me," said Jack. "I pictured you having more

friends than you could shake a stick at, spending evenings on the town, or hosting extravagant parties."

Ellie gave a nervous laugh, recalling how her life had once been as Jack described. "Most of my friends are either married or have moved away. And as far as parties are concerned, aside from the occasional night out with my assistant and her husband, it's mostly just me."

Jack was silent while he finished his beer. "What about a companion, someone with whom you share your hopes and dreams?"

Ellie shook her head, thinking that it had been years since she had someone like that in her life.

"That's too bad. A woman like you deserves to have someone."

Ellie glanced away, feeling as if the conversation had become too personal. "Tell me something—why did you never come to see me after that day?" It was a question she'd asked herself many times over the years.

"To which day are you referring?" he asked without skipping a beat.

She surmised he knew exactly to which day she was referring but played along anyway. "The day you were released from the army."

"Oh, that day." Jack was silent for a moment before answering. "Actually, I did come to see you."

"You did not. I would have remembered."

"You didn't see me," he said, and her blood ran cold.

"It was on my way out West." He looked away, appearing to be struggling with something. "After you told me you were with Michael, what remained of my world came crashing down. No matter how hard I tried, I couldn't come to terms with the fact that you'd left me for him." Jack took a breath and exhaled slowly. "So in July of that year, I took the bus to Bloomington to see for myself. When I arrived, the weather was awful; it rained most of the day. But just after sundown I caught a break. That's when I went looking for you. It took me a while, but I finally caught up with you at the diner. You were with Susan and Marjorie, sitting in a booth by the window. Your hair was up, and you had on a red sweater and matching lipstick. The three of you were talking and laughing. For a moment, I thought maybe you'd broken up with Michael, or that the whole thing had been a bad dream, but..." Silent tears filled his eyes. "A few minutes later, he walked in. He sat down beside you, draped an arm over your shoulder, and kissed you."

Ellie's heart stopped. "Oh Jack, I'm so sorry."

"It's not your fault," he said, and blinked back the tears. "Besides, it wasn't the kiss that hurt me the most. It was the look on your face, the gleam in your eye when you looked at him. It was the same way you used to look at me. And I knew right then and there that you'd moved on and forgotten all about me."

A wave of regret tore through Ellie as she watched tears streak down the sides of his face. "How come that wasn't in your book?" she asked delicately.

"Because." He dried his tears. "Some things are too painful to put on paper."

Wishing she could go back and change things, Ellie fought back tears of her own. "I can't tell you how sorry I am for hurting you like I did. I never intended for things to play out this way."

Jack nodded along. "I know."

Ellie peered into the deepening night, gathering her thoughts. When she'd composed herself, she turned to Jack and said, "What would Sara say if she knew I was here tonight?"

Jack's posture stiffened. "Does it matter?"

"Maybe. Maybe not. But shouldn't it matter to you?"

Jack appeared to be thinking. "If I were in love with her, it would," he finally said.

Ellie felt her heart pitter-patter against her chest. "If you're not in love with her, then why are you with her?"

He shrugged. "Sara's attractive, and fun to be around. Besides that, she worships the ground I walk on."

"But?"

"But she's not..." He turned away.

"Not what?" Ellie leaned closer and touched his forearm, gently prodding him.

Jack looked up at her, his face pained. "She's not you, Ellie. She'll never be you."

Ellie leaned away, taking a moment to consider his words. Before she could respond, lightning fractured the night sky, followed by the distant rumble of thunder.

"A storm is coming." She cast an eye to the south. "I should probably go before it gets bad."

Jack stood and followed her into the kitchen. "You could stay."

His offer stopped her cold.

"It's already midnight, and you've been drinking. Besides, I have plenty of room upstairs."

Ellie found herself breathless, caught off guard by his invitation. "Jack," she said, turning on her heel, "I appreciate the offer, but I'm not sure that's such a good idea."

"Because of Sara?"

Sara was the least of her worries. "That and because we may end up doing something we'll regret tomorrow."

Jack seemed unfazed by her words. "I won't have any regrets," he finally said as his eyes bore into hers.

After swallowing the lump in her throat, Ellie said, "Be that as it may, the last thing I want is to cause trouble for you. I feel as if I've done plenty of that already."

"And while I appreciate your concern," he said with a firm voice, "I'm a grown man, and I'm free to make my own decisions."

Ellie's heart burst into a jaunt as warmth radiated from her center.

A clap of thunder broke her concentration, and she looked away.

"At least let me show you the upstairs," he implored. "Then you can make up your mind."

A part of Ellie had wanted to see the upstairs since she arrived.

"Okay," she said, giving in to the urge. *What am I getting myself into?* But she knew where this would lead. She had imagined it ever since the moment she saw Jack at the ruins, had dreamed the night before of his lips on hers, his hands in places he hadn't touched in years. Suddenly, her thoughts were a jumbled mess.

Jack took her hand and led her to the upper floor, where an empty bedroom waited. "And this would be your room," he said, turning on the light.

Her eyes flitted about the room, taking in the oversized poster bed, floral drapes, and mint green walls. Clearly, it had been designed by a woman for a woman. "It's nice," she said. "Did you decorate it yourself?"

Jack uttered a small laugh and shook his head. "A woman from town—Denise—helped me with the furnishings. I may be good at a lot of things, but interior design isn't one of them."

Ellie laughed reflexively, nervously, feeling again as if she were treading into water of unknown depth. "This isn't Sara's room, is it?"

"No," said Jack. "No one has ever stayed in this room."

Ellie didn't ask, but she got the feeling Jack had designed the room for her. "Look, Jack, I appreciate the offer, and the room is lovely. It's just—"

Jack held up a hand. "Say no more. I won't pressure you into doing something that makes you uncomfortable."

Jack had always been respectful, even to a fault, but Ellie wasn't looking for respect at that moment. She didn't want him to take no for an answer. She wanted him to sweep her up in his arms and make love to her the way he had years earlier.

Turning away, Ellie took a step into the hall and stumbled. But Jack snapped into action and caught her before she fell.

"Easy."

Ellie locked eyes with him, and for a moment, her entire body went numb. At the same time, she reconsidered her decision to leave. *It's only one night. What's the worst that could happen?*

"Ellie?" His voice broke the spell.

"Sorry, I'm fine. I just lost my balance, that's all."

Jack steadied her and asked if she was okay to drive.

"I'm fine," she reassured him, "but thank you." Knowing she must go, she tried once more to leave but fell back against the door.

They locked eyes again, and Ellie felt impaled by his gaze. Before she realized what was happening, Jack had his arms around her, pulling her into a kiss.

When they parted, Ellie looked up at him through her lashes, hoping he'd kiss her again.

"I'm sorry." A look of shame crossed his face, and he turned away.

No, don't be sorry. "For what?"

"I shouldn't have taken advantage of you like that."

Ellie reached for his arm and pulled him to her. "Jack," she said, gazing into his blue eyes, "There's nothing to be sorry for. I'm not a girl anymore, and I'm perfectly capable of making my own decisions, even after three glasses of wine."

She circled her arms around his neck and drew him into a long kiss that left him short of breath.

"I love you, Ellie," he whispered against her lips. "I never stopped loving you."

The sudden sensation of falling made her clutch the door-frame. "I love you too," she said, then put a finger to his lips. "Which is why I must go." Carefully, she made her way down-stairs and grabbed her purse. "Thank you for dinner," she said, stopping on the front porch. "It was one of the best meals I've ever had. And the house is lovely." Her gaze met his.

"You're welcome." He smiled warmly. "Maybe we could do it again sometime."

"Maybe," she said, wondering if she had let a golden opportunity slip through her fingers.

CHAPTER TWENTY-SIX

Red Sky at Morning

The day of the funeral, Ellie woke to the throbbing pulse of rain. Parting the drapes, she found the world dull and dreary as a dark sky wept above her.

Taking advantage of being the first one up, Ellie locked herself in the bathroom and filled a tub with hot water. And as she sat there with her eyes closed, replaying the previous evening's events, she thought of Jack's lips against hers, the heat of his warm breath on her skin. After a sharp intake of breath, she opened her eyes and stopped herself, surprised at how easily the thought of him aroused her.

Toweling off, she went to her room and put on a robe, then searched the closet. Finding her black dress, she laid it across the bed, along with her shoes and gloves. And it was at that moment the reality of Clara's death hit her.

At breakfast, the mood was somber. Ellie and Amelia whispered about Ellie's dinner with Jack before Marie came in to get coffee.

"So how was it?" Amelia eyed Ellie over the brim of her cup.

"Fine."

"Did you get what you wanted?"

Ellie recalled the kiss, regretting her decision to leave. "Not entirely, but one thing's for certain—Jack is still in love with me."

"Is that what he said?"

"Let's put it this way: if I hadn't taken your advice, I'd still be there, and Sara would be nothing but a memory."

* * *

By the time they reached the cemetery, the rain had faded to a fine mist. When everyone had gathered, the preacher began the service. While he spoke, Ellie did her best not to look Jack's way, knowing Sara would be watching. But after what had happened the night before, it was difficult to keep her eyes off him.

The rain held off just long enough, and when the service was over, everyone hurried to their cars as the skies opened again. Ellie and her family stayed behind to say their final goodbyes. So did Jack.

"Where did Sara run off to?" Ellie asked as they sheltered beneath the tent.

"She went to take Mama home. I drove separately so I could go straight to Clara's and start preparing the food. Are you going there now?"

"I have to meet Mr. Randolph at his office. He says it's important. But I'll be along shortly." She waited for Marie to pass before going on. "Listen, about last night—"

"I was out of line," said Jack. "I'd had too much to drink, and—"

"I was going to say I rather enjoyed myself. The kiss wasn't bad either." She nudged him playfully with her elbow, which drew a smile.

"It was nice, wasn't it? It reminded me of old times."

"It might be nice to do it again," she whispered, then watched as the smile ran away from his face.

"Look, Ellie, as much as I want to, and God knows I want to, I don't think it's a good idea for us to do that again. We were dangerously close to making a huge mistake last night."

"A mistake for who?" she asked, thinking of what he'd told her the night before.

"For us both."

"Speak for yourself," she said in defiance. "You know, I woke up this morning with a feeling of regret; not for having kissed you, but for not having done more. I meant what I said about loving you, Jack, and whether you believe me or not, it doesn't change the way I feel."

He regraded her with skepticism. "If you loved me so much, why wait this long to see me? You could have made an effort at any time over the past nine years, but you didn't. Now I'm supposed to believe that after a boat ride and supper, you're in love with me again?"

"You're right," she said, feeling the sting of his words. "I know it doesn't make sense. And yes, I could have come to see you, but I didn't." She stopped and looked him in the eye. "But I'm here now, and that has to count for something."

* * *

That afternoon, everyone gathered at Clara's for lunch. Fortunately, the rain was over, and the sun appeared as the low cloud deck pushed east into the mountains. When everyone had been served, Ellie asked if Jack would like to get some fresh air.

Jack dried his hands and followed her out into the backyard. "Everything okay?"

She nodded, facing the lake. "I just needed to get out of the house for a few minutes. Being around that many huggers makes me claustrophobic."

Jack chuckled. "They mean well, but it can be a little overwhelming, especially if you're not used to it."

Ellie ventured a glance in his direction. "Listen, I wanted to thank you for today. It's very kind of you to come here and feed everyone."

"It's my pleasure, and it's the least I could do. You know," he said, "after you left last night, I got to thinking. Most people don't realize how much Clara meant to me. Outside of Mama, George, and you, she was the only other person who ever made me feel like I was worth something. She saw my potential before I did, and that's something I'll never forget."

"Speaking of last night, I hope I didn't cause trouble for you with Sara."

"She didn't ask, and I didn't tell."

Silence descended and was broken a minute later when Jack redirected the conversation. "Did I ever tell you about the first time I met Clara?"

"I don't think so," said Ellie, thankful for the change in subject.

"It was shortly after Bill died. I must have been about eight years old." Jack paused, giving a wistful smile. "Clara was looking for someone to come and help around the yard. It just so happened I was looking to make a little money, so when I heard she needed help, I walked right up to the house, knocked on the door, and asked for the job. I suspect she was hoping for someone a little older, but she was so taken by my initiative that she ended up giving me the job. I remember she and I sat right here on this swing and drank sweet tea."

"She was like a second mother to you, wasn't she?"

He nodded, blinking back the tears. "Did you know when I was writing my book, it was Clara I came to for help? When I found out it was going to be published, she's the first person I told. I'll never forget, she made me one of her famous blackberry cobblers to celebrate."

"Now that I can believe." Ellie held on to a smile for a few seconds before it faded from her face. "After that summer, she and I lost touch. Occasionally, I'd get a card or letter from her, but we were never as close as we were then. Now that she's gone, I wish I'd made more of an effort."

"She loved you though," said Jack. "In fact, she talked about you all the time. You must have made quite an impact on her." He glanced away before bringing his gaze back to her. "If you don't mind me asking, why did you never come back?"

"I was afraid."

"Of what?"

She set her gaze upon him. "Of seeing you. We didn't exactly part on good terms, Jack, and I was afraid that if I came back, I'd run into you somewhere and I just wasn't ready to face you."

Jack turned and stared at the water for a long time, not saying anything. "What will become of this place now that Clara's gone?"

"That depends on you." Ellie produced a letter and handed it to him.

"What's this?" He opened the letter and began reading to himself.

Dear Jack,

Well, it's true, no one lives forever. Not even me. Oh well, who would want to anyway?

I know you're a busy man, so I'll keep this brief. Regarding the house and ten acres, I'm leaving it all to you. Why, you ask? Because you are the one person in the world who is most like my beloved Bill. You came from humble beginnings, struggled, persevered, and made something of yourself. Whenever I needed you, you were always there, no questions asked. But above all that, I know how much this place means to you, which is why I know you're the right person to see it into the future. That said, I don't want you to feel obligated to keep the house. You've got a place of your own now, and it's a fine place, but if you do decide to keep it, I hope you get to experience the same magic I once experienced, because there's something special about this place. You can't see it or touch it, but it's there, and it's real.

By the way, as much as I loved old George, he was wrong about one thing—you got your house on the hill, after all.

P.S. As wonderful as the view is, it's better

when you have someone to share it with.

Until we meet again,

Your friend,

Clara

When Jack finished reading the letter, he began to cry. Clara was gone but had given him the greatest gift anyone ever had.

"Well, what do you think?"

Jack wiped his eyes. "I don't know what to say."

"She loved you very much."

"But what about you and your family?"

"I talked to them this afternoon, before everyone got here, and they agreed that you're the right person to have it, no matter what you decide to do with it."

"I'm going to need some time to think this over." He stared ahead as if trying to process what he'd just read.

"Take all the time you need. There's no rush."

A moment later, Marie poked her head outside and said to Ellie, "Everyone is starting to leave. Why don't you come and say goodbye?"

"I'll be right there."

"You should go," said Jack. "You don't want to keep your mother waiting. Besides, I need to get to the dock. I told Matthew I'd close tonight." He made it to the porch before he stopped and turned back. "I'll be there for a while, in case you need someone to talk to."

Ellie smiled and said, "Thank you. I might just take you up on that."

CHAPTER TWENTY-SEVEN

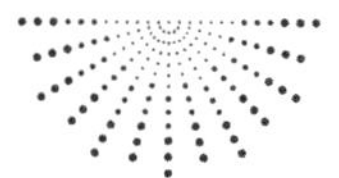

Cataclysm

After sundown, Ellie sat on the end of the dock with her feet in the water. The moon and stars, visible only minutes before, were hidden behind a thick layer of clouds, and the air smelled of rain.

"Something to drink?" Jack asked.

"I'll take tea if you've got it."

He went inside and filled two glasses. On his way out, he flipped on the radio. "Here," he said, handing a glass to Ellie.

"Thanks."

"So how are you holding up?" He took up the spot beside her.

Ellie stared into her tea and sighed. "I'm okay. You?"

"I'll survive." He took a sip of tea before continuing. "The service was nice. I think Clara would have liked it."

Ellie nodded along. "One of my biggest regrets is not returning to see her. I was going through some of her things last night when I came across a scrapbook full of newspaper clippings. Some were of Uncle Bill, others of the war, but many were of me."

"You?" Jack's face filled with curiosity.

"It seems she kept track of every major event in my life, and I didn't even know it." Ellie shook her head. "You must think I'm an awful person."

Jack draped an arm over her shoulder and pulled her close. "No, I don't. You've been busy, that's all—earning an education, building a career. Don't be so hard on yourself."

She managed a smile, but his words did little to ease her pain. "This place feels emptier now that she's gone, doesn't it?"

"Yes, it does. It gets easier, though, with time."

"What?"

"The loss."

Ellie considered all the people Jack had lost in his life. If there was a degree to be given for mastering the art of loss, he'd have earned it. She, on the other hand, was new to losing loved ones. "But it will never be the same, will it?"

Jack stared out at the water and shook his head. "No. It will always be different now."

Ellie was quiet for a moment, surveying the marina. "I still can't get over what you've done with this place. Everything is so modern. George would be proud."

"You think so?"

"Definitely."

Silence descended, only to be broken a minute later when a familiar tune came on the radio. Jack glanced over his shoulder. Then, bringing his gaze back to Ellie, a smile stretched across his face. "They're playing our song." He got to his feet and offered her his hand. "Wanna dance?"

Recognizing the tune, she smiled and took his hand.

He led her to the platform, where they danced under the stars to the gentle rhythm of the Tennessee Waltz.

"I haven't heard this song in years," said Ellie.

"Neither have I. This must be fate."

She looked up at him and smiled. "I didn't think you were a believer in fate."

"I'm not, but my opinion might be changing." In the ensuing quiet, he spun Ellie once, then held her close.

"You've gotten better at this," she commented, recalling the awkwardness of their first dance.

"It's easy when you have the right partner." He looked deep into her eyes, his face lighting up as he spoke. "Just keep your eyes on me and move with the music."

She got the sense he wanted to kiss her, but something—perhaps the thought of Sara, or what had happened the night before—stopped him.

"So what happens now?" Jack's smile faded as he changed the subject. "With you, I mean. Will you be going home tomorrow?"

Ellie drew a breath. "I suppose so. There's really no reason for me to stay. Unless you can think of one?" She glanced at him, then away.

Jack was silent for a moment as the music played on. "What if I asked you stay?"

His question caught her off guard. "Why would you do that? You made it clear that what we almost did last night would have been a mistake. Don't you think if I stayed the temptation would only grow stronger?"

Jack considered that before answering. "Isn't it obvious? This place just isn't the same without you. I'm not the same without you."

"Jack, I'm flattered, but… you're with Sara, remember?"

Regret burned in his eyes. "But if I wasn't, would you stay then?"

Ellie took a moment, wrestling with her answer. "I-I don't know. But it doesn't matter because you are."

Rain began falling, cutting their dance short.

"I think Mother Nature is telling us it's time to go," said Jack. He took the glasses inside, turned off the radio and the lights, then escorted Ellie to her car. "Will I see you again before you leave?"

"Yes," she answered automatically. "I'll swing by tomorrow on my way out and say goodbye."

A gust of wind brought with it more rain.

Jack opened the door for her, and she climbed in the car. "Well, I'd better get home before Sara starts to think we've run off together." He took a step back.

Ellie cracked a smile. "Can you imagine the look on her face if we did?"

"Oh, I can imagine," he said. "It'd probably look similar to the night she found out I was going to propose to you." Jack shut the door. "Drive safe."

His words hung in the air for a moment, then hit her all at once. Ellie rolled down the window. "What did you say?"

Jack pivoted on his heel. "I said drive safe."

"No. Before that."

"Just that Sara would be shocked if we ran off together," he shouted over the rain and wind. When she didn't respond, he said, "Is something wrong?"

"I-I don't know." Her mind raced. "Listen, I need to take care of something. I'll talk to you tomorrow, okay?"

* * *

On the drive to Clara's, Ellie put the pieces together in her head. Sara's jealously. Her mother's untimely visit. It all made sense. How could she have been so blind?

Barging through the front door, Ellie found her Marie and Amelia sitting in the living room, talking.

"Where have you been?" Marie gave her the once over.

"None of your business." She brushed the wet hair away from her eyes. "When were you going to tell me?"

"Tell you what?"

"About that night you showed up here unannounced."

Worry lined Marie's forehead. "I'm not sure I follow."

"Oh, I think you do," said Ellie. "I overheard you talking to Sara at the funeral this morning.

What did you talk about?"

Marie seemed thrown by her question. "I-I don't know. I talked to a lot of people today, about a lot of things."

"Was today the first time you'd met her?"

Marie narrowed her eyes. "Yes, why?"

"It's just that the two of you seemed well acquainted for two people who just met."

"What's gotten into you? Wait..." She paused, looking as if she'd had an epiphany. "I see what's going on here. This has to do with Jack, doesn't it? You're jealous because he's with her?"

"Mother," said Amelia, looking cross.

Her comment stoked Ellie's anger. "If today was the first time you two had spoken, how is it she knew your first name?"

Marie's scowl tightened. "How should I know? Maybe Clara told her or someone at the funeral. What difference does it make?"

"All this time, I couldn't quite figure out what happened that night, like there was a piece missing. But Jack said something to me a few minutes ago that put it all in perspective."

Marie stiffened and crossed her arms. "Do you really want to do this? Right here? Now? After we just buried your aunt?"

"Oh, I've wanted to do this for a long time," Ellie said through gritted teeth. "And yes, right here, right now."

But before the situation reached the point of no return, Amelia interrupted. "Stop it! Both of you. Less than twelve hours ago we buried Clara, and the two of you are already at each other's throats." She looked at Ellie. "What is it you suspect her of doing?"

"It's not a suspicion," Ellie growled. "It's a fact." She swung her eyes back to Marie. "She's the one responsible for ruining what might have been the happiest night of my life."

Marie threw her hands into the air. "God, how many times have we been over this? I've told you over and over that I knew nothing of you and Jack." She turned to Amelia. "Talk some sense into your sister, will you? In the meantime, I'm going to bed."

Marie got to her feet.

"Sit down, Mother!" Ellie demanded.

Marie glared at Ellie, and Ellie glared back. When Ellie didn't relent, Marie returned to her chair.

"You knew about me and Jack, and you knew about his plan to propose. The reason I know that is because the only people who knew what he was planning were his mama, George, and Sara. God knows his mama and George wouldn't have said a word, especially to you. Which leaves only one person." She let that sink in. "Sara was infatuated with Jack even before I showed up that summer, and when she found out we were together, it drove her mad. I don't know how she got your number, but she did, and she called you, didn't she? That's why you showed up here that night claiming it was a surprise, because you wanted to make sure Jack didn't have a chance to pop the question."

Marie looked to Amelia for an ally. "I think your sister has finally lost her mind."

But Amelia was unfazed, processing everything that Ellie had said. "Answer the question, Mother."

With no way out, Marie capitulated. "Fine. Yes. Sara called me and said she was concerned that you were about to make a huge mistake. Naturally, I had to intervene. I sent you here to spend the summer, not get hitched to some farm boy. Besides, you were only nineteen and had your entire life ahead of you. Did you think I'd sit idly by and let you throw it all away because of a summer fling?"

"How dare you! You had no right to interfere in my life. Even at nineteen, I was a grown woman."

"You were a child," Marie snapped. "And an ungrateful one at that. After everything I did for you..."

Fury twisted inside Ellie. "And you're a bitch! A manipulative, conniving bitch."

Amelia looked on in stunned silence.

Marie turned up her nose. "You've been waiting thirty-one years to say that to me, haven't you? Are you happy now?"

Ellie took a step forward, her blurred eyes locked on her mother. "No. I haven't been happy in a long time, but at least now I know the lengths you'll go to get your way, which is why I never want to speak to you again." Turning on her heel, she left the house, slamming the door behind her.

Anxious to tell Jack what she'd discovered, Ellie drove straight to his house and knocked on the door.

"Ellie." He looked surprised to see her. "Back so soon?"

She glimpsed the empty living room behind him. "Sara's not here, is she?"

Jack shook his head. "She decided to spend the night at her mother's. Is everything all right?"

"Not exactly. May I come in?"

Jack welcomed her inside and offered her a seat in the living room. "Can I get you something to drink?"

"No, thanks. This will only take a minute."

Jack found his chair and sat down.

"I'm sorry for barging in on you like this, but my mother and I just had a huge fight, and I didn't know where else to go."

Worry creased his forehead. "I'm sorry to hear that. What happened?"

The conversation played inside her head. "You know, I think I will take something to drink."

"Okay. More tea?"

"Do you have anything stronger?"

Jack raised his eyebrows. "Tell you what, I was just about to fix supper. Why don't you join me? I'll pour us a drink, and you can tell me all about it."

Ellie nodded, feeling herself relax.

Jack poured two whiskeys and in no time had prepared a chicken salad for them. "There." He joined her at the table. "Better?"

She nodded and took a bite. "It's delicious. Thank you."

"So what were you and your mother fighting about?"

Ellie put down the fork and wiped the corners of her mouth. "You."

"Me? I don't understand."

"Jack, this is going to be difficult to hear, but I'm just going to come out and say it." Panic swelled inside her. "Earlier, you said something that took me by surprise. You said Sara had known about your plan to propose to me. That triggered something—a memory—from the night my mother showed up. Clara and I had been in the living room talking when there was a knock at the door. When she answered it, I saw my mother standing in the doorway. We locked eyes, and I remember thinking something was off. When she finally came in, I noticed her looking at my hand, as if there was something she was expecting to see."

"A ring."

"Exactly. And the only way she would have known was if someone told her, someone who knew about your plan. To my knowledge, the only people that knew were you, your mama, George, and..."

"Sara."

Ellie watched as the pieces came together for him.

"No." Jack jumped to his feet, shaking his head. "Sara wouldn't do something like that. I know her."

"I realize it's a lot to process, but she did."

Jack took a moment to digest her words. "Why would she do something like that?"

"Simple. She was in love with you. I think she despised the fact that you had fallen in love with me instead of her, so when she saw the ring, she panicked."

A pained look marred his face. "And your mother confirmed this?"

"Yes, she did. That's the reason I exploded on her. To hear her tell it, she saved me from making the biggest mistake of my life."

Jack sat down and exhaled a long breath. "She's not wrong, you know," he said quietly.

"What?" His words shocked her. "How can you say that?"

"Don't get me wrong. What she did was inexcusable, deplorable even." He scratched his head. "But what would have happened if I'd proposed? What would you have said? What would we have done?"

"I-I don't know. That was so long ago." She thought for a moment, then went on. "Knowing me and how in love I was, I would likely have said yes."

An involuntary twitch cracked the edges of his mouth. "Which is why I'm glad it never happened."

"I don't understand," said Ellie, feeling hollow. "Didn't you love me?"

"Of course I loved you. I still—" He turned away. "Look," he said after composing himself. "All I'm saying is given everything that happened after that night, who's to say we would have made it? What if we'd ended up hating each other?"

"I don't believe that," said Ellie. "I could never hate you."

"Maybe not, but there's no denying our marriage would have been difficult, especially at the start. I mean, what if you'd quit school or I'd died in the war? There are so many ways it could have ended poorly. I'm not saying I'm glad your mother and Sara conspired against us but look at what we've been able to accomplish. It's just like we talked about."

"Only it isn't." Ellie got up and leaned against the counter, feeling a roiling sensation in her stomach. "When I fell in love with you, I saw us working together to accomplish our goals."

"So did I, but I guess that wasn't written in the stars, was it?"

"But that doesn't mean it can't be," she said optimistically. "Once, you said that we were the authors of our own destinies, free to choose our own paths." But before she got carried away, Ellie remembered Sara. "What will you do about Sara now that you know the truth?"

Jack leaned in his chair and let out a long sigh. "I don't know," he answered, appearing conflicted. "On the one hand, everyone makes mistakes, but on the other… I don't see how I can be with her, not after this. Besides," he said, staring into her eyes, "when it comes right down to it, it's you I want, and I'd give up a thousand Saras for you."

Whether it was Jack's words or the whiskey, Ellie suddenly felt light-headed.

"Are you okay?" He rushed to her side.

No. "I think I had a little too much to drink."

Jack poured her a glass of water and told her to sip on it.

"Thank you." When she had composed herself, she said, "Do you think I could stay here tonight? I can't stand the thought of staying another night in that house while she's there."

"My house is your house," he said, and went to prepare the room for her.

When Jack returned, Ellie retreated upstairs, giving him time to process what she had told him. He sat on the porch and drank a couple of beers, then lumbered to his room, where he lay in bed, listening to the rain. Armed with the knowledge of Sara's betrayal, he felt relieved, having no regrets for kissing Ellie the night before. And as he closed his eyes, he realized there was nothing stopping him from kissing her again.

Long after midnight, Ellie was jolted awake by a clap of thunder that rattled the whole house. Unable to sleep, she slipped out of bed and made her way to Jack's room, where she found him standing by the window.

"Can't sleep either?"

Jack turned at the sound of her voice. "I don't sleep well

when it storms," he said, looking troubled. "What's your excuse?"

She joined him at the window. "Guilt, I suppose."

"For what happened with your mother?"

"That, and the fact it took so long for me to learn the truth. I should have trusted my instincts."

Jack put his arms around her and kissed the top of her head. "You were young and didn't know any better."

"But that's just it." She pulled away. "I did know better. I knew her story sounded fishy. But I was so worried about her finding out about us that I failed to see what was right in front of my face."

"Hey," said Jack, taking her by the shoulders, "don't beat yourself up. Everything turned out the way it was supposed to."

The world flashed white as another crack of lightning struck.

"I guess you're right," she said. "What am I saying? You're always right." She leaned against the end of the bed. "But we lost ten years."

"True." He brushed the hair from her shoulder. "But there's nothing we can do about that now. The past is in the past, and all we can do is focus on what's in front of us."

With a finger, he lifted her chin, drawing her eyes to him. And there was something in his gaze—a confidence, an understanding—that told her this time was not going to be like the others.

Before she could utter a single word, Jack's lips were meshed with her own, stealing her breath. His kiss was light, his lips soft and warm. Pulling back a few inches, he gazed into her eyes, and she knew there was no turning back. His next kiss was consuming, hungry yet sweet, teasing her with a hint of promise and driving her body to new heights of awareness.

In one swift motion, Jack swung her up into his arms and carried her to the bed, then undressed and stood naked in the pale light. For a moment, she stared at him in silence, her heart thumping in her chest. This was the moment she'd wanted the night before. Only now there was nothing, and no one, standing in their way.

CHAPTER TWENTY-EIGHT

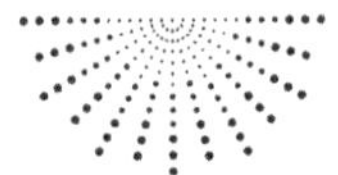

Aftermath

Ellie woke the next morning with her head resting on Jack's chest, the gentle beat of his heart thumping rhythmically in her ear. In the pale morning light, she traced a finger along his shoulder and across his chest, recalling their night of passion. Since that moment at the ruins the week before, they had been building to a crescendo, perhaps more rapidly than she imagined, and now that it had finally happened, she knew she was right where she belonged.

A little after nine, Jack got up and cooked breakfast for them. They sat in the kitchen and ate with the windows up, letting the cool morning air fill the house with the smell of rain and honeysuckle.

"Last night was fun," said Ellie, teasing him with a smile.

He blushed. "I could get used to that. Listen, I know you said you were leaving today, but given the circumstances, why don't you stay, at least until the weekend? There's still plenty I haven't shown you. We could take the boat, maybe fish, and I could cook you anything you want."

Ellie smiled at his proposition, having already decided to extend her stay. "Actually, I don't have anything on my schedule until July, so I might stay longer, if that's all right."

Jack's grin widened. "Stay as long as you like."

* * *

When Ellie was certain Marie had gone, she returned to Clara's to say goodbye to Amelia.

"I wondered if I would see you before I left." Amelia shut the lid on her suitcase and snapped the locks.

"I couldn't let you leave without first saying goodbye." Ellie leaned against the wall, playing nervously with her hands. "Did Mother say anything to you before she left?"

"Very little. I think you shook her up pretty well last night."

"Good. She deserved it. I only wish I'd said something to her years ago, and then maybe all this could have been avoided."

When Amelia was packed, Ellie helped carry her suitcases to the car.

"When will you be home?" Amelia slid the key into the ignition.

"That depends. Assuming Jack breaks things off with Sara, I'm thinking of staying for at least another week, but I'll keep you posted. Tell Sean and Christopher I said hello, will you?"

"Sure."

"Be careful and call me when you get there just so I know you're okay."

Amelia rolled her eyes. "Yes, Mother."

That evening, Jack sat in the kitchen, staring into his liquor. He'd spent all afternoon rehearsing what he was going to say to Sara, but when the front door opened, a wave of panic raced through him, causing his mind to go blank.

"There you are," she said, looking surprised to see him. She set the groceries on the counter and kissed him. "I wasn't expecting you until later."

"Yeah, well, Matthew agreed to close up, so I decided to come home early."

She smiled at him with her eyes. "I'm glad you did because I stopped to see Gary and had him cut us a couple of steaks."

"What's the occasion?"

"There isn't one. I'm just happy things are finally returning to normal."

"And by that you mean—?"

Sara cut her eyes to him. "Back to the way things were before the funeral." She unpacked the bags and asked if he wanted to eat now or later.

He downed the rest of his drink, then got up and eased toward the living room. "I'm not really that hungry."

She followed him. "What's the matter?"

He took a moment to gather his thoughts before answering. "You've always been honest with me, right? I mean, you wouldn't lie to me, would you?"

"Heavens, no." Her face scrunched up in worry. "What's got you all worked up anyway?"

"There's something I need to ask you, something important, and I want you to be honest."

Sara frowned and sat uneasily in the open chair.

"Why didn't you tell me you called Marie Spencer to let her know I was planning to propose to Ellie?"

The color left her face. "W-What are you talking about?"

"All this time I thought her showing up unexpectedly was just a terrible coincidence, but I was wrong."

"Who told you that? Was it Ellie?"

"What if it was? Do you deny it?"

"She's lying, Jack. Can't you see that? She's trying to do whatever she can to steal you from me."

"Steal me. Really, Sara? Are you seriously going to sit there and tell me you didn't call Marie the night you saw the engagement ring?" His feelings shifted from irritation to anger. "I saw the look on your face. You were angry, weren't you? And you thought if you could get Marie here before I had a chance to ask Ellie, you'd still have a shot, didn't you?"

Sara wilted under his gaze.

"Why would you do that to me? I thought you loved me?"

"I do love you. Don't you see? That's why I did it. Ellie never loved you, not the way I do. All she ever did was break your heart."

"You're right," he said, hurt by her betrayal. "She did break my heart, but what you did was worse. You had no right."

"No right?" Sara jumped to her feet. "I've been in love with you from the beginning, long before Ellie Spencer blew into town with her fancy clothes and uppity attitude. And who was there after she broke your heart, huh? Who has always been there, picking up the pieces, patiently waiting? Me, that's who. So don't tell me I didn't have a right." She stopped and took a breath, looking as if she might cry. "But none of that matters now. Ellie's gone, hopefully for good this time, and you need to accept that." She turned on her heel and started toward the kitchen.

"Actually, she isn't."

Sara turned back. "What?"

Jack shook his head. "Ellie isn't gone. In fact, she's staying."

A look of bewilderment crossed Sara's face. "I-I don't understand. She was supposed to leave this morning."

"You're right, she was. But I asked her to stay, and she agreed."

Sara's eyes grew wide with anger. "Absolutely not! I won't allow it."

"I'm afraid you have no say in the matter. And before you say another word..." He held up a hand. "Let me tell you how things are going to be from now on." Taking a step in her direction and feeling the fury boil inside him, Jack ground his teeth and clenched his jaw so tight it hurt. "You have one hour to pack your things and leave this house. After that, I don't care where you go or what you do, but you're not welcome here anymore. Is that clear?"

Sara's eyes bulged with fright as her world came crashing down on her. "Jack, you can't be serious. Please give me another chance. Are you willing to throw away what we have because of something that happened when we were teenagers?"

"Yes, I am," he said firmly. "And despite what you think, I loved you, Sara. We could have had a future together. But I won't be in a relationship built on lies." He grabbed his keys and headed for the door.

"Where are you going?"

"Out. One hour," he said, holding up a finger, "and you'd better be gone when I get back." Jack slammed the door behind him, leaving Sara weeping on the living room floor.

CHAPTER TWENTY-NINE

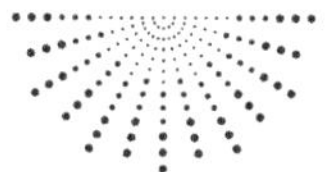

Blue Moon

With Sara out of the picture and Marie in Ohio, Ellie and Jack rarely left one another's side. It was like old times, only better. And just as they had years earlier, they fell in love all over again.

And for a while, Ellie forgot all about her other life.

One muggy June evening, they cruised far upriver to a place they hadn't been since that summer.

"That's the island, isn't it?" Ellie asked, watching as it grew out of the water. "The one where we—"

Jack nodded wordlessly, listening to the hum of the engine.

"How many times have you been back since that night?"

"I haven't," he said, fighting a tidal wave of emotion.

When he'd beached the boat, Jack lit a fire and spread a blanket. As darkness enveloped them, a full blanket of stars appeared in the velvet sky.

"This feels like a dream," said Ellie, her face red from the heat of the fire. "To be back here, with you, after all this time." She exhaled, a look of contentment on her face.

"A dream I'd rather not wake from," said Jack. "Right here, right now, I have everything I've ever wanted." His gaze lingered on her for another second before he looked away.

"Do you remember the first time we came to this island?"

The memory of that day came flooding back. "How could I forget? It's the first time I told you I loved you."

"Yes, and it was also the day you told me about the mockingbirds. For some reason, that story always stuck with me."

"Because it's true." A shooting star streaked across the sky. "I didn't want to say anything back then, but I knew it that very day. I've always known. You and I are destined to be together. It's written up there," he said, pointing to the heavens, "in the stars."

She looked at him with wonder in her eyes. "You really think so?"

"Don't you?"

"For the longest time I wondered, even doubted, but now... Back then it felt like the entire world was conspiring against us."

"But that's all behind us. Now it's just you and me, free to choose our own path." They sat in silence for a minute, gazing at the stars. "Is it still your desire to get married on an island?"

Ellie looked up. "I can't believe you remembered." When the shock wore off, she said, "Yes, it is still my dream to get married on an island."

Jack looked over at her and smiled. "I'll keep that in mind."

* * *

The next morning, Ellie was on her way out when the phone rang.

"Hello. … Zora, what's wrong? You sound panicked. … What about? … Oh my God, are you serious?"

Jack stood in the opening to the kitchen, listening intently.

"You're right. Thank you, Zora. I could never had done this without you." She lowered her voice to a whisper. "Did he say anything about next steps? … The twenty-seventh, but that's Friday. … I don't know. I hadn't really thought about it. … Yes, of course." Ellie looked over at Jack, and he saw her eyes cloud with sadness. "This is what I've spent the past two years working toward. … You too, Zora, and thanks again." Ellie hung up the phone and eased into the kitchen.

"Is everything all right?"

"That was Zora. She called to tell me I have a meeting at the university on Friday, which means I'll need to go home for a couple of days."

"I hope nothing's the matter."

Ellie shook her head. "On the contrary. I'm meeting with Dr. Dale Clement, head of research and development for the lunar program at NASA."

Jack's brows shot up in surprise. "That sounds important. I assume it has something to do with the research you've been conducting?"

"Yes and no. Since NASA opened its doors, they've been recruiting top talent in astronomy and physics from across the world. For the past two years, I've been putting in applications, hoping to land a job with them. But until today, all my applications had been denied. Honestly, I had all but given up on the idea until a couple of months ago when Zora convinced me to try one last time. I figured the outcome would be the same as before, which is why I didn't mention it."

Jack brushed back the hair from her face and stroked her cheek gently. "So why the long face?"

"I had my heart set on staying here the rest of the summer."

"But it's only one meeting. You'll be gone for what, two, three days at the most?"

She nodded, thinking. "Hey," she said, struck by an idea, "why don't you come with me? I could show you where I work, introduce you to Zora and Trey… We could make a trip of it. What do you say?"

Jack considered that. "Are you sure? My track record in Bloomington isn't exactly stellar."

"Phooey. That was a long time ago, and things are different now. Besides," she said, lacing her arms around his neck, "you know what they say: the third time's the charm."

After a kiss, Jack tossed around the idea. "It would be nice to get away for a few days. All right," he said, convincing himself it might be fun. "I'm in."

* * *

On Thursday morning, Jack and Ellie made the drive from Sims Chapel to Bloomington. After stopping for lunch at the diner, it was almost two when they made it to Ellie's place.

"Well, here it is," she said when Jack parked the truck. "Home sweet home."

Jack got out and took in the neighborhood. It had all the charm of a Midwest town. Houses of every shape and color lined the street, each with freshly mown lawns and mature trees. And in the air was the laughter of children playing in the streets.

Bringing his eyes back to Ellie's house, Jack marveled at the charming bungalow. It had been painted a shade of light blue and feature a wide porch, the columns of which were hidden almost entirely by neatly manicured shrubs. "And you own it?" he asked, mounting the steps.

"I bought it a few years ago after I got the teaching job. It's not a pre–Civil War mansion"—she grinned—"but it's perfect for me." She opened the front door and showed Jack inside.

The interior was cuter still, with solid oak floors and an open concept, featuring ample living and dining space.

"Don't be modest." He let his eyes wander. "This is a wonderful place."

He moved into the living room and noticed several bookshelves filled to the brim, and a writing desk with a stack of notebooks. By the looks of things, it was obvious Ellie spent a great deal of time reading and writing. "This is exactly how I pictured your house," he said, joining her in the kitchen. "I can see why you like it here so much."

She moved closer and put her arms around his waist. "Thanks again for coming with me," she said, looking up at him. "This probably isn't how you pictured spending your weekend, but it means a lot that you're here."

"My pleasure," he said, then pressed his lips to hers.

"I hope you don't mind, but considering it's been a long day already, I thought we'd stay in for dinner."

"I don't mind at all," said Jack. "As long as I'm with you."

CHAPTER THIRTY

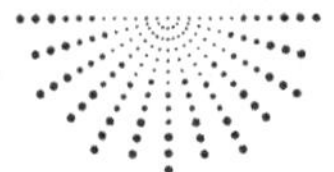

Calm ***Before*** *the* ***Storm***

Friday morning, Jack drove Ellie to the university. He parked in front of the astronomy building, where they rehearsed Ellie's answers to what she assumed would be a battery of questions. To Jack, Ellie was the smartest person he'd ever met, but, as he discovered, even she wasn't immune to doubt.

"You're going to do fine," he reassured her. He smiled, finding her anxiety endearing.

"*Fine* may be acceptable for the university," said Ellie. "But this is NASA we're talking about. I need to be flawless."

"Then be flawless. Either way, the most important thing is to be yourself. If you do that, he'll have no choice but to hire you."

When it was time, Jack walked her to the door and wished her luck.

"Are you sure you'll be okay by yourself? I don't know how long this will take."

"Don't worry about me," said Jack. "I'm more than capable

of entertaining myself. Besides," he rolled his eyes skyward and finding blue sky, added, "it's a nice morning, so I think I'll go for a walk."

After smoothing down the hem of her skirt, Ellie drew a breath and said, "Well, here goes nothing."

When Ellie was inside, Jack walked around the corner. With most of the students away on summer break, he had the campus to himself. After checking out the Kirkwood Observatory, he took a stroll through Dunn's Woods, stopping at Beck Chapel. When he was done there, he made his way to Walnut Street where he did a little window shopping before moseying over to the courthouse.

With the sun now directly overhead, Jack sought the shade of a nearby elm. Five minutes passed… ten… twenty. Checking the time, it was after noon, so he stood and started back toward campus.

While he waited for the light to change, he noticed a poster in the window of the bookstore that caught his attention. Written in bold letters was his name, along with a picture of his book. Gobsmacked, Jack went in to have a look.

"Good morning." Sam greeted Jack as he entered. "How may I help you?"

Jack looked at Sam and smiled politely. "You don't remember me. Do you, Mr. Hensley?"

Sam took another look. "As I live and breathe… Jack Bennett." He stepped out from behind the counter and shook Jack's hand. "How are you, young man?"

"Doing well, sir. How are you?"

"Fine. Just fine. If memory serves, the last time I saw you was the day you got released from the army. What's it been, nine, ten years?"

"Something like that."

Sam gave him the once-over. "I'm glad to see your hair grew back."

Jack chuckled. "Me too."

"So what brings you to Bloomington—research for your next novel?"

"Not exactly. Believe it or not, I'm here with Ellie. She has a meeting at the university this morning, and since I had a couple of hours to kill, I decided to walk around and see what's new."

Sam raised an eyebrow. "Does that mean the two of you are back together?"

"Yes, we are," Jack confirmed, which elicited a smile.

"Well, it's about time. You know, for a while there, I was worried about Ellie. We all were. She's been hanging around the store for so long, Alicia and I consider her part of the family." His smile became wistful. "She's had a rough go of it, the poor thing, but I've always said I never saw her happier than when she was with you. Maybe now she can finally be happy."

"Let's hope," said Jack.

"Did you see your poster in the window?"

"Yes, I did." Jack glanced over his shoulder. "That's what brought me in. Are you selling any?"

"Am I? I can't keep them on the shelves. You're single-handedly keeping me in business."

Jack chuckled, finding it amusing. "Speaking of that, is there any truth to the rumor that you might be selling this place? Ellie mentioned it on the drive up."

"I'm afraid so. Ellie may have told you, but Alicia's condition isn't improving, and the doctors think a milder climate might help. As much as I don't want to leave, I'll do whatever it takes if it helps her get better." He found a stool and sat down. "For years, I've poured myself into this store, worked sixty hours a week, all to make this place a success. And I've been fortunate. This store has supported a wife, two kids, college tuition, but it's come at a cost. Now with the reality that Alicia may not get better, I'm left asking myself if it was all worth it." He frowned for a moment, then said, "We take our loved ones for granted. It's not until we're faced with the prospect of losing them that we realize just how much they mean to us and how lost we'd be without them. I don't know if she mentioned it, but Ellie has shown some interest in buying the store."

"Really?"

"She was adamant that I let her know if I was ever serious about selling. Unfortunately, I may have to give her a ring soon."

Eager to keep the mood light, Jack redirected the conversation. "So business has been good, I presume."

"I'm having my best year ever, thanks to you."

"Well, I'm glad I could help."

"Hey, while I've got you here, would you mind signing a few copies of your book? My customers would love it, and so would Alicia."

That brought a smile to Jack's face. "It'd be my pleasure."

At a quarter past twelve, Jack rounded the corner. Ellie was standing on the steps, waiting for him.

"Well, how did it go?" he asked anxiously.

"There you are. Look at me, I'm shaking."

Jack took her hand, and they strolled toward the car.

"I don't think it could have gone any better," she said. "Dr. Clement said officially I'm one of five remaining candidates. But off the record, apparently it's down to me and one other."

"See. What did I tell you?" But when her enthusiasm didn't match his own, Jack suspected there was more. "What else did he say?"

Ellie walked ahead a few steps before answering. "It's just that when I applied for the position, I was under the impression I could keep my job with the university, but Dr. Clement said if I'm chosen, they would need me full-time, which means I'll have to quit teaching. And that's not the worst part." Ellie looked away. "Since the team is headquartered in Houston, I'd have to relocate."

It was one thing for Ellie to be in Indiana, but Texas? She might as well be on the other side of the world. "How long would you be there?"

A pained look marred her face. "Permanently."

It took Jack a moment to fully digest her words. "So what's the next step?"

"A final interview," said Ellie. "Dr. Clement said he'd call early next week with more information."

That evening, Ellie and Jack met up with Zora and Trey for dinner. Despite the possibility of Ellie moving to Texas, Jack put on a brave face, determined not to spoil the mood.

"So Jack, what do you think about Ellie going to work for NASA?" Zora asked.

"I haven't got the job yet," said Ellie.

"It's an amazing opportunity," Jack answered diplomatically. "Ellie is the smartest person I've ever met, and honestly, I'm in awe of what she's been able to accomplish."

"Now there's a man who knows how to answer a question,"

said Trey. "You've got to watch out for Zora. She can be crafty with her questions."

"Don't give away all my secrets," she said to Trey. Then, turning to Ellie, she whispered, "You'd better hang on to this one."

"Zora, if you don't mind me asking, what brought you to Bloomington?"

She smiled with a wry twist of her mouth. "How do you know I didn't grow up here?"

Jack cracked a smile of his own. "I know a Southern accent when I hear one. Mississippi, am I right?"

"Vicksburg." She looked genuinely surprised. "How'd you know?"

Jack's smile broadened. "I had a platoon leader who was from Jackson."

"Platoon leader?" Trey asked, taking a sudden interest. "You're a military man?"

"Army, Twenty-Fourth Infantry," Jack confirmed.

"I was in the Marines Corp," said Trey.

"No kidding. Small world, isn't it?"

"Jack, you're a writer," said Zora, "so you may be interested to know Trey is thinking of writing a book of his own."

"Oh, yeah. What about?"

"My time in the service. The things I saw." Trey's expression shifted from cheerful to serious. "My doctor thinks it might be good for me to write down some of my experiences; says it'll help with the healing process."

Jack nodded along, knowing exactly what Trey was getting at. "He's right. I could give you some pointers if you like."

"That would be great."

Their food arrived, and the conversation turned back to Ellie's interview.

"Everything sounded wonderful," she said, "except the part about having to move. If I'd known that beforehand, I wouldn't have applied. I know Bloomington isn't where I grew up, but I've spent the past thirteen years of my life here, and I consider it my home."

After dinner, the ladies excused themselves to the restroom while Trey and Jack remained at the table.

"I take it you're not thrilled at the prospects of Ellie moving to Texas."

"What gave me away?"

"I saw the way you tensed up when Zora was talking to Ellie." Trey took a draw from his beer. "It's a big step, you know, to leave your home."

"It's just that Texas is so far away. Ellie and I haven't even discussed how we're going to make things work with her here and me in Tennessee."

"Does that mean you won't go with her if she's offered the job?"

Jack shrugged his shoulders. "My entire life is there—my business, my mother..."

Trey smiled. "I know how you feel. When Ellie offered Zora to come work for her, Zora gave me an ultimatum, said she was making the move with or without me. Can you believe that?"

"What did you say?"

"I'm sitting here, aren't I?" He chuckled and took another drink of beer.

"What if you'd told her no? Do you think she would have gone without you?"

"I don't know, but I wasn't willing to find out. Zora's a driven woman and always has been. When she gets an idea in her head, she'll chase it to the bitter end come hell or high water. I tried to fight it at first, but eventually, I decided if I was going to be with her, I had to put my ego aside, hang on, and enjoy the ride. And what a ride it's been."

"And you have no regrets?"

"I thought I would, but I don't. Zora is the love of my life, and she makes me happier than I ever thought I could be."

* * *

Later that evening, Ellie stood in front of the mirror in her bedroom, taking off her necklace and earrings. "So what did you think of Trey and Zora?"

"I like them," said Jack. "They remind me a lot of us."

Ellie looked at Jack's reflection in the mirror. "How so?"

He put his hands on her shoulders and kissed her gently on the neck. "Well, Trey served in the military, just like me. And Zora's in education, like you. Besides that, Trey realizes what a treasure he has in Zora."

"That's sweet. Did he tell you that?"

"Not in so many words, but he's obviously crazy about her."

Ellie turned and slipped her arms around Jack's neck. "And she's crazy about him too," she said, gazing into his eyes.

"Are we still talking about Trey and Zora?" He grinned.

"Them, us... Hey, why don't we stay a couple more days?" She unbuttoned his shirt. "It's supposed to rain, and I was thinking we could take advantage and spend the weekend in bed."

Jack raised an eyebrow. "I like the way you think, Professor," he said, then reached for the zipper on her dress.

* * *

On Saturday, it rained, which gave Jack and Ellie an excuse to sleep in. Having nothing to do and nowhere important to go was refreshing, and they took advantage of the downtime. Around ten, they woke, and Ellie made a breakfast of scrambled eggs, sausage, biscuits with gravy, and bacon. It reminded Jack of breakfasts his mama had made him when he was a child.

"I haven't had a spread like this in years," he commented as he drizzled honey on a biscuit.

"That's the one thing I will give my mother credit for," said Ellie. "She taught me everything I know about cooking."

Jack took a bite of his food and washed it down with a sip of orange juice. "She taught you well because this food is amazing." His compliment caused Ellie to blush. "Oh, that reminds me, I meant to tell you I stopped by the bookstore yesterday while you were having your interview. Did you know Sam has a poster of my book hanging in the window?"

"Aww, that's so nice of him. Did he remember you?"

"Not at first."

Ellie reached for the pepper and sprinkled a little onto her eggs. "How was he? I haven't seen him since school let out."

"Fine, but he mentioned his wife was ill. Did you know?"

Ellie nodded, swallowing a bite of eggs. "She has Lou Gehrig's disease. Apparently, there's no cure. It's terribly sad. For as long as I've known her, Alicia has been an active, vibrant woman. This has really taken a toll on Sam. I've watched him age ten years in the past twelve months."

Jack got up and topped off his glass. "He also mentioned you showing interest in purchasing his store."

Ellie nodded. "I told him if he was ever serious about selling to let me know. It's always been a dream of mine to own a bookstore."

"I didn't know that."

"Some of my fondest memories are of me and my father visiting the bookstore near our house. It's where I developed such a love for reading and for science." She spread a little jam on her biscuit and took a bite.

Jack leaned against the counter, thinking. "But how would you manage a business and a teaching career?" he asked.

"I could be there during the summer and on holidays, but I'd need someone to run it while school was in session. Ellie leaned in her chair, letting her mind wander. "The first thing I'd do is fill it to the brim with all sorts of books. Science and astronomy, of course, but there'd be something for everyone, especially girls. I want to show young women there's more to life than being a wife and mother. Not that there's anything wrong with that of course. It's just that I want them to realize they have potential outside the home."

Jack listened quietly while Ellie revealed a detail about herself he hadn't known before. As he was learning, every day with her was a new experience, an opportunity to peel back another layer and explore the richness that made up who she was.

CHAPTER THIRTY-ONE

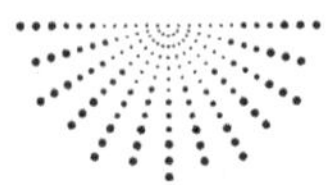

When It Rains It Pours

After the weekend in Bloomington, Jack and Ellie fell into a comfortable routine. Jack spent a few hours in the mornings at the dock while Ellie caught up on her reading. Most afternoons, they could be found on the water, catching fish, and dreaming of what their life might be like once they were married.

"And I'd like two children," said Ellie as she looked out over the water. "A girl and a boy. That way, we'd each have a best friend."

"But I already have a best friend," he said affectionately.

Ellie gave him that look. "You know what I mean."

When the sun went down, they drifted near the bluff, taking in the sunset.

"The sky is beautiful this evening." Ellie leaned back and stared into the heavens. "It's evenings like this that make me never want to leave this place."

"Then don't," said Jack. "We can stay here forever, just you and me. We've both made enough money already to last us the rest of our lives if we manage it properly. And between my house and Clara's we've got enough space."

"As tempting as that sounds, I've worked too hard and come too far to quit now. Besides, I'd be lost without my work, and so would you."

"You're probably right," he said, turning wistful. And it was at that moment that Jack felt a sense of déjà vu, wondering if this go around with Ellie would end in the same way it had before, with her leaving, and him being heartbroken.

* * *

During supper, Dr. Clement called and asked to speak to Ellie. While she talked, Jack cleared the table and washed the dishes, then grabbed a beer and headed for the porch. It was a warm and muggy night, but the sky was clear and full of stars. He hadn't much more than sat down when Ellie appeared, looking like the cat that ate the canary.

"Good news?"

"They want me in Houston on Friday for my final interview."

Jack's heart sank. "So soon? But we just got settled."

"I know, but they're eager to make a decision." She moved to the edge of the porch and leaned against the rail.

Jack rocked back and forth, contemplating how this scenario might play out.

"What are you thinking about?"

"Nothing, it's just... everything is moving so fast."

"I know, but it's exciting, isn't it?"

"Maybe for you." Jack paused and considered his next words carefully. "Look, I didn't want to say anything in front of Trey and Zora, but if I'm being honest, I'm not thrilled at the idea of you moving to Houston. I mean, we just got back together, and you're already talking about moving a thousand miles away."

Ellie took a step back. "Oh." She looked as if his words were a revelation to her. "I guess I never really asked how you felt about it, did I?" She came over and sat in the empty rocker. "I'm sorry, it's just that I've been on my own for so long that I've gotten used to making decisions on my own."

"I understand," said Jack. "And I'm not trying to rain on your parade, but I'm worried what this will mean for us if you take this job. Not only that, but are you seriously considering giving up teaching? And what about Zora and Amelia? Can you really leave them behind?"

Ellie stared at the porch, playing absently with her necklace. "I don't know," she finally said. "In my wildest dreams, I never thought I'd make it this far, so I guess I haven't considered all the ramifications." She was silent a moment before going on. "But if the stars do align, and I'm offered the job, what would you think about coming with me?"

Jack tried to process the idea, but the prospects of leaving his home, of moving halfway across the country, were daunting. "I don't know," he answered truthfully. "It's a lot to think about."

"But you will think about it, won't you?"

He looked at her and forced a smile. "For you, I will."

* * *

While Ellie was in Texas, Jack kept busy at the dock. Now at the peak of the fishing season, both he and Matthew had their hands full, which was a welcomed relief for Jack. From eight to four, he led excursions all over the lake, some as far away as

Walters Bridge, and each time he passed Parrott Island, he'd smile and think of Ellie. In the evenings, when the workday was through, Jack did some fishing of his own. But most of the time, he just sat and stared at the water, searching for guidance, and counting down the hours until she was by his side once more.

On Tuesday, after work, Jack dropped by his mama's place to check in on her and have supper. Stepping into the kitchen, Jack found a knife and cutting board and went about peeling and chopping potatoes and onions."

"Strong, aren't they?" Helen asked as the onions drew tears from Jack's eyes.

He nodded, sniffling, and drew his forearm across his eyes, careful to avoid his hand.

"Is Ellie still in Houston?"

"Until Friday." He slid the vegetables into a pot of boiling water, then immediately went to the sink and washed his hands.

"Is it harder than you thought?"

"What?"

"Being apart?"

Jack nodded. "I've tried everything I know—working, cleaning the house, cooking—to keep my mind off her, but it's impossible. Even fishing has lost its luster."

That got Helen's attention. "Sounds to me like you're head-over-heels for her."

"I am," he admitted. "I always have been."

When the potatoes were tender, Helen drained them, poured them into a bowl with the onions, butter, and milk, and began to stir.

"Grab the chicken and the green beans and set them on the table, will ya?"

When he'd done that, Jack poured two glasses of tea and set them alongside their plates at the table.

When the potatoes had been properly mashed, Helen poured them into a bowl and joined Jack at the table. "Do you want to say grace, or should I?"

"If memory serves, I believe it's your turn," he said, then bowed his head.

When the food had been blessed, they wasted little time in digging in.

"Have you thought any more about what you're going to do with Clara's place?"

Jack let out a heavy sigh. "I've thought about it," he said. "I could sell it, of course, but I can't stand the thought of some stranger living there. I could always sell my place and move, but that isn't ideal either. Honestly, I don't know what to do."

"Well, that's all right. You're a smart man. You'll figure it out."

For the next few minutes, they ate in silence, but eventually, the conversation turned back to Ellie.

"Assuming she gets the job, what do you think I should do?"

Helen sipped her tea before answering. "What does your heart tell you?"

Jack breathed a laugh through his nose. "Listening to my heart is what got me into this mess in the first place."

"Be that as it may, don't ever stop listening to your heart. You may not always agree with what it says or where it leads you, but it'll never steer you wrong."

"Maybe you're right," he conceded. "I'm just so afraid that history will repeat itself and things will end the way they did before."

"Then don't let it." Helen reached for her tea and took a sip, eyeing Jack over the brim of her cup. "Aren't you the one always saying we're the authors of our own destinies?"

"Nothing gets past you, does it?" He gave a crooked smile. "I only wish it were that easy."

"Isn't it?" She eyed him for a second before going on. "Listen, JB, it comes down to this: what are you willing to sacrifice to be with Ellie? If the answer is anything, then nothing can stand in your way, and if not, well..."

Jack looked up from his plate. "Haven't I sacrificed enough already? Besides, I've built a life here. I have friends here, family, a business. Am I supposed to just give all that up?"

"If you want to be with Ellie, you may not have a choice."

Jack felt a tug at his brow. "I thought you said love was a compromise, that to make it work, we'd both have to give up something."

"It is, and you will."

"Then why does it feel like I'm the only one sacrificing?"

Helen put her arm around him. "Darlin'," she said quietly, "life isn't a game. No one's keeping count of who's giving up more. Besides, Ellie *is* giving up something—her life in Indiana, and a career she's worked just as hard to build as you have. Not to mention, she's moving away from her sister, and you know how close they are."

Jack stared into his tea, wishing life could be as simple as it had once been, back when he was a teenager. "I just don't know why she can't be content with what she's got. She always said her dream was to teach, and that's what she's doing. Now it's this job with NASA. What's next?"

"We have no way of knowing what the future holds, but by now you should know that with a woman like Ellie, the sky's the limit. That's what makes her who she is, and I suspect it's part of the reason you fell in love with her in the first place. Even if you could, do you really want to clip her wings?"

"No," he conceded, "but that doesn't mean I'm ready to give up my hopes and dreams either. This is my home."

"They say that home is where the heart is," she reminded him.

"Yes, but what if my heart is in two places at once?"

Helen smiled sympathetically and said, "Sounds to me like you've got some praying to do." She took her plate to the sink and ran it under the water before returning to the table. "But whatever you decide, make no mistake about it: if you let her get away this time, you won't get another chance, so if I were you, I'd think long and hard about your decision."

* * *

The next evening, Jack stood barefoot in the cemetery, contemplating the future. The feeling of the earth beneath his feet reminded him of his childhood, of the afternoons spent traipsing around the woods in search of turtles and crawdads or nights by the lakeshore, digging for worms.

"It's hard to believe you've been gone eighteen years," he said, kneeling in front of Lewis's grave. "It seems like only yesterday you and I were talking about how we couldn't wait until we got older so we could get our own boat and go out on the water whenever we wanted. Those were the days, weren't they?" Jack gave a melancholy smile. "I know it's been a while since I last visited, but I haven't been thinking straight. Hopefully, this business with Ellie's job will get sorted out soon enough, and things can go back to normal."

"You look deep in thought."

Jack looked up and saw Ellie walking toward him. "You're

back." He ran to her and threw his arms around her. "What happened? I wasn't expecting you until tomorrow."

When they parted, she said, "I finished ahead of schedule, so I thought I'd come home a day early and surprise you."

Jack felt his grin widen. "You certainly did that. How'd you know I was here?"

"I was on my way to your place when I saw your truck."

They found a bench beneath the old elm and sat.

"So tell me all about your trip."

"Oh, it was wonderful." She beamed. "It was less an interview and more an orientation. I met with Dr. Clement and his team, got to tour their state-of-the-art facility, and checked out housing. They have some lovely cottages for rent. I also got to see the city. Houston is a nice town, with so many things to see and do. I only wish you could have been there."

"Does that mean you got the job?" He held his breath.

"I told Dr. Clement I'd need the weekend to think it over, but, yes. It's mine if I want it."

Pressing down his feelings, Jack said, "Congratulations. I'm happy for you."

"Thank you. You're the first person I've told."

"You'll have to call Amelia when we get home. I'm sure she'll want to know."

Ellie nodded.

"What about your mother? Will you tell her?"

"Not unless I have to. But I'm sure she'll find out."

Jack was silent for a moment, thinking and listening to the breeze as it rustled the leaves above them. "You know, every time I come to this place it gets harder and harder."

"Because you miss them so much?"

"That, and because every time I come here, it feels like another person from my past, someone I've known and loved, is here. It hurts my heart to think that all those shared memories we had—my grandparents and I fishing, George and I at the dock, Lewis and I exploring—now belong only to me. And someday, when I'm buried here, those memories will no longer exists, as if they never happened."

"If it hurts so much, why stay?" asked Ellie. "Why not start over somewhere new, where there aren't any ghosts?"

"You mean someplace like Houston?" He glanced at her before looking away. "I've considered it, but for better or worse, this is my home. It's as much a part of me as I am of it. Besides, I've learned that when it comes to ghosts, they follow you wherever you go." Unwilling to ruin Ellie's homecoming, Jack cleared his expression. "But enough about me. Let's get back to you. Given everything you've seen and heard, are you thinking of taking the job?"

Ellie drew a breath. "I don't know. Half of me wants to, but..." She fiddled with her bracelet. "It's so far away from everything and everyone I know and love." She anchored her gaze on his. "What do you think I should do?"

Jack wanted to tell her to turn it down, to be satisfied with what she had, but he decided against it, choosing instead to take the high road. "I'm not sure it matters what I think."

She leaned away as a deep frown creased her brow. "Of course it matters. Why wouldn't it?"

Jack lifted his shoulder in a half shrug as he stared into the distance. "Like you said before, you're used to making decisions on your own. Besides, you've probably already made up your mind."

"But I haven't," she protested. "That's why I asked you." She stood and faced the western sky, where the setting sun had given way to a palette of purples and pinks that stretched across the horizon.

"What if I wasn't in the picture? Would it make your decision easier?"

She turned and looked him in the face. "But you are in the picture."

"I know, but if you'd been offered this job six months ago, what would you have done then?"

"I'd have taken it," she answered without hesitation. "But that was then. Things are different now, and I would never make a decision like this without taking your feelings into account."

Jack leaned back, resting himself against the tree. "And what if I said I thought you should turn it down? What would you do then?"

Ellie looked away for a moment, then brought her gaze back to him. "Is that how you truly feel?"

Jack looked at his hands. "Maybe."

"I see. Well, I guess there isn't much more to talk about, is there?"

Jack got up and started in her direction. "Ellie, I—"

She raised a hand, cutting him short. "It's okay. I can't fault you for being honest." She was silent for a few seconds before going on. "I think I'm going to go now. It's been a long day, and there's a lot I need to think about."

Over the next few days, Ellie weighed the pros and cons of her job offer. One minute, it seemed like she was leaning toward accepting. The next, she shifted in the opposite direction, leaving Jack nauseated from all the back and forth. He did his best to be supportive, of course, but refrained from giving his opinion. He wanted Ellie to make this decision on her own.

On Sunday evening, they sat at the table after supper, discussing their options.

"I realize it's a big *if*, but if you agreed to come with me, the main facility is southeast of town, so we wouldn't have to live in the city. And the best part is"—her smile widened—"they have a lake." She'd been saving that detail as a last-ditch effort to sell Jack.

"Ellie, that all sounds great, and I'm sure it's a lovely place, but..."

"You're still not convinced, are you?"

"It's not that, it's just..."

"What?"

Jack got up and made his way to the porch. "Do you see that sky, those mountains, the water? Those things are a part of who I am. For whatever reason, God put me here, in Sims Chapel. And I know there are beautiful places all over this world. I've seen enough of it to realize that. But this is home, and it always will be."

Ellie was silent for a moment, processing Jack's words. "It's sounds as if you've made up your mind."

He turned and looked at her, his face bearing the signs of worry. "As I said before, I won't stand in the way of your dreams. If taking this job means that much to you, then you should take it, but"—he hesitated, knowing that what he told her next could spell the end for them—"I don't think I can go with you."

His words kicked her in the stomach. While she caught her breath, Ellie remembered something Sara had told her years earlier, about how it would take someone special to pull Jack away from the water. Once, Ellie thought she might be that person, but clearly she was mistaken.

"And that's it? You won't even consider it?"

"What do you think I've been doing for the past two weeks? Ever since you told me there was a possibility you'd have to move, I haven't eaten or slept. It's all I can think about."

Ellie stood, her insides on fire. "And how do you think I feel, Jack? I've been offered the job of a lifetime, a crowning achievement, and the man I love, the man that's supposed to support me, is telling me he wants no part of my dream." She paused, letting her words sink in. "If you had it your way, we'd stay here, right here, doing the same thing, day in and day out, wouldn't we?"

"No. I'm not saying that at all."

"Then what are you saying?"

"I've seen the world," said Jack. "Parts I wanted to see, parts I didn't. And do you know what I realized? That everything I've ever wanted is right here in my own backyard. I've built a life here, Ellie, and a business. Everyone and everything I care about is here. Look." He tried to reason with her. "I want to spend the rest of my life with you. It's all I've wanted since the day we met, but I won't lose myself in the process. I left this place once, and it nearly tore me apart. If you love me the way you say you do, you won't ask me to do it again."

"But I'm not asking you to leave this place, not forever. I'm only asking you to give somewhere else a chance, to give us a chance."

"Then what?" He took a step toward her. "What happens when the next great thing comes along? And the next?"

Ellie felt the muscles in her brow contract. "What do you mean?"

"Today it's NASA. Tomorrow it will be something else. You're always looking for the next great thing, another notch in your professional belt." He paused and shook his head. "Maybe I was wrong about us. Maybe we're not mockingbirds after all. Your dreams are way too big for me, Ellie. I suppose they always have been." He dropped his eyes for a moment. "As I said, I won't ask you to give up your dreams to stay with me. I love you too much for that. But if you decide to take the job, you'll have to do it alone because I won't be coming with you." Jack went inside and Ellie followed him to the living room.

"So you're just giving up, like you did before?"

Jack took another step, stopped, turned on his heel, and glared at her. "What did you say to me?"

"You heard me," she fired back. "How come you always give up so easily? How come you never fight back?"

Her question left him speechless, and it took a few seconds before he responded. "Me? Your memory seems to have failed you. I'm not the one who gave up on us, Ellie, you are."

"But you didn't object. If you loved me as much as you say you did, why didn't you put up a fight? Why aren't you putting up a fight now?"

Jack leveled a look at her, making it clear she had crossed the line. "That's a hell of a thing for you to say to me." He stepped toward her, his eyes ablaze with anger. "For two straight years, I did everything in my power—cheat, steal, broke every rule—just so I could make it back to you. And I left a lot of dead men in my wake. So don't you dare tell me I didn't fight because I did. I fought like our lives depended on it. If you want to see someone who didn't fight, take a long look in the mirror."

"I fought," she protested. "Maybe not with a knife or a gun, but I fought in my own way. But what was I supposed to do? You abandoned me, just as you're doing now."

"Abandoned you? I didn't leave because I wanted to. I was drafted to war. Unlike Michael, I didn't have the luxury of buying my way out of service. But you," he speared her with another glare, "you had a choice, and when things got tough, you chose the path that benefitted you most. Same as now."

She wilted under his gaze. "So when you said you'd forgiven me, that was a lie, wasn't it?"

Jack shook his head as his temper subsided. "I have forgiven you, but that doesn't mean I've forgotten."

* * *

That night they slept in separate beds, Ellie at one end of the house and Jack at the other. Though only separated by a floor, Jack sensed a chasm had grown between them, and he wondered if there was anything he could do, short of agreeing to move, that would bridge the gap.

Racked with guilt, he woke early the next morning and went to Ellie's room to apologize. "Ellie." He knocked softly on the door. "Listen, I'm sorry about last night. It's just that..." Overcome with a sudden sense of dread, he knocked again. When there was no answer, he entered, finding the room empty. A note on the bed bearing his name explained the situation.

Dearest Jack,

Forgive me for once again making my escape beneath the cover of darkness, but I need some time alone to think about the future. Being with you these two months has been the best time of my life, and while I wish we could stay in this dream forever, sadly, we cannot. I understand why you feel the way you do about leaving this place. I'm scared too. But with you by my side I feel as if there's nothing I can't do. I only hope you will reconsider, as losing you again is the worst thing I can imagine. I'll give you a call in a couple of days to let you know what I've decided.

All my love,

Ellie

When he had finished reading the letter, Jack balled it up and threw it against the wall, then sat on the end of the bed and wept.

CHAPTER THIRTY-TWO

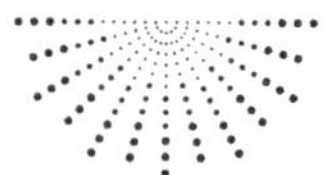

Blown Away

A few days later, Ellie phoned Jack from her house to tell him she'd taken the job. The conversation was brief and amicable, and they both apologized for the things they'd said. Ellie went on to express regret for leaving the way she had and told Jack that he was still welcome to come with her, but that if he chose to say, she understood. Before they hung up, Ellie wished him the best, and said that no matter what happened, she hoped they could remain friends. But Jack had no interest in being friends. With a woman like Ellie, it was all or nothing.

After her fight with Jack, Ellie tried to move on the best she could. With the move only weeks away, she still needed to inform the university of her decision, pack her things, and figure out how to get her belongings from Indiana to Texas. The only positive was with all the work she had in front of her, she had little time to dwell on Jack.

On Friday night, Zora treated Ellie to dinner at Sully's to celebrate her new job. They ordered wine, escargot, and chateaubriand.

"I still can't believe this is happening." Zora beamed, her face aglow in candlelight. "I'm so happy for you."

Ellie smiled in response. "Thank you. I couldn't have done this without you." She paused, turning melancholy. "You've been my friend for a long time, Zora, and I'm going to miss having you around."

Zora's smile evaporated. "Me too. I was telling Trey just this afternoon how hard this transition is going to be."

Ellie's shoulders dropped with a sigh. "I wish I could bring you with me. It'd be nice to have a familiar face close by."

"Honey, so do I, and I'd go in a heartbeat. Trey, on the other hand... I got away with it once, but I might not be so lucky the next time."

The waiter brought a bottle of wine and filled their glasses. When he was gone, Zora raised her glass in a toast.

"To Dr. Elizabeth Spencer, the hardest working, most determined woman I've ever met and a fierce friend. In the words of the great Henry David Thoreau, 'go confidently in the direction of your dream. Live the life you have imagined.'"

When the food came out, they ate, and inevitably, the conversation turned to Jack.

"So what happened with you two? I thought things were going great."

Ellie shook her head. "I guess when it came right down to it, he wasn't willing to give up his life in Tennessee. I can't say that I blame him though. It's a lot to ask of anyone."

"But you both seemed so happy."

Ellie turned wistful. "We were." She thought of the time they'd spent together over the summer. "Not to sound unappreciative, but part of me wishes Dr. Clement had never called."

Zora's eyebrows shot up in disbelief. "You know, it's not

too late to change your mind. I haven't said a word to anyone at the university."

"I can't do that, not after accepting the position. Dr. Clement and his team are counting on me. Besides, I want this, and I feel like if I walked away now, I'd always wonder *what if.*"

Zora wiped the corners of her mouth and cleared her throat before speaking. "Can I be brutally honest with you?"

Ellie chuckled. "It's never stopped you before."

"You're like a sister to me, so I say this with as much love and affection as I can muster. I just think that sometimes you're too driven, that you don't take time to stop and smell the roses. It's okay to be content with what you've got instead of always complaining about what you haven't got. Lord knows you're smart enough to do anything you want. I truly believe that. But at some point, you need to think about the future, about what your life will be like when your career is no longer the most important thing."

"What do you mean?"

"At some point, you'll find someone you want to spend the rest of your life with. If you're lucky, you'll get married and start a family, have a couple of kids and a dog. Work will become less important, even for you." While Ellie processed that, Zora went on. "My point is if you're always chasing the next thing that comes along, you'll continue to push away those who try to get close. And if you're not careful, you'll wake up one day alone, and it'll be too late to do anything about it."

Once Ellie had digested her words, she responded with a question of her own. "As long as we're being honest, what would you have done if Trey had decided to stay in Mississippi?"

Zora leaned back in her chair and laced her hands in front

of her. "You don't know how many times I've asked myself that very question. Fortunately, he decided to come with me, and everything worked out."

"But if he hadn't?"

"If he hadn't, I would have stayed."

"Really? That surprises me."

"For me, it's quite simple," said Zora. "As much as I love work, it's temporary, but love—love is forever."

* * *

A week passed, then another, and still there was no word from Jack. Ellie assumed once he'd had time to process, Jack would change his mind, but with her move now only a few days away, she wondered if she hadn't miscalculated.

On Friday morning, Ellie was busy boxing up the last of her belongings when the telephone rang. Hoping it might be Jack, she rushed to pick it up.

"Hello."

"Hey, it's me."

"Oh hi, sis. How are you?"

"Fine. Listen, I have a favor to ask, and before you say no, promise you'll hear me out."

"Okay," she said uneasily, settling into an open chair.

"Mother has requested to come and see you."

Ellie could hardly believe her ears. She sprang to her feet, putting a fist on her hip. "Absolutely not! I have nothing more to say to that woman. Besides," she said, examining the half dozen boxes scattered around the living room, "I'm in the process of packing up my entire life and moving halfway across the country. The last thing I need is a distraction."

"I understand," said Amelia calmly. "You're angry and busy,

but as your sister and your friend, I'm asking you to hear her out. Besides, you owe me one."

"For what?"

"Covering for you while you snuck off to Jack's, remember?"

Damn. She sat back down, feeling her pulse return to normal. "Do you really want to waste your favor on her?"

"Considering where you two left things, and the fact that you're moving to Texas in a few days, yes. You know how much I detest discord."

"Fine," said Ellie, realizing she had little choice. "But if she so much as looks at me the wrong way, I'll—"

"I'll keep her under control," Amelia reassured her. "We'll be there in an hour."

While Ellie waited for them to arrive, she wondered what her mother could possibly have to say to her in person that couldn't be said over the phone.

Just after noon, Ellie heard a car pull into the drive. Taking a deep breath, she crossed the floor and opened the door.

"Hello, Ellie," said Marie, looking stiff and solemn.

"Mother. Won't you come in?" She stepped aside.

Amelia entered next, and Ellie glared at her.

"How's the packing coming along?" she asked as she stepped into the living room.

"Nearly finished." Ellie cleared a spot for them on the couch and offered them a seat. "So what is it you wanted to talk about?"

Marie cleared her throat before speaking. "First, I came to apologize… for the way I acted when we last saw one another. I was completely out line."

Ellie let out a mirthless chuckle. "You… apologize?"

Marie seemed to overlook her question. "I shouldn't have

said what I did, and I was wrong to interfere in your personal life. It won't happen again."

Ellie eyed her surreptitiously. "Why the change of heart? Is this because I'm leaving?"

Marie asked Amelia to give her and Ellie a moment alone. When Ellie gave a nod of approval, Amelia retreated toward the front door.

"I'll be just outside if you need me," she said, then stepped out onto the porch.

"Believe it or not," said Marie, "I've done a great deal of soul-searching over the past couple of months, and what I discovered was just how poorly I've handled things with you over the years. I want you to know it was never my intent for us to wind up here, with you hating me."

"I don't hate you, Mother," said Ellie, feeling a tinge of remorse for the things she said. "It's just... You don't know where to draw the line. Ever since I was a child, you've watched over me like a hawk, making sure I didn't step out of line. 'Chin up. Back straight. Read this. Don't say that.' It was exhausting. And the worst part was you only did that to me. Amelia got to do whatever she wanted."

Marie was quiet for a moment, then said, "Did you ever stop and think there was a reason I treated you different from your sister?"

Ellie shook her head.

"When you were little, maybe four or five, I knew there was something different about you." She gave a little whisk of a smile and continued. "On warm summer nights you used to lie in the backyard and stare into the sky, connecting the stars like dots with the end of your finger. Sometimes you'd lie there for hours, not uttering a single word. And I remember this one time you said, 'someday, when I'm older and smarter, I'm going to learn the names of all the stars.' It was as if you could see your entire life up there in those stars. That's when I knew you had something special inside you."

"If that's how you felt, why were you always against me?"

"I wasn't, but I knew from experience that if you were going to be great, you'd need someone to push you. God knows your father couldn't do it. You had him wrapped around your little finger. Still do. So I took it upon myself."

Ellie thought about that for a minute, remembering all the times she and her mother had butted heads when she was growing up. "Father may not have been much of a disciplinarian, but it was he who got me interested in astronomy. That book he bought me, *Seeing Stars*, lit that fire inside me."

Marie smiled. "I hate to break it to you, sweetheart, but that also was me."

"You? But I thought... Why didn't you say anything?"

"Because in your eyes your father could do no wrong. When you thought it was he who bought it for you, your face lit up like a Christmas tree. After that, I didn't have the heart to tell you otherwise, so I let you think it was him."

Ellie was silent for a long time, processing her words. "Thank you," she finally said, "for telling me the truth."

"You're welcome. And just so you know, if I could take back what I did that summer, I'd do it in a heartbeat. On the bright side, at least things worked out with you and Jack in the end."

Ellie turned and stared into the kitchen.

"You are still together, aren't you?"

Summoning the courage, Ellie turned to face her. "I don't exactly know how to answer that," she said dismally. "I don't know if Amelia told you, but Jack isn't coming with me to Houston."

"No, she didn't." A deep furrow ran across her forehead. "Are you okay with that?"

Ellie gave a half shrug. "I don't have a choice. Apparently, there's nothing I can say or do to change his mind."

"I see." Marie sighed. "Well, for what it's worth, I'm sorry. I know how much you love him."

A painful silence descended.

"I am doing the right thing, aren't I?"

"Only you can answer that," said Marie, dodging the question.

"Figures."

"What?"

"I thought if anyone would understand, it would be you."

"I do understand. And under normal circumstance, I'd tell you to take the job and never look back. But things have changed, haven't they? I don't know if it's because of Clara's death or the fact that you and Jack reconnected after all this time, but I've realized life is too short to throw away love, because once it's gone, we can never get it back. If I were you, not that I'm trying to tell you what to do, but I'd give him time," said Marie. "If memory serves, it took you a little while to get used to the idea of moving away from home too."

Ellie snapped her head around. "Did not!"

Marie raised an eyebrow.

"Okay, so it may have taken me a few months to get used to this place, but at least I tried. Jack won't even give Houston a chance."

"Does that surprise you? He's a man. If you haven't noticed, they're notoriously hardheaded."

They laughed.

"Besides, the poor guy must feel as if he's caught in a tornado. He doesn't see you for ten years, and then you appear as if from nowhere, fall in love all over again, only for you to spring it on him about a job that's going to take you halfway across the country. It's a wonder his head isn't spinning. Give him some space. I'm sure he'll come around."

"And if he doesn't?"

"Then you'll do like you always do and land on your feet. Regardless, one day, when you have children of your own, they'll look back on your career, whether it be here at the university or with NASA or wherever, and marvel at what you've done."

CHAPTER THIRTY-THREE

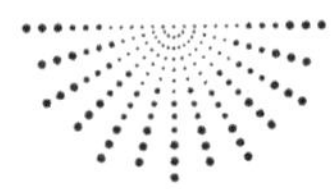

Bright Horizons

Since accepting the job with NASA, Ellie had kept the news limited to her family and close friends, but there was still one person she hadn't told.

"Hello. Is anyone here?" Ellie asked, finding the bookstore empty.

Sam appeared from the back room, looking surprised to see her. "Ellie, my dear, how nice to see you. This must be fate." He gave her a hug and offered her a seat. "I was just about to call you."

Her eyes wandered around the room. "What's with all the boxes? Are you going somewhere?"

Sam's smile faded into a frown. "I'm afraid so. Alicia's taken a turn for the worse, and the doctors say if we have any hope of prolonging her life, we need to move as soon as possible."

Ellie was stricken with grief. "Oh, Sam, I'm so sorry. You and Alicia are like family to me."

"And you to us," he said. "Which is why if you're still interested in the store, it's all yours."

Her heart stuttered, and she had the feeling of falling. "Sam, I-I'm flattered. You know how much I love this store, but I'm afraid I must decline."

His face fell the slightest bit. "I don't understand. Have you had a change of heart?"

She took quite a long breath before she answered. "No, but I've recently been offered a job in Texas, and I've decided to take it."

"You're leaving Bloomington?" He propped himself up against the counter.

Ellie nodded in response. "My flight leaves Monday morning. That's why I'm here—to say goodbye."

When the shock wore off, he said, "I never thought I'd see the day. What about Jack? Is he going with you?"

Ellie looked at the ground and shook her head. "No. I'm going alone."

Sam cocked an eyebrow in surprise. "Do you mind if I ask why you're leaving? I thought you loved it here."

"I did. I mean I do. It's just... I received a once-in-a-lifetime offer, one I couldn't refuse."

"And Jack?"

The mere mention of his name was enough to make her heart ache. "Jack loves me. I know he does. And I love him too. But his life in Tennessee means more to him than I do."

Sam reached out and patted her on the shoulder. "Well, I'm sorry to hear that, and for what it's worth, I liked him. From the first time I met him, I've always believed the two of you were made for each other."

"You're not the first person who's said that to me recently." She recalled the conversation with her mother. "So who will you sell the store to?" she asked, changing the subject.

Sam returned to packing. "Marge Nantz has expressed

interest. So has Richard West. Worst case, I'll take out an ad in the paper. Given the location, I don't think I'll have difficulty finding someone."

The thought of the bookstore belonging to someone other than the Hensleys made Ellie want to cry. "What will become of all the books?"

"That will be up to the new owner, I suppose. Are you sure there's nothing I can say or do to change your mind?"

Ellie smiled politely. "No, but thank you for asking." Her eyes wandered. "I'm really going to miss this place."

"Me too. This store has been in my family for over half a century. But I guess that's life, isn't it? One minute we're set in our ways, and the next we're trying something new. People are resilient like that." He picked up a box and set it on the counter. "Oh, I almost forgot…" Sam disappeared behind the curtain and returned a minute later, holding a small, tattered book. "I was saving this for when you took over the store, but given the circumstances, I'll give it to you now."

Ellie examined the cover. It was a copy of *Seeing Stars*. She had mentioned it once to Sam years earlier, had told him how it had ignited her passion for science and astronomy.

"That's the one you were telling me about, isn't it?"

"Yes." She nodded. "It's nearly identical to the one I used to check out at the library when I was in grade school."

"Not just nearly," he said as a smile broke across his face.

Curious, Ellie opened the back cover to the checkout card and found her name. The last entry was from December 15, 1941. "Oh my God." She slapped a hand over her mouth. "Where did you get this?"

"From a friend of mine in Chicago."

Ellie blinked her eyes to keep the tears in place. "I don't know what to say."

Overcome with emotion, she threw her arms around Sam as silent tears fell from her eyes.

"You're welcome," he whispered. "Maybe someday, when you have a daughter of your own, you can give it to her," he said as they parted.

Ellie dried her tears and smiled. "Yes, I think I will. Thank you again."

"Don't mention it. Besides, I should be the one thanking you for all you've done for me and Alicia. Your generosity and smiling face will stay with me wherever I go."

When Ellie got home, she sat in her bedroom and cried. Jack was right. Everything was happening so fast, which made her question her decision to leave. She debated calling him one last time to see if he'd changed his mind but decided against it, thinking that if he wanted to talk to her, he would reach out.

Sunday was spent tying up loose ends, and when she was satisfied that she'd done all she could do, Ellie sat down to one last dinner. Over a plate of spaghetti and a bottle of red wine, she reminisced about all who had visited her over the years. It was Amelia who had been with her the day she moved in and again following her breakup with Michael. Then there was Zora and all the times they had sat in the kitchen, trading stories over glasses of wine. And more recently, the weekend she and Jack had spent together. Scanning the empty room, she felt a stab of loneliness at the realization that her life would never be the same.

Upending her glass of wine, Ellie pushed those thoughts out of her head, clinging to the hope that what lay ahead was better than what she was leaving behind.

* * *

Monday morning, after loading the suitcases into her car, Ellie made a final sweep of the house. In a few minutes, she'd be on the road, headed toward her destiny. She had just said her final goodbyes when she heard someone knocking at the door. Thinking it might be Zora, she went to answer it.

"Jack." Her jaw went slack when she saw him. "W-What are you doing here?"

"I'm probably the last person you expected to see, but I couldn't let you go without first telling you I'm sorry." His eyes were full of regret. "For everything. And if it isn't too late, I'd like to come with you."

"But—"

"Please just hear me out." He took a moment to gather his thoughts. "Look, I know what I said about not being able to leave Tennessee, but I was wrong. All this time I thought my life was there, in those hills, on that water, but I finally realized my life is wherever you are. And if that's Texas or Tennessee or Timbuktu, I don't care, so long as we're together."

The breath left her chest. "Jack, I don't know what to say."

"Just say you'll think about it," he pleaded. "That's all I'm asking."

"It's not that. It's just..." She dropped her eyes for a moment, then met his gaze. "I phoned Dr. Clement this morning to tell him I'd had a change of heart."

Confusion flitted across Jack's face. "I don't understand."

"I'm not taking the job," she explained.

"But the suitcases," he said, nodding toward the car.

Ellie chuckled, finding the timing of Jack's visit remarkable. "I was on my way to see you," she said, overcome with emotion.

"Me? Is this because of what I said? Because if it is, I—"

"No," she reassured him, "it isn't. At least, not entirely." She offered him a seat on the porch swing. "The truth is these past couple of weeks have been the most difficult of my life," she admitted. "I went back and forth, wondering if I'd made the right decision. Then I was reminded of something recently that helped put things in perspective."

"And what was that?"

"Believe it or not, it was something my mother told me. Apparently, the fight we had caused her to do some soul-searching of her own. After we reconciled our differences, she made me realize that everything I ever wanted was right here. Well, almost everything." She set her gaze on him and held his hand. "Jack, I'm sorry for saying those awful things to you. I didn't mean any of it. You're the most wonderful man I've ever known." She swallowed hard at the tangle of words stuck in her throat. "When it came right down to it, more important than work or prestige, I couldn't stand the thought of spending one more day without you. Can you forgive me?"

A tender smile crossed Jack's face. "I already did," he said, and then he leaned in and kissed her softly on the lips.

CHAPTER THIRTY-FOUR

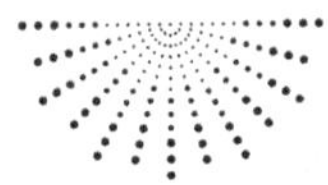

Cloud Nine

Now that she'd decided to stay in Bloomington, there was one final piece of business Ellie needed to take care of.

"I'm headed out," she said, grabbing her keys on the way to the door.

Jack looked up from his notebook. "Do you want me to come with you?"

"I'll only be a few minutes. You stay here and write, and when I get back, we'll have lunch."

"Yes, ma'am." He raised a hand in salute.

The drive to Sam's store took less than ten minutes, but it was enough time for Ellie to prepare a statement. She wanted the store, plain and simple, and she only hoped it was still available.

"I've changed my mind," she said as Sam welcomed her inside. "I've decided to stay in Bloomington after all, and Jack's here with me. I apologize for all the confusion, and if it isn't too late, I'd like to buy the store."

Sam frowned heavily. "Ellie, I hate to break it to you, dear, but I already sold it. When you said you were leaving, I put a sign in the window and had an offer within twenty-four hours."

Ellie wilted. "Can I ask who you sold to?"

"An out-of-towner… said he wants the space for an appliance store."

Ellie collapsed into a chair, shaking her head in defeat.

"Ellie, I'm terribly sorry. If I'd known…"

"It's not your fault, Sam," she grumbled. "If anything, it's mine. I'm the one who couldn't make up my mind. I only wish I'd come to my senses sooner." To have come this far only to have her heart broken left Ellie feeling hollow.

"You know, you could always try to buy it back," he offered. "It might cost you a little more, but everyone has a price."

She looked up, feeling a tinge of hope. "You think?"

"It's worth a shot." Sam checked the time. "In fact, he's on his way here now to look around the store."

Ellie roamed the shelves, gently dusting the old books and straightening knickknacks. The inside looked as it always had, with books as far as the eye could see.

When the door opened, she looked up and saw Jack.

"Fancy running into you," he said as he walked in, a smile stretched across his face.

"I thought you'd be writing."

"I was, but I had some business to take care of."

"Look," she cried, pointing to the SOLD sign in the window. "Sam sold it already. Can you believe it?"

"Oh, Ellie, I'm sorry." Jack comforted her. "Did he say who bought it?"

She shook her head. "Someone from out of town." Dejected, Ellie sat down on one of the comfy reading chairs and stared out the window. "You don't know how much I wanted this place, Jack." She felt as if the air had been knocked out of her.

Jack sat down beside her and draped an arm over her shoulder. "I know," he whispered, pulling her close. "Do you want to go and get some lunch and we can talk about it?"

She shook her head. "I'm waiting to talk to the new owner. Sam said he'll be here soon. I'm going to offer him above asking price to buy it back."

Jack raised a brow at her. "It really does mean a lot to you, doesn't it?"

"You have no idea," she cried. "This was one of the main reasons I chose to stay." She sighed heavily. "But I guess it doesn't matter now, does it?"

After a long pause, Jack said, "Years ago, someone wise once told me that the key to a woman's heart was an unexpected gift at an unexpected time." He took a key from his pocket and slipped it into her hand.

"What's this?"

Jack smiled tenderly. "The key to your heart, I hope."

Ellie tilted her head quizzically.

He nodded toward the door. "Go on, give it a try."

Ellie stood, slid the key into the lock, and turned the knob. The key fit. "I don't understand," she said, glancing over her shoulder at him.

He joined her at the door. "I wanted it to be a surprise."

It took a moment, but Ellie finally put the pieces together. "Wait. You're the guy from out of town?"

He beamed a smile at her. "Guilty as charged."

Tears pooled in her eyes. "Oh, Jack." She threw herself into his arms. "Thank you. Thank you. Thank you." She kissed him over and over. "How can I ever repay you?"

"Funny you should ask." From his other pocket, Jack took

out the little black box he'd been holding on to for twelve years and dropped to one knee. "Elizabeth Grace Spencer," he said, looking up at her, "will you do me the honor of becoming my wife?"

For a moment, Ellie was light as a feather, her senses upended. Her eyes switched from Jack to the ring, and back again. "Yes," she said as tears of joy blurred her vision. "A million times, yes."

CHAPTER THIRTY-FIVE

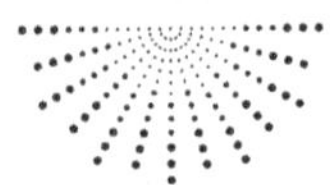

Written in the Stars

"Are you nervous?"

"A little," Ellie answered, her foot tapping nonstop against the hardwood floor. "But not about getting married," she clarified. "I'm just afraid I'll forget my lines."

Amelia smiled amusedly. "You'll do fine. Just don't forget to breathe. Besides, once you see Jack, everything will click into place. Trust me. There." She put the finishing touch on Ellie's updo. "Now you look perfect." Amelia reached for a mirror and held it up for Ellie to see. "Jack's going to have a fit when he sees you."

Ellie beamed. "As he should."

When Amelia had finished getting ready, she turned to Ellie. "I want to thank you again for choosing me to be your maid of honor. I don't know if you realize how much this means to me."

"You're welcome," said Ellie thoughtfully. "And just so you know, it was the easiest decision I've ever made."

They embraced in a long hug that had them both on the

verge of tears. And it was then that Ellie was most thankful to have Amelia in her life. She was more than just a sister; she was Ellie's best friend. Unlike the many friends and acquaintances that had slid in and out of Ellie's life over the years, Amelia, through all the ups and downs, had never left her side.

As they parted, a knock fell upon the door. Marie's voice followed. "It's time."

"One minute," said Amelia. "You have something new, borrowed, and blue, but what about something old?"

Ellie reached into the drawer and pulled out the arrowhead that Jack had given her the first time they visited the island. "This," she said, holding it up for Amelia to see.

"All right then," said Amelia. "In that case, I think you're ready."

When they got to the dock, a half dozen boats were waiting to ferry the wedding party to the island. The guests were already there, including Jack, who at that very moment stood on the beach, watching the sunset.

"I wish your daddy were here to see this," said Helen as she scanned the horizon. "He'd have been so proud."

Jack lifted his gaze to the heavens. "I'm sure he's watching. Mama," he said, looking at her, "are you happy with the way things turned out? I know how much you adored Sara, and..."

A warm smile touched her lips. "JB," she said tenderly, "I couldn't be any happier that I am at this very moment. Ellie is the love of your life, the same way your daddy was mine. And despite all the trials and tribulations you've endured, it was all worth it 'cause, in the end, you got what you wanted. My only advice is to hang on for dear life, son, and enjoy the ride, and never take a single day for granted because none of us are guaranteed tomorrow."

Jack put his arm around her shoulder and kissed her on top of the head. "Well said, Mama."

"I have something for you." Helen reached into her purse and took out an old wristwatch that looked as if it had recently been shined. "This belonged to your daddy." She handed it to him. "He left it with me for safekeeping just before he went to war. I think he'd want you to have it."

"Mama, are you sure?"

"Positive." She helped him put it on. "A perfect fit."

Jack held it up in the dying light, marveling at the way it sparkled. "Thank you, Mama."

"You're welcome. Oh, and one more thing." This time Helen handed Jack a small cross, which had belonged to Lewis.

"Mama, I can't." Tears filled Jack's eyes.

She placed it in the palm of his hand. "Now," she whispered, "they can both be with you today."

Jack placed the cross in his pocket and dried his eyes. "Thank you, Mama. This means the world to me."

When the boats appeared on the horizon, Jack retreated to the forest and took his position beside the preacher. While he waited for Ellie, he looked around the clearing and saw the tree that bore their initials and the rock they'd jumped from to reach the lagoon. Then, as his gaze settled in the direction of the beach, his cheeks rose in a smile as he remembered the first time they'd made love. The island—a place of firsts—was special for many reasons. It was where much of their story had already taken place and where this new chapter was ready to be written.

Softly, a violin began playing, and everyone stood. A minute later, with night closing in, Ellie appeared, and as Jack's gaze settled on her, time stood still. All at once, he remembered the thousands of wishes he'd made on shooting stars. It had been this moment, right here, right now, that he'd so longed for. Only now it wasn't a dream. It was real. She was real—the woman that had convinced him love at first sight was possible.

When Ellie joined Jack beneath the arbor and everyone had been seated, the preacher began the ceremony. "We are gathered here today in the presence of God at the invitation of Jack Edward Bennett and Elizabeth Grace Spencer to share in the joy of their wedding."

Jack and Ellie traded glances, smiling at each other the way they had when they were teenagers.

"Jack, will you have this woman to be your wife? Will you love her, comfort her, honor and keep her, in sickness and in health, and forsaking all others, be faithful to her so long as you both shall live?"

"I will," said Jack, peering deep into Ellie's eyes.

The preacher asked Ellie the same question.

"Of course I will," she said, looking up at Jack.

When the exchanged of rings had taken place, the preacher announced, "By the power vested in me by the state of Tennessee, I now pronounce you husband and wife. Jack," he said, "you may kiss your bride."

Softly, tenderly, Jack kissed Ellie, much the same as he had at that very spot thirteen years earlier. And as they parted, he whispered into her ear something that had been on his mind since the day she returned to Sims Chapel the summer before. "Mockingbirds."

EPILOGUE

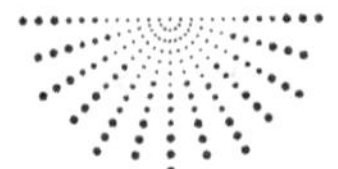

MAY 2020

The ride across the water is quiet, familiar. Above me, whispers of dying fog, like ghostly tendrils, glitter in the morning sunlight. In a wide arc, I circumvent the sandbar and turn north, setting my sights on Mama Holler. The warmth of the sunlight against my face eases my nerves, and for a moment, I forget about the task at hand.

Passing the island where I'd taken Ellie the day we met, the last seventy years—our wedding, the birth of our daughter, birthdays, anniversaries, winters in Indiana, summers in Tennessee—flash before my eyes. Mama was right—it came and went in the blink of an eye.

"How many times do you suppose we've navigated these channels and coves?"

I turn my attention to the bow and find her sitting in her usual spot. "Ellie?"

"What do you think, hundreds? Thousands?"

I nod in response, not believing my eyes.

"And how many fish do you think we've caught?"

"I-I don't know. Why do you ask?"

Ellie takes in her surroundings before resting her gaze on me. "Curious, that's all. I wonder if Mama Holler still has fish? It seems like forever since you've taken me there."

I squeeze my eyes shut to stop the tears from falling.

"Listen," she says in a tender voice, "I know how hard this is for you, but I want you to have the peace of mind of knowing you're doing the right thing."

I swallow the lump in my throat and nod.

"That island is the place where life really began for me, for us, so it's only fitting that should be my final resting place. There I'll have unobstructed views of the heavens so I can always see the stars."

"Ellie—"

She reaches for my hand. The touch of her skin against mine causes the hairs on the back of my neck to stand on end. "Once, you told me that God chose only the strongest to carry the heaviest burdens. I don't know why he chose you, but he did. Which is why I know you can do this."

The roar of a passing boat draws my attention. When I look back, the seat is empty. Scanning the horizon, I find my destination and draw a steadying breath.

Landing the boat is simple, getting out is the challenge, but I manage both with little trouble. Now on the beach, the ground has a familiar feel beneath my feet. I grab the bag from the boat and cross the beach toward the woods.

The first step is the hardest, but after that they come thoughtlessly, automatically, and before I know it, I'm standing in the clearing. It is quiet here, making it easy to hear the ghosts whispering in my ear.

To my surprise, the arbor, weathered from decades of wind and rain, still stands. My spirit soars, if only for a moment, as I recall the night we got married. I find the poplar tree with our initials and run my fingers over the deep cuts in the wood, and the hair on the back of my neck prickles.

"I know you're here," I say as I lift my eyes. "I can feel you."

As if on cue, the wind whistles back.

After composing myself, I do as Ellie directed and scatter her ashes, a little here, a little there, but all in places with unobstructed views of the heavens. Upending the urn, I breathe a sigh of relief. My work here is done.

I turn to leave and notice something off to my right, glittering in the sunlight. Drawing closer, I can hardly believe my eyes. "How did you get here?" I ask, feeling light as a feather. I kneel beside Ellie's memory box and lift the lid. Inside, there is a letter with my name on it, along with the arrowhead, and the bottle of sand I had once given her.

My beloved Jack,

We meet again. If you're reading this letter, it means my time on earth has reached its end. Gone? Certainly not. I've simply flown away for a season, just like the mockingbird you once told me about. What, you didn't think I'd let you get to heaven first, did you?

Right now, I know you're hurting, but do not despair, for our adventure has only just begun. I suspect by now you've noticed the gift I left for you. No doubt you've turned the house upside down looking for it. It's funny how an object, even one as small as an arrowhead, can come to mean so much. Seventy years ago, at this very spot, you unearthed it for me. It's been around the world and back again, but it's now where it belongs. I hope you don't mind, but I'd like you to return it to the earth so that someone else will come along—perhaps another young couple in love—and discover its magic. Maybe it will mean as much to them as it has us.

Thank you for all the adventures and all the memories, which I will carry with me into this next great journey.

You were right all along. Our fate is not determined by the universe, but by us. We are the authors of our own destiny. And I thank God every day that he made you my keeper of stars.

Until we meet again,

Ellie

I step out of the darkness and into the light. At the bottom of the hill, I give one last glance at the trees, and knowing this will be the last time I set foot on this hallowed ground, I thank God for the opportunity to have discovered this place.

Back in the boat, I start the engine and ease away from the island. Turning for home, I look to the west. The sun breaks free of the clouds, dispensing rays of golden light that spill over the surface of the water. Riding south, away from the island, I smile through blurry eyes, knowing that the end is only the beginning, and the greatest adventure is still to come.

END

PLEASE LEAVE A REVIEW/SHARE ON SOCIAL MEDIA

Thank you for reading ***The Keeper of Stars***. If you have an opportunity, please leave an honest review on your preferred platform. For those on TikTok, feel free to share on #BookTok. In the meantime, please check out Buck's other stories at:

www.buckturner.com

Made in the USA
Monee, IL
22 January 2024

52216712R00164